Child of the World

Child of the World

Anthony LaBranche

Tony LaBranche

Writers Club Press
San Jose New York Lincoln Shanghai

Child of the World

Writers Club Press
an imprint of iUniverse.com, Inc.

For information address:
iUniverse.com, Inc.
5220 S 16th, Ste. 200
Lincoln, NE 68512
www.iuniverse.com

ISBN: 0-595-17126-5

Printed in the United States of America

For Tillie
May the road be not too rocky

CHAPTER ONE

1

Far beneath me outlined against the gray limestone horizon, Canada geese are flying unencumbered in huge V-formations, eighty, a hundred of them. Viewed from above, they look like Japanese squadrons on their way once again to Pearl Harbor, the toylike 1940's aircraft shrunk to the size of twenty-pound birds, their drivers perched atop the airborne tin flivvers we marvel at in old newsreels, riding so they can angle wings downward like a stiff paper glider and drop their violent birdseed droppings. But the wings flapping below me are pliable and curvaceous—they arch from a supple living body, not an odd mechanical contraption of man.

I'd volunteered for an animal survey and relocation project in Thailand. I suppose that's what people do who are feeling dispossessed from their current lives. Relocate themselves into the lives of animals through some project or other. These northern geese, some of them, would be dead before I returned, patches of gray and white bobbing like crashed hang-gliders on the polished surface of the black water. They knew where they were going, that seemed certain, but not why they were going there or what the cost might be.

I turned back from the window, twisted into my seat and tried to rest. At night the silent body rests, having rid itself of the busybody me, at least for a while. It lies there stretched, victoriously me-less, ticking away its mute body time and storing up its uninflected documentary footage which silently it will continue at the next opportunity. The busybody me in the meantime has been asked to vacate the body-room for a few hours and go babble elsewhere like a vagrant high on canned heat. Fly off to a fictional place made of words, postures, gestures where it can babble over and over to itself that it exists, truly exists. So it tells itself.

Would Thailand be a fictional place of constant babble or would something happen there to restore the mute body?

The night before I left, the wind gusted so fiercely the cars parked up and down the street rocked back and forth setting off their alarms. I looked out. No one was trying to steal them. Just the wind. I turned from my bedroom window and crawled back into bed. I lay in silence waiting for it—my recollection of meeting two weeks ago some one on the lakefront beach—in fact as it now approached me I was slipping back toward it. Miraculously it was still taking place, that meeting, neither of us grown older, not an hour, not a minute.

Tiny spiraling shells, the soft colors of sandstone, a parcel of *columellae* have dropped into a backwater trapped on the beach and are lolling gently back and forth under a thin ripple of waves. Not far off, a dead seagull, a small one dressed in gray and white, its head twisted under, sleeps half buried in the sand.

I bend over to straighten its neck, but I can't go through with it. A freshwater clam, shut tight and sturdy as a rock, oblivious of the gull, lies squirting and thriving nearby in the same pool.

On a further stretch of beach down a short way about two dozen gulls are closing now into a circle, squatting against the cold ruffling breeze. They have their own dead creature to attend to, a monster twenty-pound grouper washed up, its ribs sticking up out of it like a dismantled shipwreck, all sharp ridged teeth and blank eye sockets. The gulls peck listlessly at it whenever they wish; its spiked dorsals have petrified and slumped under the desiccating sun and no longer are a defense for the creature.

A kid of about nine stands at the water's edge. As it drifts out he picks up an empty clamshell. In response I pick up one. He picks up another, then discards it and watches me. I start to pick up another but stop.

"Why are you collecting...?" he asks sharply as I bend down. I jerk bolt upright.

He doesn't care about those useless language stunts but cuts right to the point. And there's never a complete answer to a cut right to the point. That's written gospel. And trying to answer a cut involves lying.

"I suppose you want me to explain." I'm shaping my speech a bit stiffly, after what I've been thinking, like we're two adult figures in a novel who happen to be standing right here where the author want us to stand and just happen to be talking reasonably like the author wants us to.

That won't do. We're confronting each other like two school bullies. And he doesn't think I can explain things anyway, not really. I look down at the dead gull lying between us. I'm trying to make sure the boy isn't myself. I want to make sure he won't reveal to me why I've decided I must go away to some distant place for however long.

"Well, why are you?"

He adjusts his baseball cap and looks out over the water. "Don't you have a family?" he asks.

I retreat, digging my toes into the sand. Yes, no, I think. It's high time to shift the topic.

"I bet you're going to become a scientist," I attempt gingerly, in order to pull us out of the hole. But he sees through the ploy. I get a shrug for it. He's thinking over his question about a family. "Computer whiz?" I ask. Worse shrug. "Surgeon?" Nope. "Poet? Philosopher?" No reaction at all. I listen to my queries flapping and drying in the lake-front breeze. The two of us are standing with our toes digging into the wet sand, and who the hell wants to become a poet or philosopher?

"We had to learn all about poet and philosopher stuff in class."

So did I, I pondered, but it didn't take. I had to wait until philosophy itself came along, and that wasn't exactly in class. She wasn't exactly a philosopher. I'll tell you about it...one day.

My young inquisitor examines me sharply. He's not going to trust anything I have to say about families unless I shape up.

"Scientist, I guess." He chooses to play along with me for a bit longer.

He confirms this by rubbing his nose with the hand that holds his plastic bag. But the hand really isn't a hand; it's a tangled clump of knuckles and stumps of cartilage turning in on themselves with undecipherable random purpose. A steel brace runs under his forearm and wrist and circles the heel of the stump to lend it rigidity. At one side of the bright steel band there's a clip which might receive a pen by means of a slotted holder. My toes dig down further.

He ignores me, since I'm scrutinizing him, but his toes are digging into the wet sand the same as mine. He gazes out over the lake toward the horizon. Under heavy puffs of churned-up clouds, the water spreads dark purple, not rough. In the near distance two tugboats are nosing along a barge laden with huge blocks of granite, purplish under the sea-reflected light. The blocks are to be placed, by means of a tall yellow crane on the barge, along the shoreline as a breakwater to hold the lake away. I wonder if there is another meaning to them. Hold the lake away. In the wake of the tugs shepherding the barge the water spreads out a smooth velvety purple. Some lake gulls follow the barge lazily, marking time mid-stride in air.

The tugs themselves look like quaint 1920's Brooklyn Bridge jobs, built probably in the late '50's. Their radar antennae have been stuck on as an afterthought like a glitzy diadem mounting the clumsy perpendicular foc'sle painted barn red, Depression style, tiered with tiny white portholes and window boxes. I imagine temples in the remote East might look like that. Obligatory truck tires dangle along the hull all the way from midships to upswept bow. The tugs nose the barge a little, then rest, then nose a little. The headway is almost imperceptible.

The boy observes the mysterious, unhurried, nautical movements, and touches his nose again in deliberation with his free hand.

"Scientist, I guess," he repeats with only distant conviction.

"I don't have a family," I offer all of a sudden, "not exactly. My parents aren't, you know. And a friend and I…we had to go separate ways, a little while ago."

"Why are you collecting then?" He's not to be diverted into any false sympathy for me. He lifts his sack slightly to emphasize the sharpness of the question.

"I practice drawing them."

He doesn't seem satisfied with that. "We do that twice a week." He examines me as if I were a hack comedian put on the spot and saying the first thing that flies into his head then covering it over by mugging down to his audience. "But first," he continues, "you've got to collect them. I have a pen that fits into this clip." He raises his stump to show me the brace around it, partly because he knows I've been staring at it. He wants to situate me as precisely as he can.

"How do you…" I start, then I stop, unable to resist staring at the stump and its clip. Any curious question coming from me would now seem out of place. My toes dig deeper, to the second joint. The sensation of wet sand makes me question why I've told him I have no family and how I could have spared him that piece of information.

"I've only got half a family." He examines me steadily, divining the crux of our conversation. "My dad's gone. Somewhere. But I don't miss him that much."

It begins to dawn on me why he's bothering to talk to me.

"Somewhere," I mutter gloomily and start to hand him my shells. He takes them looking at them quietly and without responding to me.

"It's not so bad. But you got to keep busy," he says.

Next thing he's working at opening the plastic bag with the clip on his stump, fumbling away, just as I drop a couple of extra shells I've been holding out to him. They hit edge first and wedge into the wet sand. We pretend not to notice. But we both notice.

"Nice shot," he says finally. At last we're becoming human. The words seem to be coming actually from our bodies.

I don't know if I should bend over and pick them up, but I'd call attention to the fact that he's not doing so well with the plastic bag.

"Good luck," I say, "good luck." I say it twice because I mean it for both of us. I turn and start trudging back toward the dead gull. "They're yours for keeps, to remember me by," I shout over my shoulder without turning around. After I go about eight steps his voice overtakes to me.

"What're you going to draw without these? You dropped'em. You forgot'em. You can't forget'em."

"I didn't forget them," I toss over my shoulder. "I draw from memory."

I turn back to face him. His nose is getting the same treatment again. He thinks for a bit. "If memories are so important as that then why don't they stick around? So you can examine them. Collect them, and then they'll not never go away."

That'll not prevent them, I think.

"I know, I know" I reply, figuring I should stoop down now and pretend to look for more shells where I'm standing. There seem to be none around. And it's obvious he doesn't want me to leave.

"I'll remember you, I'll remember," I say, but it's more of a mutter. He looks at me, incredulous, underneath it partly believing me.

I turn to leave, glad that he has my shells or at least the better part of them. I wouldn't have done anything with them, he's right, just put them away maybe occasionally recalled them. I'm beginning to trudge in earnest along the dark wet sand toward the dead gull. But his voice still follows, more insistent and admonishing now because he too has been considering something all this while.

"Hey you really should take a trip." He's waving the bag of clamshells. I wasn't aware I'd told him I was preparing to do just that.

"Know why? Because you'll always find some one out there who's willing to talk to you—and the way you are—hey." He calls louder, "Hey."

"What?"

"Maybe even take care of you. Seem to need it."

Two weeks later I started my journey.

2

Bill Avery, the American field representative of Animals International, whatever they might turn out to be—I'd joined up with them through a poster tacked to a Berkeley bulletin board—bestowed a blandly humorous eye upon me. (He pronounced it *Every*, like Everyman I thought, French-Irish he said, my condolences, I replied.) He had a sort of pale watery sharp-toothed Irish look under violent red hair and crooked teeth and an alert jesting gaze on the lookout for some angle or witticism that would score a put down for his side. Whichever side that might be at the moment. I'd always cherished an aversion to the O'Finn's, something instinctive, no dismissive and you'll soon see why. More often than not they made the best writers in my composition class back at the university, which both pleased and galled me because they knew I knew it. Later I found out his tap roots were French-German, not Irish. Matter of fact, though I claimed mine as French-German they were more Irish than his. And that provided the clinker. Somehow I'd missed out on the dratted gift-of-gab gene pool, so it seemed. In any case he could guess all this from the first five minutes of our encounter, and it explained why he took immediate delight in bugging me.

Right now he was squinting at me over a parcel of burnt fish on his platter. "Shore now, yore going to be in difficulty boy," he declared with theatrical muggery then a sigh, observing my painful efforts to navigate the sea of cultural differences surging around me in the shape of charred fish. I sat, wishing his carrot color hair were edible. I hadn't noticed a vegetable since I arrived.

"Likewise," I replied. "By the way I'd like to eat some of your hair. I haven't seen a vegetable here yet." It helped just to say it.

He flagged down a waiter—we were seated on a veranda of that fancy hotel I couldn't afford, The Oriental, overlooking the Chao Phraya mother of waters which in Conrad's day was the lifeline of the kingdom. Almost immediately a plate of pale green somethings appeared before me. Bill stared at them. "Go light on the bacteria for now. On the other hand you might as well introduce yourself to them. They've persisted hereabouts longer than you will."

"Thanks. You were saying about the field project."

"I was saying that's about as much cooperation," he crunched some charred seafood, apparently part of a huge shrimp, "as you can expect from authorities, which means army, police, same crooks basically. They make it sound like they're co-operating—form before function you know—but the elephants and other creatures aren't so convinced." He saw the question in my eyes. "They say they're relocating them—the animals not the vegetables. To where, is the question you might ask. But nevertheless and because. There's money in dead animals, or parts of'em. And this country is the conduit for the mayhem committed in other parts of the world too, China, Burma, Africa, you name it. This joint runs on money, mostly U.S., or should I say it runs on the people running after money, and that's everybody. Matter of fact, if I were an elephant I'd stay away from the army and the police and anybody with more than a cap pistol. You know, even in the National Parks they keep losing their ivory tweezers," he imitated tusks with his fingers. He paused, Celtically, for effect. "Stay away from the world." He checked the angle of his fingers. "I don't mean to be prejudicial."

"Of course you don't," I agreed. "Why should you? You've been over here six years observing the crinkled bumwad of civilization and editorializing upon it."

A long-tail boat growled in the near distance off our elbows; I looked up in time to catch a single incandescent eye glow white then fade into red filament, finally closing its lid down into a dark nothing.

Stay away from the world, I thought, even as you're sailing out to meet it.

The vast riverfront restaurant where we were seated was festooned crazily with Christmas tree lights and red paper lanterns dangling over the tables encumbered with chattering diners. Between tables at intervals, and ignoring all but the vaguest fire precautions, smoking barbecue grills whose flames burst upwards periodically—we'd been invited to a drunken hobos' Christmas party in sweltering June.

He read the expression on my face. "You're thinking, if I may use the word loosely, now you've successfully arrived here, that the good old U.S. seems less so than any other country a smoking bucket of you know what."

Another long-tail growled downstream in the dark, and the several spotlights of long-tail boats answered from their secret locations winking on and off as they drifted cautiously with the flow of the dark water.

"Something like that," I said peering out into the darkness punctuated each minute by a spotlight gliding into view from a different location.

The river, lukewarm and muddy, seemed to carry on its strong back all sorts of floating plant life mixed with animal and human refuse. A mist was close upon it and drifting toward us, and with it arrived large flying contraptions too elaborate and rudderless to be classified as insects in the Northern Hemisphere. I hoped one might carry away what was on my plate. Sharp-edged packing crates, teakwood logs, derelict from the rickety floating riverfront warehouses, drifted just under the surface.

The long-tails, fragile as pencils, threaded their way among them, winking their single eyes on and off to one another in a perfected, secret code, while their long thin bodies slipped between night air and the mist. I brought my attention back to dinner. The charred shrimp on my plate, hiding under their hot sauce and chopped greens, were the size of beef tenderloin and as tough as dog.

"What about the trade in live exotics, birds, monkeys, tigers, so forth?" I asked, staring at my plate, wondering what I was actually eating. Bill looked at me quizzically. And why not. What appeared to be extraneous parts of unpeeled shrimp, a half dozen or so of legs dangled from his lower lip. He wiped them away with a clenched thumb and forefinger, watching as I observed him aghast.

"You gotta keep chompin' mate" he chomped, as if to certify that he did possess table manners, "if you're going to make it over here."

"I'll remember that. You've got to keep on chomping."

We fell silent for several mouthfuls. The dark water sucked and gurgled at my elbow.

"Most everything that passes through Bangkok, every endangered species does, has been killed several times over," he explained equitably. "They lay more flat that way." He reflected for a moment. "People lay more flat that way too."

What the hell am I doing here, I asked myself. Part of another shrimp dangled from a corner of Bill's mouth. He was having his own trouble with our high-toned culinary outing. He raised both eyebrows, mumbled the morsel as if he were plucking a chicken then swallowed. "Sorry chief, been gone too long from manners. Shlimp are supposed to ray more flat that way too, when they kill'em. Like these 'ere shlimp. But apparently they don't."

"Lie more flat," I said. "Not lay."

He looked at me thoughtfully. "Well maybe *lie* that way. Some people would say *lie* that way. But I don't like the word. Gets us into lying, don't it?" I nodded, after a pause. "Which is another favorite local pastime.

And we don't want that do we? Worse than laying, another favorite local pastime. Unless you forgot your condoms."

I nodded again in silence.

"Hey you're not enjoying…" I'd pushed my plate to one side—like one secretly tries to push away a lie. "But you're not supposed to say anything about it, the trade in poaching," he continued undeterred. "You make concessions; you find the art of accommodation or you don't last long. Like a fish floating between cool and warm currents." He extracted from between his teeth some sort of bone which surely didn't belong to a shrimp.

"Accommodation," I murmured, pushing the plate further away, "Question. Who wants to last long over here? What's the point?" I looked up at the red paper lanterns swaying above our heads.

"Exactly," he accommodated. "You're a rapid scholar, prof." I wasn't sure how he meant that. He folded his napkin, as if by some stroke of insanity we might return, or as if he were secretly pleased about something. I hoped they might wash the napkin before re-issuing it. "Now, did you enjoy the meal?" he inquired politely. "Well, better luck next time."

I must have been gazing almost transparently at him, because he read the words off my mind. "Yes," he continued, "I agree. It's too bad we don't have the heroism of the old colonializing explorers and novelists, now so unfashionable. They had good syntax too. Too bad," he repeated meditatively. "The heroism. Of course," he roused himself, "in this currently enlightened era, and mind you take note of it, of so-called historical revisionism, it may eventually become too bad that it's too bad. And after that, another too bad. Now let us continue our tour. I'll be your whad'um call it."

"*Vademecum*," I replied. "Come go with me."

        ★   ★   ★

Supper now finished, after its own manner, we strolled back down the street leading from the grand Oriental Hotel, once Conrad's dusky stopover, preserving in his memory a heavily draped Edwardian drawing-room with overstuffed chairs, Victorian globe chimney lamps and a simple wooden dry bar. Obviously a corner into which the western imagination could tuck itself away over a cigar.

The modern hotel was painfully aglitter in polished marble, multibucks a night, catering to upbeat business conventions of marketing analysts and video hawkers. The street leading to the hotel was vendors' alley, and we looked over the bizarre bargains offered to us—wallets, belts, shoes (lizards and 'gators would give the skin off their backs for them), endangered ivory doodabs, endangered seashells and tortoise combs, and the endless other toiletries and knickknacks made out of long since evicted creatures. It was a trade our great grandparents had fostered, and currently it seemed to be doing fine.

"If you want a good deal on any of these things" Bill observed caustically, gesturing with what appeared to be an ivory toothpick at the faces of the vendors whose mute sour scrutiny of us had descended to our hiking boots, which registered indisputably low value with them, "if you want a good deal, exclusive of course of bimbo, that's never a good deal, we can buzz down to Chinatown." Silently I agreed we might, or we mightn't. "This is ivory by the way." He waved his toothpick while his eyes swept down the line of squalid hawkers, now frozen in their postures of attentive disregard. "Took it off a retired poacher," he announced loudly in Thai, translating for me while gesticulating at them with the pointed end of the instrument.

All of a sudden I caught wind of what he was about, and consequently of what I might eventually be about. Or thought I might be. My feelings about not staying in Thailand were beginning to shift. "I trust the donor has reconciled himself to its absence," my vademecum continued. He proceeded to translate all this into Thai for our audience. As we continued down the street, turning to me in a voice almost as loud, but in our secret, communal, international, intercultural tongue, the English, "We're not supposed to say a thing about this sort of stuff, you know. Out loud. Not a thing."

*   *   *

So we walked on. Tumbling vines covered the terrace walls of the restaurants and hotel patios that crowded the banks of the river. Tendrils drooped and detached themselves, falling into the rapid current and circling in a vortex for a while. Then these derelicts collected others like themselves and together they drifted downstream in a long trail, stretching out on the warm muddy stream for twenty or thirty feet, still growing as they drifted. The long-tail boats steered clear of them to avoid becoming snarled. We watched two long-tails suddenly leap forward neck-to-neck sending up their rooster-tails of spray, what a welcome relief, racing for the dare of it.

"You like animals and such?" Bill remarked neutrally as we watched them.

"When they're on the hoof. I haven't seen much of that so far. Including our trip to the local park. By the way, is that why I came?"

"Oh well, these will surely still be on the hoof. Pottery hoof." He thought over the anomaly. "And why not, they're pottery animals." We ambled down the street past the row of endangered wildlife vendors.

"They don't sometimes slap the wrong labels on the wrong item, do they?" I demanded, sighting down the row of stands. "Like Louis Vuitton watches, Rolex suitcases, Adidas dentures, boy for girl, girl for boy?"

"Not too often. Sometimes. Give the *farang*, the consumer, what he's anxious to have. Or thinks he's anxious to have."

"Sell the *farang*, the foreigner, what you tell him he's anxious to have. God, all those lovely animals. How contemptible."

"Not very," Bill chuckled, turning his own scrutiny upon the vendors. "Not so very as other things. Let's not get irritated because the East isn't what you want it to be. They think they're giving us what we want."

"I'm not so sanguine about that," I objected. "Something disturbs me about it, like I'm disturbed by your fish floating between the cool and warm currents."

He shrugged. "Well, try to keep your balance between cool and warm. Our shop is the next one down, and it's owned, incidentally, by the wife of the Police Superintendent. Cool, huh? Might do some good to purchase a thing or two there, if you're contemplating getting your passport back. Just consider your state of quarantine."

From the window of our designated shop a great porcelain lion looked out fiercely at my crotch, pottery wrinkles around his smooth nose, a knobby stony porcelain mane, bright red malevolent eyes matching his tiny malicious ears, an open orange-pink mouth with symmetrically distributed chompers. Hanging from his neck a large sign in green read WELCOME.

"Attraction, repulsion," Bill commented, and started to push the door open.

"Beautiful," I countered.

"No, scary."

"Beautiful, and scary. Like an angry Pekinese." A couple of tuk-tuks sputtered sedately down the street, each replete with an overweight hotel-bound Mr and Mrs, or MrMrs. I stared after them. "I don't believe these beautiful orientalizing monsters have any appetite, really, for us westerners. Wouldn't taste right. We're too mean and low to digest well in their mythological tummies. We don't believe in anything, we don't sit still, we don't meditate. And we'd be the wrong diet for the wonderful soft fiery nap of their skin, that wrinkled bulldog skin on their furrowed brows. We're too far down the mortal side of mortality."

"Let's hope you're right."

"Wah-house sale, wah-house sale." A small boy with one heavily drooping eyelid, ran up to us from the interior. He had been sweeping the floor on his hands and knees. On the way over he paused to finger in demonstration one of the priceless pottery beasts on the rump. He held the door open.

"You want to step inside and meet Dragon Lady?" Bill inquired politely.

"Wah-house," the boy announced from under his heavy eyelid.

"Yes I know, warehouse sale," I replied irritably, "or whorehouse, same thing here." Turning to Bill in exasperation. "All you seem to do over here is to visit trinket shops." The boy froze in his partial intuition of our confrontation and in his sense of how different from his world we were at bottom, a dark maelstrom visited upon him from a turbulent foreign land. I looked at him as if he were at the root of our stalemate. Under my glance he started to edge toward the protection of one of the larger lions, still shifting his dirty hand along its rump.

"What the hell are we doing here?" I demanded suddenly. "I'm already tired of this tourist crap. And I've been here only a day, two days." For some reason the boy's dirty hand on the lion had done it, broken down the barrier between my being a respectable pigeon of a tourist and being, what would you call it, a vademecum type of individual. "How do we get in touch with what's really going to happen... if anything at all?"

"I said I'm giving you slow warm up. It'll get warmer soon enough." As if to illustrate this bit of wisdom, Bill let go of his own porcelain creature, on warehouse sale, which he'd been favoring since we entered. We went to the door—the boy had retreated in dismay. Bill turned and closed it quietly in the face of the silently frowning flower-pot king of beasts.

We resumed our walk, and his hand reached out to touch me. He turned away half smiling, apparently to relish his small recent triumph. "After all, ye don't want Yale college or Harvard yard to be thy only whaling-ship. Dost ye, professor?"

*   *   *

The river taxi deposited us suddenly and precariously on the boat landing just off the Ratchawong, slowing just enough so that we could leap to the rickety surging pier made of teak logs bound together with hemp. From there we wandered into Chinatown, streets that wound past hole-in-the-wall shops illuminated by a single lightbulb, each specializing in some particularly desirable product, metric wrenches, toilet seats, plastic hose, pharmaceuticals, ready-made false teeth—these last halted me and gave me a moment of joy after the vendors at the Oriental.

"Contemplating getting your own replaced over here?" Bill inquired neutrally.

"Not if I can help it. They'd have to knock mine out first," I blustered, mostly for my own benefit. He glanced at me sympathetically. My ears tingled. "Anyway I guess they'd have to," I added.

"I realize that," he smiled sweetly. "Talk to the police; it's easily arranged."

But what I found myself burning to acquire, I shortly discovered with surprise, were the slender polished driveshafts for the long-tail boats, and then—figure this on our return via rickshaw—the Volvo engines that powered them.

"They're not Volvo," my guide corrected me, burping faintly, "they're modified Toyota. Everything here is Toyota. They trade elephant tusks for them, or lizard skins, or tiger skins." He waited, "or anything endangered. I mean dead or alive." A dark thought began to take shape, moving slowly from behind me along the brightly lighted streets. Bill caught it also and looked to cheer me. "Or sometimes Namibian sea-lion organs."

"Namibian what?"

"Hey, let me know if I'm sounding too much like yer wady-mekong, whatever that old word is."

"I told you, it means 'go with me.'"

"I know what it means, I just never get a chance to use it. Now you're my chance. Like *periphrasis*, a sin of evasion which politicians and telephone solicitors and doctors commit lasciviously day in day out. No one owns up to it simply because they can't get around the word either to spell it or understand it or even pronounce it. The doctors can, maybe. I said Namibian sea-lion organs, from Africa; they're supposed to prolong sexual potency. Big item in Japan." I was silent; I didn't particularly see why Japan needed it. I heard they were overcrowded. "You eat'em," he reassured me, "not wear 'em."

"I don't do either," I remarked loftily. "I'm old-fashioned." Two wizened four-foot tall women in pantaloons and straw hats turned in front of us and gazed stonily into our conversation, as if they hadn't been eavesdropping all the while to determine whether or not we were in the market for Namibian sea-lion organs.

"I know you're old-fashioned. You've been amazingly chaste for the ten minutes you've been in this country. Smart fellow. Bound to change." He nodded significantly to the women; it sent them scurrying with pinched looks on their way.

Our discourse had blossomed just to that point when we came abruptly upon the next item I knew I needed as much or even more than I needed the marine engine—a huge cardboard fold-out placard, three-quarters lifesize, of a kind that stood in the display windows of provincial hardware stores in Nebraska in 1952, depicting a modern kitchen dinette with family seated therein. There were other cardboard slices of domestic life, among them Pa driving the whole bundle of family to the A&W Root Beer in something that resembled a red toaster on wheels. Beautiful residual scenes of outdated American bliss, something we had forgotten and believed the rest of the world never knew.

Yet here they were reconstituted along with automobiles that resembled toasters and tucked away in the midst of Chinatown, possessing their own foreign out-of-place reality amid the unreality around us. Next to the cardboard scenes, a heaping pile of shiny Sloane valves for toilets. Why were these unlikely *membra disjecta* reminders of my far away country? I looked off in order to sort it out though I knew I couldn't. Across the street the pink gingerbread rooftop of a temple poked above the stone wall guarding it.

"They sure know how to sell you stuff," Bill remarked airily, eyeing me as we sauntered. "I notice that along with toilet and engine parts you're also showing an interest in the broiled octopus on sticks." We were in fact starting to enter the avenue of street food, and yes I'd been checking out the barbecues. The area was overhung by dense bluish smoke that stung the eye—was it burning pig fat, like they smeared on parasols to water-proof them? "This is a daring if not dire inclination of yours. Why do you think this area is adjacent to the wholesale plumbing parts?"

"I haven't the faintest," I grumbled, "I'm a chronically fatigued and hungry tourist not a philosopher or medic." I looked back at the octopus. "Probably something to do with ants and unclean fingers."

"You can try one if you want," he cautioned cheerily, "but ten to one you'll end up with some clever bacteria, not ants, and be obliged to take a turn at the British Nursing Home on Convent Road, where a great many pretty English-speaking nurses will remark upon the complexion of your stool. Then consequent to your urging upon them a consider-able remuneration in return for your life, they'll send off to London for a pill, while you remain consecrated to your toilet."

The food vendors had set up their charcoal grills belching blue smoke, smackdab in the middle of the sidewalk so you had to edge along through the billowing stench. Ancient, unwashed fingers tumbled animal and fish parts around on the grill.

"Don't get your hopes up," he cautioned again. "Actually none of the nurses speak English."

"Why bring us to Stinkville then?" I gagged. I took out my wild west bandanna and folded it in front of my nose.

"To show you it's no worse," Bill maneuvered through the stench, "and no better, than where we et. Or almost et."

"I ate street food in India," I muttered defiantly, "and didn't get sick."

Bill raised a sympathetic finger. "Probably a different kind of shit they wipe their hands on before they prepare it. Anyhow, seafood is seafood. Take care."

"That's not in the guidebook," I grumbled somewhat darkly. "That seafood is seafood, take care."

"What's a book?" Bill stopped and turned to me with vehement seriousness for the first time since we'd met. My jaw dropped beneath the bandanna, and I inhaled a good bit of pig fumes and other odors. "This is a book, a real-book," he indicated the pile of Sloane valves blinking at us under the street lights and the greasy cooking grates nudging each other to crowd alongside us. "Translating itself each minute into the next thing. All your so-called books are just amateur distillations of this, pickled in this or that middle class opinion about people's noses and the dirty washrooms, with a certain silly extrapolated diction compressing two hundred years into forty-seven seconds or whatever it takes to read a paragraph. You read it; you forget it, because it just repeats your own idiom anyway." He paused.

"What of it?" I mumbled furtively.

"This is the real-book," he pointed at the grills heaped with smoking parts of creatures, "because it writes itself, prints itself, binds itself, then dissolves and throws itself away before it forgets itself like a book-book does." He stopped and contemplated steadily the traces of my open mouth working behind the bandanna. "Have you ever thought about how much you dislike—and distrust—characters in a book. Have you thought about it really?"

"They're just...after all," I stammered, taking down my protection and pointing back at the pile of Sloane valves.

"They're just what?" He waited for me to continue. A wave of blue smoke from the octopus pit stung my eyes. "They're just repulsive," he continued, as if that were agreed upon by both of us, "and we're glad to let them forget themselves. You know why?"

"I don't think I do." I wiped my sooty face.

"Because they sit, stand, talk, doing only what the author allows them to, only that." I stood waiting for myself to say something or to act, like a real not a fictional person. "Tell me, how intelligent is that, really?" Not very, I thought to myself, if I had to answer truthfully, but how could I tell anyone that? Especially since any one who read books was always polite company who didn't want to hear it.

"You can't treat your reader—that's all the rest of us—with contempt." I fished it up from somewhere, probably because I'd heard it so often. "It's not very ingratiating."

"Why not? Is life ingratiating? What does the reader expect, some sort of safe territory to spraddle his ass on? The whole book game is an industry of indirect contempt and distillation, call it humiliation of the true book." He swept the alley with a glance. "The book, the written word doesn't really care about this." He indicated the alley. "It holds everything, the book does, you, me, this stinking alley, perfectly still and snapshots it, so that some alienated fools driving around in Oldsmobiles or Subarus somewhere safe can feel comfortable that they know and understand all about me, you, the octopus here, the child-labor question, pickled by the know-it-all author in some comfortable detail that will uphold our politically righteous values. It makes the whole concept, and the industry of literature seem frivolous." He desisted. "Did I say flatulent? Sorry prof. I know that you're a prof."

"Not really," I answered, "not a prof... in good sooth." Even then something inside of me had started to change at the instant of my wise-crack. No I wasn't a prof, not in sooth, and yet I still was. And I couldn't be sure if either being one or not being one was any good. He seemed placated and resumed his discourse after a while.

"I'll send you to a sweatshop where children make jewelry boxes out of crushed eggshells, pieced together." I looked at him. "Piece by piece. Small work for small eyes, I guess. Go ahead and take a snapshot of it; all the animals, the people, the toilet valves, the eggshells stay absolutely still, so that we can feel comfortable looking at them. That's a book.

They like to read'em in the States. And no matter how well defined and polished they are, they haven't a goddam thing to say. There's been child slavery over here for centuries, probably ever since the place fired up," he indicated the street behind us. "It's part of the place; it's wrong; it's part of the place."

"There is no shit," I replied, "man will not do."

"Or eat," he eyed me sharply, "if he's a politician. When the time is ripe."

I should have known already I was in deeper than I'd bargained for. But after all I'd raised myself on books. And they don't tell the truth, do they?

*   *   *

"Incidentally I thought we were here about the elephants," I piped up out of nowhere. He gave me a startled look. "To help the elephants. You recall?"

"You did? Well dang me, you'll get your elephants." He was simmering down, but almost bitterly. "Something grandiose to feel magnanimous about, those big jobs getting bumped off." He glanced at me like I was a bit of a poseur, so convincingly that momentarily I felt I was.

All along he'd been taking care to march us safely out of the food sector, and now we'd arrived at the extensive walls of a giant wat, the temple precinct that housed a complex of buildings ornate in speckled blue and gold. Without saying anything I tried the gate. It was locked. "I suppose you find that revolting. Of course it's revolting," he continued, then paused. Gripping my shoulder in a hand so iron that it startled me. "Right here you've got another of those value-institutions, been around for ever, significantly locked up. And now I've sermoned your head off unto apoplexy, as if I were the professor not you. Here endeth."

"Yes, why don't you shut up," I replied ingratiatingly.

We followed along the high impenetrable walls of the wat. You could see tall towers and the immense stupa or dome poking above them, gigantic vegetable shapes shimmering like hometown chorus girls in bright sequins and broken pieces of English colonial blue and white crockery, glimmering untouchably behind the walls, a china shop Coney Island all locked up and the visitors could go to hell. The tops of the walls were thickly strewn with jagged glass and razor wire.

"Holy cow, these religious people are unmerciful," I reflected aloud, trying another gate. It didn't budge.

"Oh you get used to it, work around it somehow." Suddenly he'd returned to his sanguine self.

"I thought the Orient was supposed to be accommodating."

He gave me a charitable look. "You're so crabby it's a sign you must still be hungry. No wonder, you didn't touch dinner. In good sooth," he continued even more charitably, "you look about ready for the noodle shop. Incidentally, they tell us not to say Orient any more. Sounds imperialist. We say Eastern, or Asian."

"It does? We do?"

"We do. Lays more flat that way. But it doesn't sound as good as Orient, does it? Come on, I know a relatively safe establishment for noodles and seafood. I called them earlier while we were at the hotel and they're expecting us. Relatively safe, for the Orient."

"Sounds imperialist," I remarked lamely, traipsing after him. "I enjoyed your lecture on books though, I really did. If you think about it…"

"If I think about it…"

"If you think about it, everything you said about what books do could also be used as an argument in their behalf."

He pondered. "Yep, I imagine so."

"And what you said about child slavery…" I didn't finish.

"Let's get going. You won't find this establishment dull. Like a locked up temple."

*   *   *

We turned aside and two steps up into a smoking, greasy room with plastic-covered tables that apparently had not been cleared the latter part of this century. Nor had the sawdust floor, judging from the litter of paper and food on it. Red lanterns dangled once again precariously over the heads of the noodles-and-seafood eaters, roasting them in a harsh lurid light, like an Oriental version of Van Gogh's Potato Eaters. At gutter level by the entrance, an expired grandfather rat, decently composed, was posted as quiet sentinel unnoticed and unadmired by all save me.

The toothy old proprietor seemed intent upon ignoring us, but after a short while a young woman with strong northern features, as much Chinese or Laotian as Thai, came to our table and cleared it meticulously, murmuring some sort of apology to us. Bill spoke to her in Thai, indicating yours truly, the prof. She bowed, smiling. Her eye caught mine with sudden and unusual pride. It silenced me. I saw how remarkably beautiful she was.

"Doc, meet Alice." Bill noted my breathing hiatus and he grinned. I unbent my head some and bowed. For an instant I felt I was near not to the Orient, wherever that place was, but to some ground closer to home. Her features seemed almost Native American, no Tibetan. I don't know. In an instant she vanished, leaving behind two glasses of dangerously contaminated water. I looked at mine.

"I asked her to keep the bacterial count low on yours," Bill remarked. "I'm referring to the water. I'm not commenting on your eye noticing her eye noticing yours. And so forth. I can't vouch for that."

"And so you're not," I glanced in her direction in spite of myself, "vouching. Just grouching."

In a short while she returned, this time with the noodles, but appearing ever more so between woman and child and as if she'd passed through adolescence in the interim of her absence. Then she vanished again.

"We'll see," my mentor observed, "what comes of this intrigue in the mysterious Orient," he clacked his chopsticks together dexterously and cackled in accompaniment, "as no doubt you'll keep calling it."

"Nothing will come of it. That's why it's called the mysterious Orient." I tried to concentrate on a particularly troublesome batch of noodles. Second round of the evening. Looking down beneath them I spied what I thought might be a fish eye looking up at me.

"That's octopus," Bill said encouragingly, pointing a stick. I didn't see why it had to be.

"Cooked?" I queried. "Nothing will come of it," I insisted again, staring back at the octopus. "Nothing ever does in the mysterious, disappointing countries I've visited. What is there to come of it?"

What indeed. The meal progressed without incident. And nothing did come of it, or should I add nothing good. Just as we were finishing the last noodle, I felt a rush of warm stale air beside me, and the sharp, thin flavor of a body from a distant land. An old villager in ragged billowy pants and a wide-rimmed peasant's stood beside the table. He bowed and in the same instant placed a bundle wrapped in dirty rag on the table in front of me and was gone.

"I eyed it apprehensively. "What's this? The bill, or is he depositing garbage?" I picked at the heavy sodden bundle. My curiosity got the better of me, and using a paper napkin as a bacteria screen gingerly I started to unwrap it.

The ugly snout of a black automatic appeared. Bill got up.

"Where are you going?" I quavered.

"Pay the bill," he burped faintly, searching for his toothpick. "Excuse me."

"Holy Jesus what am I to do with this?" I indicated our gift. The noodler next table over coughed a couple of noodles onto his sleeve. No great loss.

"It's one of those nights," Bill observed absently, looking first at the recuperating noodler then around for something to pick his teeth with, having misplaced his ivory. The discourse on books seemed to have dissolved all enmity and passion in him. "For starters you might wrap it up again, and when you get outside into a dark spot use your red Oshkosh, USA, bandanna to wipe it clean of prints if any are on it, including your own." I nodded. "You like salted shark?" he inquired politely. I shook my head in vigorous negation. "Good, then I'll get some, and we'll wrap our two gifts in a bundle together, and you'll not feel badly on the way back in the river taxi if the whole smelly package slips overboard." He paused. "Unless you want to keep the fish." I shook my head. "Salt shark's not bad." I shook again. "Hey, maybe this is a good sign. You seem to get all sorts of responses over here, prof. In the Orient."

"Do I?" I quavered uncertainly. He paid the bill, and carrying our parcel calmly under his arm, together we left.

*   *   *

It was late, and the benches of the river taxi carried only sprinklings of passengers huddled in small groups. I looked up and saw the night slowly filling with a million stars, and beyond, far beyond, millions of trillions more if you wanted to go there. The night wasn't so sinister after all, just passionless and unregarding of human fantasies and sufferings. The buoyant river swelled up and down like a sturdy child quietly breathing in its crib. We could just make out the mahogany pencils of the long-tails gliding past us at trolling speed nearby in the darkness. Next instant one of them would leap out of its jungle in a frenzy of acceleration, one bright eye staring, reddening for a moment, then fading to oblivion. Against the purple skyline their gigantic rooster-tails of vapor and spray drifted long after they had passed, rising to the level of what I knew were orange temple rooftops on the horizon of the far shore. I sat clutching my smelly parcel, wondering what it was that I was obliged to let go, why I had been chosen to let it go so soon upon arriving. Bill gave me a nod. I let it plop into the water.

We disembarked at the Oriental Hotel, the taxi-stop that served my sector of town, I mean the Eastern Hotel, the Asian Hotel, whichever has the proper ring to it, you decide. We stepped back into the western world, beginning at $240 a night. Dragon ladies extra. Marble parquetry and brilliantly lighted crystal chandeliers scraped at my eyes, after the half-light of Chinatown, and looking down at the knees of my once-white trousers I saw how seedy and disreputable I'd already become. Bill snorted at a tiny anxious bellhop who gave ground reluctantly. A few young, high-grade prostitutes wearing evening gowns that actually were fitted to them rather than borrowed from a roommate or street vendor, looked at us with every sign of undisguised negativity and then turned away. After all, they'd been introduced into the sweet life with real westerners, not strange packrats like ourselves.

Introduced into the sweet life. There was no sweet life. Only an anxious one. I mean earnest one. Maybe they're the same. Some years ago a chance meeting had shown me as much. It was responsible ultimately for sending me… here.

Sharp klippety-klop—woman's heels on the cement path winding through the park. A figure steps into the fluorescent glare, print blouse with roses faded into it and a short white skirt made even paler by the unnatural light. Bordering the path, huge concrete tubs hold dark leafy shrubs sharply defined under the slender lamp mounted at the center of each tub. I wait. Moths zip all around her then disappear into the dark only to return on the night cricket's song.

"Gotta clean off this here clog. Must have stepped in it." She hikes a bare leg onto the rim of the nearest tub. Looks up at me apologetically. "Gotta clean off. Stepped in…something."

A deep blue tint has spread along the horizon, as if dripping from a painter's brush, and all around the city's rim far below pairs of tiny Christmas tree lights drift along the parkways dotting the empty notebook of night.

Dark hair, early thirties, plain features, gray eyes under the fluorescent glare. Tearing a leaf from a tub she begins to look things over. Bare all the way up. The clog she's hoisted on to the tub sports ruffs of colored gauze mounted on its backstraps recalling a bridal figurine stripped off a glitzy wedding cake or a winged messenger from a 1960's sitcom. She gazes steadily at me. I step back to allow the breeze.

"Most likely you thought I stepped outta a fairytale book or somewhere, not outta some dogdo."

Not exactly, I say to myself staring at the stretch of leg extended between us. If so, I'd like to see the rest of the fairytale.

"But we're in Pittsburgh, ain't we," she soliloquizes rather openly and looks off, perhaps to give me more time to check things out. Down below, a few dark barges are balancing on the shiny metallic surface of where three silver rivers join. Our park seems rotary powered by the white moths.

"I think it's 'aren't we,'" I say after a while, "not 'ain't we.' Lord knows why. And I've got to get back," I nod uphill, "to the Conference Center. I'm searching for a job, teaching, editing. I'll do anything."

She gives me a deep look. "So ain't I" she states flatly, "lookin'." Behind our contradictory voices the park lies starched and silent under its lights.

"We say 'so aren't I' or simply 'so am I'" if we wish to employ that idiom," I observe hollowly. Underneath she seems so civilized in a curious way, beyond what currently passes for civilization.

"Anita," a voice roars ungrammatically from way up in the lobby of the Conference Center. We stare at each other. "What about two hundred bucks?" The voice announces.

"I'm a writer," I volunteer suddenly. Hell who isn't, or ain't? I think. And so what?

"So aren't I not," she enunciates. "You may perceive."

Fact is I'd just delivered a paper 'Hawthorne and the Recumbent Female Adolescent Nude,' which was not so good as that sounds, to a recumbent afterdinner audience. And I tell her so because every writer loves to do that. Also because I'm beginning to suspect there may not be a twiddle of difference between us.

She shakes her head. "What a world. I hope they catch that Hawthorne guy. Molester. Any chance of it?"

"Very slim," I respond gloomily.

"Anita," the voice resonates from the marble lobby. "I can go two-fifty."

"Well don't get a hard on over it," she bellows back. "I'm having a conversation." She turns back to me, confidentially. "Anita's my name."

"So I imagined. That's not a train schedule he's taking about, is it?"

She shakes her head and smiles at me. "For two-fifty I shouldn't let him take me out for coffee." She lowers her leg from the rim of the tub. Together we look at the moths zigzagging into the light then retracing a spiral way out. "But of course I don't have much free will in this case."

I should have seen the old academic ploy, but I just didn't expect it from… "You don't have no free will?" I explode suddenly impassioned and ungrammatical. I'm falling into the trap, but I can't hold back. "You always have free will, as long as you will yourself to be free."

She squints at me with some care, meanwhile removing her leg completely and all that went with it from the rim of the tub. I guess I was trapped. "If you're willing to hear what I've got to say on this particuliar subject, or any other, free for nothin' naturally." She looks at me solemnly. "I've already got two-fifty in the bucket," she reassures me.

I swallow once and nod. I'm trying to recall how they would reply in one of those old-fashioned dialogues where they sit around dressed up in sheets and headwreaths, sipping watered down wine and gazing at the nether parts of girl flute players and boys.

"I can't do your answers for you," she remarks a bit scrapingly. "Your questions neither. And if you think this is hard, wait till you get out into the real world. You've got to get out and run a test on these guys, to see if they're real. Now I'll ask again do you want to try," she almost whispers softly, "then I gotta go."

I nod yes. Because of our different professions naturally we had to go separate ways. But that was not the end of it.

Bill had been eyeing me a bit suspiciously. I'd been out of bounds for a considerable period, but still he was one heck of a mind reader. "Bet you wish you had your Volvo engine now, to trade in on one of these beautiful girls," he remarked drily, with a sweeping gesture to the gallery.

"Toyota," I corrected. "No, not one of those I don't." I didn't add that I already had a girl, up there in my mind I did, but he remarked my hesitation.

He smiled to himself. "Even a Volvo would cut a better bargain than the package of salt whatnot we lost overboard." I think he made the empty remark in order to comfort me.

"Indeed," I lamented somewhat lazily, exhausted by the soiree, and relaxed and at ease now that I'd let my thoughts wander elsewhere then gradually find their way home. "What can you buy nowadays with a piece of salted shark and a Czech…protuberance ?"

"Beretta," he corrected, "It was a police issue Beretta."

I stood on the marble floor under the glaring lights, in sudden disarray. "You couldn't have seen the entire…you knew it when you brought me there."

"No I didn't." He looked off, then around us. "Not exactly. Well, I might have inkled that something like that could happen."

"And you also set me up with what's-her-name."

"Alice. You know perfectly well her name, even if you're a daydreamer. She asked me if we could trust you. Of course we could. Absolutely, I vouched."

"Absolutely?" I barked uneasily. "Why?" But beneath all the noise I was making, for the first time since my arrival I felt homesick, terribly homesick.

"Because from all the signs, prof…" He didn't finish. We walked to the door. On the way he stuck his tongue out at a pair of bored, lackadaisical hookers who were hovering nearby uncertain whether to give us thumbs down or not. They moved off, astounded, ashamed. But the last one turned in parting, as if in sudden reconsideration, and caught me watching her rear end. I guess it must have been my daydream that set me on. I looked up into her eyes with an inadvertent longing that was beyond me, I don't know how it arose, and she recoiled then responded toward me all in one instant. Maybe it wasn't me, maybe she was responding to any individual soul stranded in her bizarre country.

"Why? Why could you trust me?" I had to halt in order to fumble out the question.

No reply. Bill and I started wandering again down vendors' lane, wonderfully deserted now. The night was soft and calm, as if it might heal the scar left by our disruptive plunge into Chinatown. In the distance an occasional long-tail. "From all signs, prof," he resumed quietly. I waited, anxious for a sign of what was going to happen to me. But of course there was no bottom, so it turned out, to his irony. "From all signs, prof you're going to be an immense success over here."

3

Sure as shooting I got sick from the shrimp dinner, or the noodles, take your pick, and for a while I lay in bed convinced my entrails would feel better if they dropped out entirely not just part way.

It was right after my visit, next morning, to the eggshell box factory where they manufactured small round jewelry boxes, all speckled with gray and white pounded eggshells, where you might store your pills or false teeth. I was allowed into one room only, bright and clean where none of the teenage girls appeared to be doing any work, except smiling for visitors, if that's work. They sat in white-scrubbed smocks before a long empty table, in a long empty room, hands folded, staring straight ahead emptily, a scene startlingly reminiscent of a Dickensian orphanage. Well, they were awaiting more eggshells, one of them told me. It took a long while, I was informed, to do even a single one of those little sets of light, nesting, eggshell-covered boxes. I suspected frankly they were manufactured elsewhere, under darker conditions, and that the present workshop was merely a front, not worth wasting eggshell supplies upon.

I'd heard stories before arriving in Bangkok about the sweatshop industries—but once there, no one seemed to know anything about that strange rumor, or about the glass factories, or the shirt makers, the confectioners, the paper cup makers and tinfoil manufacturers that paid the workers pennies for piecework, then, locking the doors on them from outside, took back most of the pennies for room and board.

Anyway, my sickness came between me and this glittering industrial world made of eggshell. To be sure I spent moments trying to balance all our shenanigans of the first night, but I was too clouded to make any headway. I retreated into my sickness. I was living in a tube stuffed at one end with tissue paper; I was insulated from hearing anything properly, even the long-tails. I could hear them grumble somewhere in the distance, then they lifted off without me. I watched from my window the cross-river ferry drift and flounder back and forth, an absurd miniature 1920's tugboat, converted to a passenger vessel through the ministries of blue and white paint liberally applied, a Popeye anchor on deck and what appeared to be recycled wooden window-boxes with lattice work for seats. Suddenly I recalled the tugboat on the Chicago lakefront whose maneuvers I'd watched in the company of my young tutor. The passengers wandered aimlessly and dangerously upon deck, soiling their pants by sitting on coils of tarred hempen rope. The whole operation seemed pointlessly funny, held at arm's length by my stuffed cognition. Then suddenly I became aware that it was pathetic, somehow, and potentially deadly if one of those tubs capsized. I crawled to the toilet, crawled back and sank down on my bed, then back to the toilet.

Finally, after eight days the pills were flown down, as Bill foretold, from London, and several conferences were held at the British Nursing Home clinic, attended by every pretty nurse in the eastern hemisphere, concerning the peculiar contents of the stool that I delivered there in person and on the spot, explosively in a tiny thin-walled cubicle situated at plumb center of the waiting room. Gradually I began to mend, and become whole again.

It was still and always Christmas morning, in small corners of the city. Looking down from above I could spot on the patio of a modest residence or on the rooftop garden of a hotel, miniature Buddhist spirit-houses, tenderly gaudy and decked out with tinkling wind chimes, red threads and recycled Christmas tree lights still blinking from the night's vigil. The morning air hung hazy and polluted, polished white and shimmering by fluorocarbons. The major intersections were filling with tiers upon tiers of yellow Toyota taxis, airconditioned and expensive, going nowhere, and propane-powered three-wheel autorickshaws, tuk-tuks, each sporting mag wheels, custom pinstriping and a gaudily fringed old-fashioned canopy that could be raised or lowered under rain or shine. Like their grown cousins, the long-tails, these minimonsters could whiz under their old-fashioned canopies like a cricket down an empty side street, radio booming, nearly airborne. From my window high up I could see them. Racing away. Racing away.

Emerging from my sickness I found I could relax once more at night, and things began to regroup themselves as if preparing to make sense— not sense in a seriously pragmatic way, but the kind of whimsical sense that informs a dream through and through and upon our waking leaves only its taste behind. And I had some dreaming to catch up with.

"You're being awfully silent," she remarks amiably, determined to be no longer a mere adjunct to my silence. "Plotting the insides of a novel?"

But I was just speaking with Anita's voice inside my head—some sort of internal support system—as too often I did, and as she warned me not to. In reality she was sitting quietly and seriously amid the torn

leather of her bucket seat, her short black evening dress soaked with the rainwater dropping steadily on her white thighs, and nary a word of complaint.

We followed the twisting boulevard, soaked and slippery, downward into the city. The windshield leaked where it joined the roof and the side windows leaked on all sides and so forth in all the corners of my old crate, more like a World War I airplane than a car.

Now and then she fought off the defective shoulder harness which threatened to coil itself around her neck each time we stopped for a light. Suddenly she grappled it with both hands, as if it were a boa constrictor, and started to gnaw on it with her two great front teeth.

"What the hell is this?" she demands, "Some new form of bondage?"

I look over at her, startled. She smiles back amiably, knowing she'd knocked at the door of my daydreaming "I was just making up a line for you in my head," I confess. "I suppose that's a kind of bondage. I had you say something silly like 'Awfully quiet. Plotting a new novel?' Maybe that's bondage."

Anita sends me a fishy look and pommels my arm so it hurt. "I thought you were awfully quiet. Plotting a new novel?" Then a moment later she rescinds. "You're forgiven. Because I have a life inside me too." She pauses, as if bringing her secret life up on the screen. "Even if you're slippery," she contemplates, "like this street. Speaking of which. I knew an artist once. Had him as a boyfriend. Artists are slippery." She pauses in reverie, as the sitcom unrolls inside of her. The windshield wiper clacks.

I look as much like chopped liver as I can, sitting bolt upright in my seat. "What the hell do I look like...?"

"Now why are you making me do this comedy patter?" Anita intones. "Men. What hath God rot."

"God what?"

"God rot," she intones again, as if she'd enunciated properly.

"God rot? Is that a kind of hoof and mouth disease? God rot? What corncrib did you bail out from? Oh that's right, Pennsylvania. Where we're presently sliding down the road."

"Oh come now," Anita lets go of the seatbelt and grabs my arm with both hands, "let's exhibit some hands-on tolerance of our cultural diversities." She lets it sink in. Then somewhat proudly, "Do you like that one?"

"What one?" I reply, actively feigning ignorance, at the same time endeavoring to hold our swaying hulk to the white line.

"God rawt, rawt, raww-t" she trumpets in my ear so that the car swerves. "There. We're no longer culturally diverse. Nor vocationally."

I watch the road, looking straight ahead. Something white moves in the dark beside me in the passenger's tunnel, a leg possibly. "You could always be a dreamer," she says, shifting her leg. "That crosses the boundaries."

"Pooh," I goad, "Pooh. Women have no use for dreamers." Suddenly it flashes before me that before night was out I might lose her.

"Pooh?" Anita queries, "I won't yet comment on the rest of your stupid statement. But I do understand Pooh?"

"They have no use for dreamers," I state, more weakly.

"And most men," she meditates, "believe me." She looks down at her damp dress. "I'm a mess for this date. I think I'll just cancel, and argue with you. Continue educating the world from the bottom up..." she trails off, brooding.

I consider what I'd said, in the light of her soaked dress and all. "I'm sorry. I guess I should have opposed dreamers to non-dreamers."

"And not women to men, men to women. Kind of a criminal oversight, considering how much they are opposed from the beginning."

I think it over for a while. "I'm a child, most of the time, Anita, trying to save scraps of my old truths, unless I'm talking with you."

Anita smiles; something for an instant glows in the dark down by her legs. "I'd like that," she breathes, after a while.

"Like what?"

"I'd like it if you remained a child, and saved bits of truth like insects flattened helter-skelter in a schoolbook or seashells jumbled into a box. However you'd have to become a child of the world, if you were to be my child. You know the phrase 'a man of the world.' Well, you could never manage that, believe me. But a child of the world. Here's my little child of the world—it's got some bite to it." She sucks her tooth, then turns to me.

"Well," I concede somewhat put off, "tell me how to start being …and I'll start today."

"You're starting," she almost yodels in my ear, "this is a start," turning in her seat so that her whiteness rises toward me in the dark. The car swerves.

"It is?" I ask cautiously.

"It is,' Anita reassures me. "The first step is wonder—quite different from your daydreaming, you know, what you've been doing for the last scary five miles down this waterway. Well maybe we shouldn't pick a dreamer, we should pick a wonderer. And that's what you're doing right now—even in the dark, you're positively a picture of wonder," she laughs. "Hey, check my hick accent, will you, *pitcher* of wonder." She hesitates. "Pour me a little out of your pitcher of wonder," she raises a half-cupped hand to her mouth, "so I can wonder too."

We skittered down the rainfilled street to the clack of both wipers.

∗   ∗   ∗

"Hey man if you wanna celebrate being alive again," Bill peered intently at my inward doubt that I should see any reason to, "we can saddle up and go down to Chinatown. I can get us some real deals on bacteria—just a joke, just a joke." I declined to find the humor in it. We set off; it was a nice day, chilly, below 90, and maybe he did want to celebrate. I carried a little bottle filled with fizz water to settle the stomach. "Glad to see that," he commended. "Get you suited up for our visit to Khao Yai National Park. There's been elephant poaching going on while you were on vacation. You recall you demanded something or other about elephants. As I told you, it's not a perfect world, and it hasn't got any more perfect while you were recumbent."

When we reached Ratchawong, Bill let me wait outside, a striking touch of delicacy, while he ducked into what I imagined was the restaurant we ate in that first night. By daylight not much of the area looked familiar to me. In a few minutes he reappeared.

Alice was with him.

"I owe, we owe," she stammered "Many apologies. For the restaurant that night."

You've got that damn straight, I remarked to myself. Between most probably poisoning me and letting me stroll around with a police weapon tucked under my arm, for which I'd likely spend my short life in prison.

"Uncle didn't know. Because you're a friend of Bill, he thought…" Her voice trailed off into a frown around her eyes. "He was just saying welcome."

With a police issue weapon, I continued to myself. "What welcome was that?" I asked aloud.

She looked more than a shade hopeless. A motor scooter dodged dangerously close-by, sneering at our silence.

"He was saying…" She stopped.

Yes, go on. I mouthed the words to myself. "I could use an explanation," I murmured aloud, though perhaps inaudibly. What were he and the company of his corn-popper saying? Somehow I bet I'd never get a clear explanation.

She chose to ignore the doubtful frown spreading plainly over my face. I didn't like that. Rather, I didn't like myself for expecting more from her. But hell, how I missed the old days of dialogue, when people could talk, really talk. I couldn't live like this. I couldn't.

I confess I don't like living in a world that refuses to answer the questions that trouble me, or doesn't even try to answer them. Something haughty and condescending—I mean dead—about it. Though why the devil should it bother to answer them? They're only my questions.

Alice bobbed a few times, a hurt expression spreading downward from the top of her forehead. Before I could open my mouth she had vanished.

"I don't like a lack of explanation, or a good try at it," I announced to Bill, since he was the only audience I had at hand. Bill evidenced all the surprise in the world that I still knew how to speak. "Something dead-end about it."

He indicated that we should continue our stroll. "You got the last words right, OK. Dead end. Describes a lot around here."

For a moment I couldn't tell whether he was joking or warning me.

Suddenly I wanted to tell her directly and frankly about a great many things—like the gun she'd handed off to me, and about this street carnival where we seemed to be living in flagrant disregard of common sense, and why I no longer could use the word *Oriental,* and the doll-girls back at the Oriental, and why I was starting to like her so much for no reason. But...

"I knew you wanted to see her, so I brought you direct. Direct," he nudged me for emphasis.

"I'm puzzled," I heard myself say not unexpectedly. I looked back at the street hubbub taking place behind us but it seemed to have fallen quiet, gone mute. Figures moved about as if they were on old black and white celluloid, rummaging among their great, silent piles of wares. I turned back to the two of us standing alone in their midst. "I'm sorry," I said, unable to come up with anything better than that, "I guess."

"Alice swears you didn't get the bug from her—from here, I mean," Bill piped up oafishly. Then from behind his shoulder as if by magic her face reappeared anxiously. I was thrown off entirely by the sudden apparition. Something in it prevented me from speaking my mind, or rather, started to change what my mind had to speak. I said nothing. In the bleak interim they exchanged a few words in Thai. Possibly, I imagined, myself as main topic.

"This is hopeless," I interrupted suddenly, looking at her. "Don't you think I see... ?" I looked back at the street carnival, then turned to her. "You don't understand a word of what I say anyway." She stepped forward in a posture of resigned attendance. No doubt there was a considerable something in my face and voice that transcended the barrier of language, but it still didn't keep me from being anything but a clown. I made a grandiose exasperated sweep of the arm. "But still you don't have the right to play dime-store tricks on a *farang* just because you're standing on your own home turf." My grandiose speech was undercut by the shrill cries of a shopkeeper pushing an itinerant noodle-vendor off the sidewalk and into the path of a swerving autorickshaw. "If you seriously consider this to be anything like a home turf," I mumbled to myself drawing a breath, sorely offended.

"Why do you stay then?" Alice asked in perfect English. She looked at me calmly, commiseratingly. Something about her response kept me from falling overboard but also from answering. At that moment I perceived she was in fact very beautiful, indescribably so, but only for an instant, then the worry lines flooded back.

"I don't know why I stay. I'm sorry I came." My words sounded more sincere this time but just as hollow. "No, that was mean of me; I apologize."

"I do not want you to go," Alice stated simply. "I want you to stay. And keep from being hurt."

Meanwhile Bill was dancing around our spot in the alleyway blocking traffic, with his hands gyrating at ear level and trying to keep from exploding. He exhibited every semblance of a frustrated film director trying to manage two novice actors from disparate cultures while endeavoring to keep the sidewalk clear. We both stared at him until he stopped.

Alice indicated the street uproar which seemed to have subsided once again in order to give place to us. "I know this is bad to you. And I know why you stay then."

"She says she's sorry too," Bill interpreted idiotically, dancing some more. We ignored him, and he muttered something apologetic to himself. Another silence prevailed. Whatever should be said next, was no doubt too difficult to say. "And she knows why you stay, then," Bill piped up. We didn't answer him.

"You do know? Then answer me this. Why are we given," I exclaimed vehemently, "why are we given each so small a segment of life you, me, both of you, all of our segments so different."

This time there was a considerable pause. In response to my tangential inquiry Alice smiled faintly, made a bow and took her formal leave, as if that were a satisfactory response since no one knew how to continue anyway. Bill smiled sideways at me like it was finally clear I was the one who was mad, crazy and idiotic, not he.

"Well I guess that means we don't know the answer to your question," he observed, watching Alice's sternside retreat and sucking on the ivory toothpick, which he had reclaimed from some contraband market and in secrecy had been consulting the while. "Can you let us have a hint? Or are you always so obscure?" He removed the ivory from his mouth and examined it. Probably I had gone mad, for certain. And yes I was always so obscure.

"I just had to know," I maintained stubbornly, "why we're so different…never mind."

"Don't apologize to me." Gently he took the knapsack out of my hand and slung it over his shoulder and we started off again. "Strictly speaking, on certain days—and this is certainly a certain day—I agree with you. We're all so different." We walked toward the end of the block. I couldn't field a reply to his comment. I'd been thinking anyway about her last words, *I know why you stay then.* She did? She probably did, already. And I wasn't sure. And that's where I stood at the moment.

* * *

We found ourselves before the Wat where the locked gate and razor wire had denied us entrance the first time. Bill had further business to conduct elsewhere, he claimed. I thought maybe back at the little noodle house. I could meet him later in an area he referred to delicately as fishgut row, the wholesale fish market. I knew where to go; we'd availed ourselves of their gourmandize earlier.

The temple grounds, I confirmed this time, were unrepentantly Coney Island, glittering, soaring, flashing, tinkling, exhilarating. Yet to one side of this carnival, an L-shaped viharn, a cloister within whose shaded corridor sat thirty-two identical Lord Buddhas, clad in gold, waiting for me to kneel and join my hands and mind their silence. One golden hand of each statue, the left one, rested palm upward on a folded ankle, the other draped itself easily over the right knee, calling on Earth to witness. I sat back and rested, wondering how the call worked, exactly. As the moments drew longer, I found myself drifting down into my own thoughts.

Those thirty-two benignly seated figures, were they identical or not? Was Alice's remark about me just polite or something more? The further I scrutinized each lip, each eyebrow, the more surely I detected the faintest individuality among them. I couldn't say whether they'd been cast out of the same mould or not. Maybe I was still queasy from the bug. But short of devising some measuring instrument—I couldn't do it by eye—how embarrassing the West was, I thought, measuring, always measuring—I couldn't come up with a way of determining the quotient of individuality each possessed. I wondered how the Asian, hell the Oriental viewed Western faces. Was it all a bewildering variety, or just a monotony of too obvious differences?

It made me angry, peaceful, no angry, that in the presence of those seated golden figures it was a niggling matter whether I would ever be with her or she with me. Alice, I mean. Or something better, if something better still existed in the currently available world. Angry, I guess, it made me angry. Because what would it mean anyway if we were awarded that vanishing instant? Yet it wasn't niggling, and the seated images claimed it was, and disposed of it just like that.

I got up, shook myself, stretched out a cramped leg and rotated a shoulder. It was time to rejoin Bill. I turned back to the images. They waited, and didn't wait. "There's a line between us," I threatened aloud. "Stay on your side of it."

       *   *   *

The sun had dropped to where it starts to turn blood-red, declaring its nearby kinship to us. I set off. At the end of ten minutes I came upon the designated spot in fishmonger alley. I stopped, peering down the stands. Fifteen yards away Bill was in deep conversation with a wizened old man. Was it the old peasant who'd dropped the gun on the table? It might be. I couldn't say for sure. A better look at the stranger revealed his features to be Burmese, not Thai. Maybe he was Karen, according to photos I'd seen, a tribe from the Burma border. He was muttering to Bill using his right arm as a crank or roller to get the words out, more muttering, more cranking. That old Karen stranger with eyes squeezed nearly shut didn't abate for one instant but kept up the repetitive motion-phrases until I felt my mind was being tumbled on a lottery wheel as I tried to imagine what he was saying. I felt how cut off and excluded I was, a leftover number spinning on a lottery wheel, totally ignorant of my surroundings and ignorant of any language I could speak aloud to make my feelings heard.

Something behind both speakers caught my attention up short. The fishmongers, to show the freshness of their catch, had settled upon the practice of hacking the heads off the larger fish alive and suspending the heads with twine drawn through the pulsing gills. Very much an Eastern demonstration, I thought. I stood at a distance from the two men, helpless against their impenetrable dialogue, and I had a sudden crazed feeling that I had been transported to this country not to listen to human speech, which in any case I couldn't understand, but to the severed fish heads suspended on their nooses that were straining to tell me, if only I would listen—*if only I could hear them*—transfixing me with a bulging circular eye clinging in disbelief to the memory of its hacked off carcass... Small bubbles issued from the rhythmically pumping gills and from a mouth struck mute at the verge of its final outcry.

CHAPTER TWO

1

The bus ride to Pak Chong was interminable, but then I transferred to *songthaew*. I must expose the nature of this contraption hiding behind a term that designates, in Thai, "two rows of seats" facing each other, mounted on the platform of a Toyota pick-up truck with a tall birdcage body overarching it. This jury-rigged brainstorm was designed to transport a dozen and upward of tiny traveling citizens, rapidly, conveniently, agonizingly through hinterland and cities, but in actuality it is a species of mixmaster or osterizer, contrived to shake the visitor out of any false sense of security. I had to charter such an osterizer to take me the remainder of the distance to Khao Yai National Park, where Bill had asked me to meet him at the guest house. My driver hand picked me, detaching himself from a gang of loose trousered hoodlums who loitered about their gaudy vehicles deployed near the bus stop which was the most convenient place to sell dope. He was fourteen, no maybe seventeen, recently escaped I feared from a Hong Kong racecourse or a correctional facility.

"You want girl?" he howls cheerily, to set me at ease, as we drop with a grind into third, and we negotiate squealingly a hard, washboard, uphill corner. After all I was alone in the back bouncing around like a grape, and probably lonely.

"Hadn't much thought about it," I yell back, a partial lie, through the birdcage's trapdoor. Maybe he figured her extra sixty-five or seventy pounds would help to settle things down back there. Or that I would feel reassured if an international commodity were ready to hand. Picking up self-confidence now from its insane pilot, the truck screams toward the Park, front Bridgestones scrubbing and chattering like monkeys as the young daredevil, courting my reluctant approval, cranks her into the turns at full throttle. The suspension hammers the seat beneath me, and the birdcage sways and teeters and follows the best it can, with me in it. Everything lies quiet in the still brown heat enveloping us And still we fly on like a horrible intrusive crustacean or invading insect.

"Girld very good friend," he encourages cryptically, out of a temporary yet deep meditation, just as we reach seventy, conferring on the word a new plural form or perhaps an honorific intensive. I don't feel I can debate the topic adequately, given his already covert operations upon English morphology, and to boot I have my own reservations as to whether his proposition is always unconditionally true. So I keep silent in the back of the birdcage and hang on bravely. Earlier in the day I'd stopped off at Ayutthaya, the ancient capital of Thailand, a town entirely encircled by the Chao Phraya river and its rivulet cousins, upstream from Bangkok and renowned for its gangster community and rotten food. Testimony to the latter were the 'floating restaurants' on the Pa Sok section of the river, so called I imagine because of the condition in which they left the visitor's stomach (I did not try them). One of the wats originally boasted a sixteen-foot standing Buddha clad entirely in gold, unfortunately for him, which Burmese invaders, when they took over in the eighteenth century, chipped off and melted down leaving him in his skintight long johns. I discovered too late (happily) that I could have come upriver by boat, endlessly, from Bangkok. Pressing onward by bus we'd stopped also at Lop Buri, noted for its ugliness and hordes of tamarind tree monkeys growing fat on tourist handouts. The

Chinese street food was reputed to be delicious there, but I didn't dare sample it either.

Lurching further down the road (we were headed southeast now), the bus paused at SaraBuri, the shrine that houses Buddha's footprint, huge and identifiable through its 108 auspicious distinguishing marks, like an FBI printout, not a single one of which I was able to discern. Once again in the bus—I won't say a short distance, it seemed for ever.

But now the damp smells of jungle pour through my shattered window, and a green moisture seems to dissolve the wrinkled tightness of my face, forever the peering, simian-like tourist. The dampness doesn't smooth out wrinkles; it turns them inside of you. That's how the jungle ages you. With internal wrinkles. When you emerge into broad daylight of friends and acquaintances next morning, they gather round to look at you, and my god their intimate x-ray eyes see a withered prune. All along you have been growing aged in the dark silent underbrush that during the night conspires toward a decay beyond your control.

Then the hills. The tangled jungle already is changing, becoming drier, and as we climb more and more bright red flowers, flame-of-the-forest, appear when I look up and around me. Then we arrive at Pak Chong and I get out, queasy and uncertain, not at all prepared for what next I might endure, this torturous passage via another *songthaew*.

I can't forbear dilating once again upon what it is—a chopped and lowered Toyota pickup, mounting on its back two facing rows of church pews, and overarching all—an elaborate iron grillwork cage, constructed to restrain the bouncing passengers as loosely and uncomfortably as possible and to act as a funneling device, a grillwork butterfly net, for the assorted insects and small birds one might suck in at shoulder height above road level.

"You no want girld?" This time he turns his head all the way around, grinning at me through the dainty grillwork, now openly resuming his original inquiry and at the same time intuiting my unreasonable opposition to it, just as we enter a particularly vicious blind left-hander.

Looking past him, I observe the tachometer needle dancing beyond six thousand. I smile, shake my head, and indicate the road ahead, hoping my refusal might restore his attention to that bothersome detail. Instead it sets him to ruminating once again upon where he has failed.

"Boy? Giraffe?" He turns around for each of these, letting the truck have its own head. The latter suggestion embodies a joke, I now suppose. Upon my refusal he drops "her" down a gear, so to speak, and double clutching and stripping a few teeth off the helicals, assaults the next grade in earnest, now flat out pilot trying to pump her to seven thousand, no more a procurer. The engine screams, the birdcage whistles, and I can't hear his next remark. Outside, I can see wonderful changes streaming past the birdcage. More spiky plants, dangling orchid-like blossoms, and further up, mountain pines and teak, so inaccessible they're protected from renegade loggers, at least for the time being. I was a bird, an old bird, cruising along in my container, white, internally wrinkled, peering with red eyes out of my birdcage on wheels.

"We came near," the pilot issues ungrammatically through the grate, in the backward proleptic tense, "to hotel." In testimony that he has performed expeditious service, he locks the front wheels full over, scrubbing about half an inch off the rubber, and lifts the inside right rear tire above which I'm uneasily perched, sending me rocketing over to the opposite *thaew* of the *songthaew*. "Girld at hotel," he screams through the grillwork, one hand on the wheel, in a final stab at a satisfying synthesis of his two vocations, flying and pimping, "waiting all along with Mr Bill, Mr George."

I was certain I wouldn't be equal to meeting any girld, whether she was in the singular or plural. Maybe barely Mr Bill and Mr George, whoever he was.

"Watch the damn road," I howl back as I shoot across to my original homebench. The jungle bends around me for several milliseconds, enwrapping me, then straightens out and divides itself, as it should, on each side of the birdcage. Very suddenly, as if through some magical reversal of inertia, we arrive at a row of bungalows, and we cease. The motor shuts down, chugs a few times, overheated. There's a silence, and the chatter of strange birds, perhaps it's monkeys.

"Here," he grins, handing me down, glued to my sack, "hotel. No charge. Friend of Bill."I guessed as much.

*   *   *

"So greetings, professor," (I'd acquired this obnoxious soubriquet that stuck like glue for the duration). "I am Kristen." A tall handsome blond man stepped toward me, no by golly, a woman, and she towered over me. She bowed formally, decreasing herself somewhat, not a great deal. I couldn't tell if this was an Eastern accommodation or a vestige of Old World upbringing. I ducked my head and shook hands with her.

Bill grinned. "She works with *Radda Barnen*. That's Swedish for ah, you know, that outfit in Connecticut USA," he emphasized the last, "What's it, Save-the-Children. She's a Swedish," he added and superfluously, modestly, I gave her another nod, "Quaker," I gave her another nod, more pronounced this time. She curtseyed half an inch. Hair streaming down but bound behind her head in a bandanna, feet turned at angles beneath the faded dungarees, there was something vestigially undergraduate about her except at the moment she started to speak. Then it was all vehemence cloaked behind politeness and reserve.

"Well," Bill looks back and forth between us, "if you two have finished your aerobics, let's get down to the game park and see what George has waiting for us."

"Let's go," Kristen volunteers with enthusiasm, and in colloquial English too, shocking the hell out of me, "By golly I'm dying to see the elephants."

"By golly," I echo faintly.

It took almost ten minutes of hammering and coaxing to get the old Land Rover chugging. "I'll show you how someday," Bill yells in my ear—apparently he was, I feared, the secret mentor of my Hong Kong pilot. We all jam into the front seat, me in the middle.

We tottered on our way, magisterially, earnestly, uncomfortably. Immediately I felt at peace. In the bosom of this old clunking dinosaur it was like being part of a strange new nomadic family, perhaps survivors washed ashore from the wreck of the good ship *Occident* upon Orient waters. I started to nod off. What clever rascals we were, I drifted, to have survived, poor yet free. Not entirely poor. We had Kristen's golden hair, I could just glimpse out of a corner of my eye, if those Burmese did not try to steal it. I began to sway to the lurchings of Rover. We passed a waterfall, I could hear, and half-rousing myself I saw the embankments alive with white and purple orchids.

"Ho, now. Here's George." Bill exclaims, for the benefit of rousing me all the way. A slender figure leans toward us as we pulled into Park headquarters, "George Magrehbi."

George was decidedly not a Swedish Quaker. "Very good, very fine, professor," he beams at me with two darkened front teeth, which seemed already well acquainted with my titular handle.

"George is from Bengal," Bill adds informatively. "You know, where the tigers used to come from. Fact is he's here studying the movements of animals in the park."

"Very nice elephant," George lights up, "no tiger." He bows to Kristen. "Madam Kristian."

Kristen steps over to him and put both hands on his shoulders. "Hello George. Saver of animals."

"Thank you, memsahib," George beamed at the honorific.

I wasn't entirely ready for this mawkish performance, whether it was for my benefit or not, but I got over it attributing it to the varieties of our ill-matched cultures. I thought of Alice and feared we also were ill-matched inhabitants of ill-matched cultures.

"Can't break him of those *sahib* cognates," Bill ruminates disconsolately. I remained skeptical. "A good seventy, eighty years out of date."

"Thank you, sahib." George's way of acknowledging Bill's complaint. He shoots me a glance, perceiving I half suspect his major pastime was to needle Bill. Then to Kristen, handing her at the same time a small paper bag, "Madam Kristian, for the big snakes, the great snakes that hang from the trees."

Kristen peers inside and shrieks in horror. "Small mouse, memsahib," George comforts her regarding the contents of the paper bag, at the same time glancing at Bill, scoring two for two. "Very good lunch, very good for snakes." His two dark teeth smile to themselves happily and then to me, honorifically I thought. We set off.

✶   ✶   ✶

After a mile or so we got out of the Rover and started to walk. About twenty yards uptrail Kristen let the mouse out of the bag. After listening carefully to her explicit instructions it hopped away into the under-brush, soon to be devoured by whatever if not by a snake. The gibbons followed us, observing every breach of etiquette, including defecation, as they swung overhead urging us forward, mocking us that we were going forward, hooting 'we told you so, we told you so.' Pointed hacksaw fingers of jungle plants ripped at my trousers. After about half an hour, drenched with sweat we reached a deep bluish plain, part water and reeds, rimmed round with limestone bluffs pushing upwards under fes-toons of vines and shrubbery, like ragged dromedary humps. In the middle distance the grass turned less dense and more trampled, and gradually we could make out the shapes of two huge, soft brown cattle. I didn't know there were cattle in the area.

"Gaur," Bill remarks matter-of-factly. "Water buffalo," he adds for my benefit. "Unreliable. We better go around." We went around for a half hour or so. We were now at the foot of a hill which as it rose shed bit by bit the spiky tropical foliage we had been passing through, replacing it gradually with a soft deciduous cover of light green leaf and the pale smooth tan arms of sandalwood trees, then further up, in surprising contrast, a small darkwood forest of huge teak. "Probably the last in the country. There's a bit more around Chiang Mai up north. The elephants have been rolling those teak logs around for so long I thought we might catch some who had come back to pay a visit." Bill wiped his forehead. "Even though they're officially off-duty in the Park." He ruminated, "It's said they never forget a trail after they've been on it—even if only once."

"Very good workmen," George's two darkened front teeth concurred, "very good companions."

"I have to pee," Kristen declares suddenly, just like that, "I have to find the toilet."

"Oh sure," I agree looking around. She strikes out to the west of the trail without answering me. A gibbon swings overhead hooting.

"It's not us," Bill reassures her.

"I don't mind that company," comes the muffled voice, "I know you boys are too polite to climb trees. I mean too clumsy."

"What do you do about mosquitos?" Bill yells after her. A brief silence.

"Whaddy'a mean, what do I do about them?" she yells back. Another brief silence. Kristen rustles about in the shrubbery. "I let'em bite. They have to have lunch too."

"Awfully religious of you Kristie," Bill mumbles down low so she doesn't hear.

"What?" There's considerable rustling of undergrowth. Some creature now separates itself from Kristen's corner and is heading toward us, I mean toward me in particular and it's really moving.

"Pheasant, guinea hen," I call out. Nothing flies up. Just a turmoil beneath the underbrush that's drawing nearer, as I stand rooted in my little clearing. With an insect like prehensile motion George reaches his long pole over and raps on the snout a little brown pig now thundering along at a good rate toward the space between my knees. With a grunt it diverts course, scrimmaging and snorting under the greenery like a runaway snowblower. George beams, highly pleased with the wildlife demonstration.

"Very good piglet, yes?"

"No," I protest. I'd caught a brief glimpse of long hair and tusks.

"Boar," Bill calls out from uptrail.

From behind the nearby bushes Kristen giggles. A red flower the size of an artichoke frames her golden head now bound with a bandanna, with the flower behind it. She rises modestly yet confidently from hiding.

"Mate" Bill hollers again, whatever he means by that. At first I thought he meant Kristen, then discarding that as altogether too forward I imagined, for a ridiculous instant, that he might be playing a private game of chess on the checkerboard greens of the hillside. Another small thunder of underbrush rolls downtrail toward us. Kristen, now gracefully emerged from her bower, with a brusque unladylike motion whacks the second pig squarely between the eyes with a hefty banana branch. The sow peels off to our left, squealing. I stand defending my spot, eyeglasses fogging.

"So there," Kristen puts down the banana stem and readjusts her flower.

"By Jove", Bill remarks from his observation post uptrail. "Come on, doc-sahib," he yodels, "don't rust out there, composting a lecture on something."

*   *   *

About halfway down the far side of the hill we caught sight of three vultures, and Bill quickened pace. In the distance, another alluvial plain with palmyra palms. Our trail was showing more red mud and bamboo, and before us, an instant flash of electric blue parakeets.

"They might be down at the watering hole," he remarked as we stumbled along behind him. In another ten minutes we broke into a clearing. Two vultures flapped up, then two more. A tremendous stench greeted us. At the edge of the clearing, legs splayed outward stiffly, head plunged into the soft mud, the elephant was waiting for us. Its bottom jaw with its tusks had been sawed off, probably with a chain saw, and its trunk half cut through and left dangling to one side, red end exposed. The ears drooped down to cover the eyes. Several small birds hopped along its back, as if pretending it was still alive, picking intently, eyeing me, then hopping down the other side and out of sight. George leaned on his long staff. I approached and, forgetting for a moment the smell, examined the roadmap tracery on the leathery skin. I didn't look toward the head. I tentatively moved down its length pitched into the mud like a giant contraption dropped from another planet that had malfunctioned and neglected to spread its wings. When I reached the end I was staring into the narrow face of a mangy dog.

"Wild dog, careful." Bill throws a branch at it and it disappeared. "Usually there's more than one."

We didn't see any others; this was a solitary.

Bill examined the length of the elephant. "Believe it or not, there be bullet holes."

"Bullet holes?" I ask, joining him and looking down at the torn hide. "Then this is one of the Queen's elephants that jumped parole?"

"If you prefer, this one may have died, not just of AK-47 but of natural causes, or of grief."

"Grief?" I exclaim. "Over what?"

"Or poison, if you don't like that. Can't say. Take your pick among all of them. In any case the ivory salvagers came."

"Natural causes, poison or grief. Those are the choices I have?" I demand. "What the hell is going on over here? Or do I take this as an instance of things laying more flat that way?"

He stared back at me, a different person for the moment. "Sorry. Anyway those are the choices you have. Over here," he went on, somewhat drily, as if I should know it by now. "And we're too late, whichever choice it was." I wasn't entirely satisfied with his reply, but I tried not to show it. Yes, I did. It just slipped out.

"What's a book?" I echo distantly, looking down at the scene spread before us. "And what fills up a book? Natural causes, bullets, grief?" Bill looked away. "Bullets? What if I choose those?" I continue bitterly. "And you, and Kristen, and George?" I stooped to examine the huge creature and the entry holes Bill had pointed to. It occurred to me that the pachyderm had been in its sad state for more than a brief while. Maybe that's why I'd been brought to see it—to witness a small drama about poachers. How much more poignant I thought, to that end, if death had been caused not by a hail of bullets or of politics but by grief. Grief transcended all wars and their politics. And grief came from living too long and, like an elephant, never forgetting. I wondered that people didn't see it. Maybe they did.

I bent down and examined the wounds carefully. "By the way. The only problem with the bullet theory is these wounds were made after it was already dead." I looked up at Bill. "Like for a window display."

Bill shrugged and looked around. Kristen was ten yards off. I think she was listening to us carefully.

"Target practice. They need target practice," he remarked drily.

"They'd better brush up on it damn quick if they intend to hold me in their sights. I plan on dying from grief."

"Hey guys, quit arguing and get over here," Kristen calls suddenly from the underbrush.

She's standing under an empty strangulation noose dangling from a branch. The fine bamboo snare had been cut, and the victim taken away. But the noose was still discernable, swaying emptily. From the undergrowth about twenty feet away a squeaky chatter calls up to us, and there squatting, blinking with fear, a baby gibbon too frightened to move. Kristen bends down, the concern on her face makes her sharp chin meet almost the tip of her nose.

"Watch out. Bites." Bill warns.

Kristen takes off her shirt. She has only a striped bikini top underneath. She reaches down and in an instant has wrapped the baby gibbon in her shirt.

"Let's have your backpack, George. We can get this one to the park headquarters."

*   *   *

The return trip seemed endless. I brought up the rear, following the swarm of insects which hovered over Kristen as she marched glistening white in front of me. There was something deeply urgent about her taking up the young ape. I couldn't help but pity that all her strength had such fragility hidden within it. But it wouldn't take long for me to discover why.

The path was dry as dust. Our newly adopted co-traveller seemed, after a period of adjustment, the most contented of all of us, discussing matters to himself while we remained silent. His head popped out of the sack several times a minute; the rest of the time he seemed to be setting up house in the backpack. I watched for a while, trudging along in thought, intrigued by the choices Bill had laid out. Intrigued by the image of the empty noose still swaying where we'd left it and by the suspicion that this whole operation had as much to do with show business as with animals.

At last it dawned on me what he was doing, the gibbon I mean, waving his arms and gesturing periodically as if he could command by signs all the intent and meaning in the world. He'd found the remainder of our lunch and was helping himself to a picnic. All the way back to park headquarters, he was lunching al fresco, not forgetting to toss the remnant scraps and peelings of his feast toward me as I stumbled along at the rear. He watched to see if I would pick them up and join in. Like he was saying hey, that wasn't my mother after all, hanging on the line. Just old aunt Hilda visiting. But you fell for it hook line and sinker, you gringo sucker. Hey, I know what I'm doing, do you?

I nodded back to him. You take care of yourself. Maybe I have something to do other than take care of myself. Perhaps that's the difference between apes and human apes. At least I think so. Hey, my partner replied, at least have some lunch before you begin.

We passed silently and quickly along our good narrow trail cut through the soft low jungle. A few peacocks burst overhead to the right and left of us.

2

The chedi (say *jedii*), stupa, or what we'd call the pagoda of the temple was conical, tiered and crusted with jagged crockery. It recalled the huge anthills we'd encountered in the Park, buttressing a tree and reaching ten feet upwards and twenty to twenty-five in diameter, housing a trillion trillion industrious white ants. The chedi showed itself the product of this same industry, but in broken bits of English porcelain repieced together like a spectacular jigsaw, tier upon tier, bits of the old crockery Empire crazily preserved. At one corner of the wat a solid unornamented pillar of dark brick, and unceremoniously fixed to it at navel level a solitary sunflower, life size, of white and tan Copeland spode with an earthenware center, something as childish and fanciful as the paper flowers you find in a San Diego street fair.

Alice tapped me on the shoulder and redirected my attention to the jigsaw towers. She stood patiently beside me, a small, quiet sturdy presence. Bill had said she wanted to show me the temples.

"They look like the anthills in Khao Yai Park," I remarked sourly, thinking back on the adventure. Then with some faint notion of redeeming myself, "But I like your beautiful elephants on the marble walls inside, traced in silver and mother-of-pearl." I waited. Nothing. "Even though they're the only elephants that can stay alive in your country," I added obtusely. "What do they stand for?"

Alice took my arm, which surprised me no end. My monologue ended right there. We started to walk slowly. "I wish to explain," she began painfully. I couldn't tell whether she meant to apologize for the elephants, the unwelcome pistol, the even more unwelcome meal or maybe for my feeling shipwrecked in her country. "They stand for," she continued earnestly, "they mean that the elephant you found dead, still lives, now again."

"I doubt that" I replied before I could catch myself. "Nothing lives now again. Anyway forget the elephants," I observed angrily, at the same time recalling the decimated creature we'd found in Khao Yai. "I mean forget not them but all the pretentious claptrap…both sides of the ocean." She lifted her eyes. I could see in them, at least as well as I could see, that she was in fact apologizing for something. I paused, not knowing whether I should acknowledge it or not. "Where did you learn…western talk," I inquired finally, regaining a small measure of control, "so well?" She smiled at me.

"The elephants. Perhaps they are also a reminder," she continued discretely yet doggedly, "that you can put on your shoes now. I don't want you to get something bad in your foot. We're not in Japan here, or at a mosque."

I'd forgotten I was in fact carrying my hiking boots. "My feet got hot," I grumbled, looking down. "And where did you learn to speak English so well?"

"I don't want you to get something bad in your foot," she repeated, ignoring my question. "Here, I'll help." She dragged away one boot in both of her hands as if it were a log, and led us to a low wall where we could sit. Funny, the different use of hands, I thought, in the Or…

"Where did you learn English so well?" I insisted. "You understood Bill and me all the while at the restaurant."

She let my comment pass. "I am still trying to understand you. How you can hate me so much and still love me." There was a dreadful silence. I felt as if I were sitting in only my underwear. It was all I could do to balance on the wall without toppling off. She continued deliberately, but painfully shaded. "And when you are not angry, you are even harder—more difficult, is it?—to understand. Because then…"

"Humpf," I remarked irritably, but meaning mostly myself. "Humpf. Is it because you meet so many *farang* like myself?"

"I wish to explain that night. I didn't mean to upset you—it got beyond my hands when I asked uncle, I call the old man, what I should do, to know you well enough…to trust you. So he came up with the gun."

I collapsed further down on the wall. "The old bullshitter" I muttered to myself, relieving myself once more of the fright I had been thrown into and my subsequent sense of shame. "Could have said oriental bullshitter, too," I muttered to myself even less audibly, now full of hurt feelings. "Asian, Asiatic. Eastern, what does it matter?" I cried aloud. "Is it because you meet so many *farang* like myself?"

She held my arm as I sat, steadying me, and with her other arm she balanced her half of the boots at a safe distance from our noses, totally unembarrassed.

"Humpf" I repeated. Again meaning myself. "Or was he warning me off, to get away while I could?"

She shrugged. I don't think she fully understood.

"That depends on how you see," she answered politely.

"Everything depends on something else over here. What a load of baloney," I muttered to myself.

"That depends," she said, suddenly joyful. Enough so that I was thrown off.

We both worked at installing the boots. Alice squatted in front of me tomboyishly—there was certainly nothing fancy that way about her— in her short green dress which unabashedly revealed everything up to the works and balancing on her orange high heels, perfectly intent on wedging my feet back into my heavy Americans. She laced up one boot, I did the other.

"But I knew from the start I could," she resumed finally.

"Could what?"

"Trust you… without all that. And now I am ashamed."

Something about the row of identical Buddhas I felt staring at my back made me feel uncomfortable. There they sat, without ever crossing the line I had drawn dividing us in that original challenge, inhumanly indifferent to our story, whether we might ever be friends, or lovers or nothing at all. They were simply idiotic, sitting there. Maybe they were benign. It angered me. It defeated me. I got up and started trudging toward the exit gate.

"Would we feel happier if I bought us each a set of wind-up mechanical teeth that laugh? That's real western technology. I know where to find 'em, just down the street." Even to my own ears it sounded blustery.

"No, I think no," she replied shyly.

"Some cardboard kitchen dinettes," I persisted foolishly. I don't know what got into me, but I suppose it was the best I could do at that moment to try to heal us. "So we could cook an edible American meal at long last, even if it tasted like McDonald's wrappers. Or maybe a plaster-of-Paris Buddha wrapped in a yellow see-through scarf, so that we could…" —believe all that stuff, I said to myself—"So that all will be right and well?"

Alice shook her head apprehensively, at the same time managing a faint smile. "So that is how you find it here." She retrenched her idiom, taking my arm for support. "You must believe no matter how bad it is— this is—it is still our actual moment."

"Yep. It's our actual moment." I looked around us. "It's our actual moment." Inside of me a voice piped up *what a horrible moment*—not her moment, our moment, but the moment of the world she lived in. "It's the actual moment," I repeated in order to stop any chance that the word *horrible* might leak out.

She shot me a look edge with compassion, and yet she couldn't possibly have seen through all that clumsily churning western irony. The voices inside of me began to subside. We reached the gate.

"I'm not going to answer you until you're polite," she replied with sudden, unexpected affection and at the same moment slipping more easily into western idiom. "We orientals, as you keep calling us when you are offguard, are a very polite people." I stopped and looked at her amazed, speechless, and in spite of myself delighted. She tugged me along on our way, and she stumped alongside on her wobbling high heels, touching me, reassuring me with the pressed length of her whole body from moment to moment as naturally and unassumingly as a moist breeze upon the cheek. "What is this *edible* you are speaking of? Let's go by the river. Maybe we'll hope you don't fall in." She beamed up at me as she bobbed along. "See how polite?"

✱   ✱   ✱

"Right over there, across the river," Alice raised a small brown arm— I noticed traces of several old bruises on it—"is Wat Arun, Temple of Dawn." She confided, "Dawn is always just across the river." I didn't reply. The heavy dark silhouette looked foreign and medieval against the hazy blue sky. We stood still and looked at it. "All the thousands of people who are asleep..." she began.

I don't like it, to tell the truth; it looks too...it looks awfully much like an Indian temple. The stones of it."

"…or who never sleep," she persisted levelly, "there they meet, sleepers and non-sleepers, in the dawn." She finished, and turned to me triumphantly, "you see… in the dawn".

"I see," I allowed drily. "That helps me to like it a bit better. But I still don't like it." A strange sense of loyalty started to creep over me regarding my not unexpected predilection to western architecture. From across the river a fragrant breeze sprang up. Unattainable. Unlike anything on our side. "It looks too…foreign," I protested, gazing at the stones.

"Foreign. Well, Arun, Aruna is an Indian god," she remarked helpfully. Then standing tip-toe, which did not make her that much taller, "Aren't I a good tour-guide? A waddimekong?"

"Stones always look better *in situ*," I persisted. "*In situ* means in their proper place."

"Proper place," she echoed.

"When you take them to your home they lose their colors. Like flowers. You wouldn't believe that stones could lose their colors, like flowers."

"Yes," she replied quietly. "They always look more beautifully when they are at their home."

"I think if I were a god I'd prefer one of those little Thai temples in front of Aruna," I insisted perversely, "made of wood. They look from a distance like Viking-prowed outhouses."

She frowned meditatively. "What is that? I thought you spoke earlier that you found the Thai designs too…" She couldn't retrieve the word.

"That the people who made those designs reminded themselves they lived…preferred to live in a manner superior to the natural world."

She puzzled over that for a while. "So that is what it looks like to western eyes." She glanced down and straightened her dress. Western eyes. I feared she'd guessed at that moment what was at the back of my thoughts, that for all their oddities of architecture and custom, eastern faces appeared as ornamental as a row of inscrutable, stony lookalike Buddhas, and hers was among them.

"I didn't mean…" I continued, trying to justify myself.

"Boy," she looked at me glumly, then caught my eye, making sure I noticed her handling of the vernacular, "boy, if that's how you say it, you westerners are difficult to please."

"That's how we say it. Boy, we westerners are difficult to please," I conceded. "But we are easily poisoned off by the food, which is a great convenience. And now you're beginning to sound very western." Suddenly it occurred to me that without doubt she had been Bill's lover. What did that mean for us? She took my arm again, delighted by my compliment to her command of idiom.

We passed a street vendor's noodle stand, and I pretended to ogle his particularly suspicious concoctions. Alice squeezed my arm firmly, pulling me away from the vendor who stopped ladling and for an oriental moment looked at us in amazement.

"Come, you see. I am a westerner too. Can't you tell?" She gave a small hop, then pretended to trudge as if she were wearing hiking boots. "The women, they push and pull their men like soldiers." I looked at her dubiously. "I'll feed you when you've deserved it," she corrected herself, "you-all" (she enunciated each word distinctly) "deserve it. Now that's western, isn't it?"

"Very western indeed," I approved drily amidst my surprise. "When can we dare to eat?"

"I have friends who will feed us" she explained."They live in Thonbury. That's across the river," she looked at me, "where the dawn is. You see, I try to be a good friend for you. Because you are a friend to me."

I didn't answer. I wasn't certain that was the term I'd use. "Thonbury," I said finally. "Where the dawn comes up."

"Across the river," her face might have reddened a bit, I couldn't say. "Oh you." Alice suddenly put her arm around my back. "How do they call it. 'The white man is a burden'?"

"The white man's burden," I corrected promptly.

"Oh sorry, I see." She laughed and shoved me a little as she broke loose from me, "I didn't know. The white man's burden." We looked at each other; I wondered how many different ways each of us meant that. All of a sudden, she raised the palm and fingers of one hand first to her mouth then to mine. "All these sayings, all these things we talk back and forth…they are not what I hope we could say."

CHAPTER THREE

1

Kristen had developed a desire to inspect closeup for herself the crushed eggshell lacquer boxes I told her about, especially the hemispherical set of three, softly speckled gray and white and nesting within one another. She'd already visited the workshop once, but they had been out of them. One of the girls told her that she should come back in a week.

"That's what they told me also," I replied. "Aren't the chickens laying this year?" We lurched along in a tuk-tuk reeking of propane. Bill was somewhere up north. "Everything else is," I added gratuitously.

"Furthermore," she meditated dourly as we plunged swaying down Sukhumvit past the girlie bars and the Arab dominated hotels, "I don't think it's eggshell boxes that they make there."

"Oh then, this is a great place to get them," I muttered. "What do they make?" She was silent. I thought to myself, will this be part three of my trial run?

When we arrived we found several rows of a new batch of teenage girls occupied in burnishing the boxes. They sat bolt upright at a long heavy wooden table, their hands folded before them when not busy scrubbing. Identical outfits of black skirts and starched white blouses, fishbowl haircuts. Yes, it looked for all the world like that scene from a Dickensian orphanage.

It came about that there were three finished sets of boxes we could purchase; actually, the third set was incomplete I later discovered when we got it back home. The center of the nest was empty. The coop had flown the coop, as it were. While Kristen chatted partly in English, partly in Thai with one of the girls, very pretty with a serious northern village face, I sat looking with a kind of remote longing through the great open heavy wood-framed window. There were red flowers in the garden, and from nearby the high-pitched chatter of school children broke upon my ears then trailed off.

"Not a day for mass production," I looked down sleepily at Kristen's small bundle of treasures she had managed to wheedle from the sales office. "They're not going to snatch it away from Honda, nor even GM when it's not on strike." We went out. "Don't tell me it's the chickens again."

"We'll go round to the back," Kristen said suddenly. I trailed after her. We passed through a hidden garden, its foliage growing more tropical and entangled as we continued. At the far end, a dilapidated wooden structure, heavily walled in roughhewn timbers, apparently deserted. Kristen walked around the building through bushes that clung to her dress and cut at her legs.

"Why?" I followed grudgingly. "Why are we doing it?" But I was beginning to feel caught up, despite myself. She paused and stooped toward a smudged window which arose from the dirt at ground level. She wiped at it with her kerchief.

"Look."

At first I didn't see anything. It was dark inside; the only light came from the dusty window and fell in a faint pool on the dirt floor. Then a child's face emerged from the shadows, and the pool of light grew larger, whiter. Caught in the glimmer transmitted through the dusty window, a tiny girl's face stared up at us in surprise. Or perhaps this was a dream, it began to dawn on me, an old grief-soaked dream emerging from the shadow that the image was my sister, punished for something I'd done, and shrunken down to this child or it was myself, shrunken down to a little girl and punished in her place, or an earlier Kristen punished for I don't know what. The little girl was squatting on the earth next to an iron stanchion, a pile of white powder before her on a tin plate on the dirt floor. Looking harder, I saw a heavy shiny chain around her right ankle, one end fastened to the stanchion. She looked up surprised and frightened. A patch of darkened earth between her legs marked where she must have peed. I stood up, suddenly dizzy.

"I don't think it would be hard to get in, but we'll need bolt cutters for the chain."

"Where do we get that?" Already we were turning toward the street.

Where else? I thought to myself. Chinatown. Even if we had to buy a Toyota engine to go with it.

*　　　　　*　　　　　*

We were back an hour later, looking for all the world like a pair of safecrackers, this time in a taxi. We walked down the alley and approached the building from a different angle. Almost immediately two men in light tan uniforms, caps, white braid on shoulder, whistles, pistols, stepped out from the shrubbery and stopped us. Guess who. They spoke to us in Thai, which didn't much impress me. Kristen listened attentively while I looked them over. They felt my gaze and responded by swishing some clubs around, harming the air, as if they were the Asian Keystones.

The chief was a short, powerful man, extra braid on his cap, extra moustache, extra room in his pocket for graft, who wasn't bothering to smile as he lectured Kristen. All right, I said to myself; I didn't want his smile of approval. Better to have his enmity. His sidekick was a bit taller, but more angular and frail, of no particular age, a bumpkin Barney Fife from somewhere upstate leaning on his long baton like a cowpoke, with three of his front teeth missing and a worried look about him, as if anticipating that the rest might follow soon. The chief raised his voice and his finger to include me, in Thai. He paused and felt his moustache to underscore his point whatever it was.

"Hurrah for the republic," I announced suddenly, smiling in his direction and repressing an urge to reach over and tug his pet facial hair. Kristen shot me the queerest glance. At the present moment we were not standing in a republic nor anywhere near one. She looked at the officer, who looked at her, then at me, then at her again as if all this demanded some explanation, or perhaps apology.

"Does he understand any English, Kris?" I asked.

"I don't think so."

"Money?"

The chief gave me a considerably dirty look for one who didn't understand English, unlimbered his walkie-talkie, mostly I believe, to show it off, and pretended to consult with another opaque dimwit who spoke static at the other end, even though the light didn't stay on to show it was working. Depending on how technology was used—I meditated upon the Sony—it was all in the use, I pondered, whether it was malign or just silly.

Meanwhile the assistant Keystone twirled his club clumsily, remaining amidst this international crisis a certified bumpkin. Kristen's patience was wearing thin. The chief consulted his machine some more, while private Minus-tooth glanced apprehensively about, wishing not to be here, then briefly at my bolt cutters which were about half his size. I looked down at them and raised a finger to my front teeth, nodding to him. A terrible recognition befrowned his face and he looked away. "Stay cool," I advised him, "it won't hurt. You may feel a little pin-prick." I turned to Kristen. The chief gestured to me to put the bolt-cutters away. I couldn't exactly comply. He spoke to Kristen in Thai.

"We can't stay here. It's against the law to interfere with some one else's property," Kristen informed me.

"Even when it's three years old and chained up in the basement mixing coke," I replied. "We learn new things each day," I added, angry now because I knew somewhere deep down that we'd already lost.

"It doesn't matter," Kristen continued, trying to sound equitable, "that's the law, he says." She indicated the officer. I could see he was beginning to get into a lather. "And he says for you to put those cutter things down on the ground." She sounded quite reasonable now, which generally I took as a sign that she was hopping mad. I stood wrapped in indecision, and Chief took a step forward.

"Civil rights have made great strides here since the '84 rebellion," I announced to the world, appraising his step forward.

Chief nodded authoritatively, appearing to agree with the gist of my statement and patted the flap of his white pistol holster, indicating the Beretta. Kristen froze. So did bumpkin.

"Very handsome," I replied, soothing the waters. Pointing at the Beretta, "I got one of those for an early Christmas present" I added amicably, "*fabriccata in Italia.*" Kristen grabbed at my elbow. I avoided her lunge and even while reassuring her turned to the officer and smiled at him, bowing slightly. "Yep, I had one of those for a while. Goes good with salt fish." There was silence all around. "Are you sure he doesn't understand English, Kris? I keep getting glimmers of yes and no"

"Very little. Not much, I don't think," she gasped. Her eyeswere widened anxiously. "What's gotten into you?" she moaned. "You say such weird things. I didn't want it to come out like this." The Chief produced a pad and began writing.

"Am I going to get a receipt?" I jibed. Turning to Kristen, "What do you mean you didn't want it to come out like this?" Up to now I'd had only the faintest glimmer that all this had been so spontaneous... When she remarked that it wasn't eggshell lacquer boxes the girls were making what had she meant? And how did she suspect? Or did she know? My mind was freewheeling now toward any number of unfounded suspicions. And why were the police waiting for us?

"Am I getting a receipt for visiting this country?" I insisted a bit more lamely since the game was getting cold.

"No, you're getting a ticket," Kristen snapped acerbly, jolting me back to the moment. I stood by neutralized as the Chief spoke to her in italics. "And now he wants your passport."

"These are the reasons for consulates and embassies." I blathered to myself, handing it over. At that instant it broke clearly upon me that being a smart ass did no more than to betray that I was a smart ass on the defensive.

Chief worked at jotting down the number and searched randomly through the visas, holding them upside down and any which way. Other countries, other scripts, were a puzzle to him as much as they were to me. After a short while my attention wavered, and I signaled Kristen that we should go. He was still writing as we retraced our now guilty steps. Apparently the ticket wasn't mine to keep, nor the passport. And I didn't want to bother him for it in the middle of his writing a novel about me. As we reached the street I turned and gave our two new acquaintances a wave of the hand. "Peddling dope for profit is one oriental business over here, Asian, Asian I mean. But peddling children to do the labor is quite another," I announced in a holler from a safe distance and in a language they couldn't understand. "There's a line between…"

Kristen pulled me by the wrist into the street. "God, you're a child," she exclaimed, her face dark with emotion, then her voice softened and all my momentary suspicions softened with it, "and twice as difficult to look after."

"I'm not entirely childlike, stupid maybe. Can you imagine, on the basis of this minor episode, how many years we'd be spending in prison if I'd reported the pistol Alice's so-called uncle laid on me?" We reached the street and I turned to holler at the Keystones once again.

"Let it go," Kristen pleaded, drawing me away. "At least you don't pay the taxes to support them."

"The hell I don't. I'm not so sure about that. I was under the impression that our federal tax returns supported the world. Sent M-16's all over the place."

She seemed not to hear. "There's nothing we can do now." She was dragging me along. "We're the ones who stepped over the line, legally. Any further trouble we make only creates more harm. But you know, these people just move the children around from basement to basement, worse than animals."

"And so," I retorted bitterly, "UNICEF is preserved, after a close call, for one more day. They almost had to do something."

"We've got to find a phone," Kristen interrupted my fretful lament, "and report it."

"Report what and to whom?" I snapped back. "Tell me, exactly what the hell was this exercise for, if all we're left with is a pair of bolt cutters and a telephone call? And we even lost the bolt cutters." As soon as I spoke the words it suddenly flashed upon me that perhaps indeed the whole thing was a game pretending to represent life, such as you'd find in a video arcade. And even so, as phony as it was the game was beginning to command my full attention.

I followed her down the street, half-heartedly searching for a phone, past the girlie bars venting into our shimmering noontime heat the dank sweaty halitosis of a thousand bum lays and shriveled hearts. All of a sudden it started to sprinkle, large warm drops. From a nearby crowd of pedestrians the thunder of heavy, agonized, immature male voices answered the rain. Two hulking undergrads, unmistakably American male species, *homo insipiens macho erectus*, recently unpastured from some cow college—how did they get here? Fat thighs splitting their gaudy bermudas, hefty Reebocks pumping. They were blustering along, towing a pair of skinny fourteen year old Thai girls chattering shallowly and apprehensively to each other and waving their toothpick arms. The two lads confronted us with a red, angry, beerful glare as we stood aside to let them pass.

Everything we'd been through flew for the moment out of my head. No, I'm not American, I said to myself, staring after the baleful collegians. I'm not American really. Not in this case, nor in many other cases as well. And yet I'm an American. "You're a Quaker, aren't you Kris?" I remarked out loud to Kristen. "Quakers condemn violence?"

"Yes," she replied, staring after them along with me. One felt our eyes at his back and turned his beefy, terrified, resentful face over his shoulder. "Yes," she repeated, turning her lip under and biting it. "This goddam doakey world." I drew back from her sudden vehemence. "This goddam doakey world," she repeated, "what does it care?" She pulled angrily at a strand of bright hair. Right then I didn't know which side I stood on, the Quaker or non-Quaker, regarding any of this. "It's all for violence."

In my eyes too many unexplained things were happening, and happening all in a row. I hadn't the nerve to suspect that all to come would be...let's say, that there would be other bizarre confrontations, other bizarre...

"This whole thing is entirely out of control." So speaking I tried to sound as if I were perfectly on the level.

Nobody answered.

2

The representatives of UN agencies are actually nominated by the countries involved, and they are expressly forbidden to engage in any activity without the approval of the government of the host country.

Bill looked up from the mutilated pamphlet, which held the Official Word. We were at lunch in our favorite riverfront restaurant. Kristen had already gone north, still angry and depressed, as if she and Bill took turns like two buckets in a well being here or away. I couldn't fathom the whole thing and I honestly couldn't drawn any conclusions about who was in the right, who in the wrong, whether things had been planned to happen just that way or whether it was by courtesy of chance, fate, or half a dozen conflicting interested parties eager to cancel one another out. I held no firm ground in this hothouse atmosphere because in truth I had no firm ground in myself. Not yet. Maybe I'd grow. But I knew I was a thing apart from whatever went on, and I had been from the outset.

"That means you can't go around liberating children since children are considered property, chattel." Bill looked at me in one of his implacable moods, "like women are." **Practically speaking, the organizations can choose between behaving as they should or packing up and leaving, and UNICEF in reality is silenced with regard to human rights violations.** He put down the document and took a bite of his lunch.

"I hope that's written on rice paper," I remarked affably, "in the event our table is raided. All that crap sounds like something you'd get off the internet. I'm tired of these beneficent committees and their representatives. All they do is flap idly in the wind."

He ignored my remark. "Now take fish," he continued judiciously, some of which just then happened to be working its way toward my mouth during this late lunch on the day following armageddon with the Keystone officers. "Which is not an idly flapping topic."

"In or out of water?"

"Now take fish. They don't show their age like humans who get all droopy and deformed, dried up in wrinkles so tight over the face that it brings out unexpectedly ugly contours in the person you think you know... Tastes good," he declared tapping his plate, "this time around."

"It's a good thing it doesn't happen to fish. They get eaten instead." I looked at his plate and at mine. Then leaning toward him in confidence, "Tell me the secret reason. If every one's so highly principled nowadays, how is it that human relationships are so scummy?" I lowered my fork. "Is there anything else I should be mindful of?"

"While we're young," Bill persevered, undeflected, "the skin covers our multitude of structural flaws. We look rosy, smooth and squeezable." I looked around us then at him and shook my head. Neither of us looked young, rosy or squeezable. "But the constant pull of gravity over the years changes that and pulls down the facade…into a broken horseface."

"A broken horseface." I saw myself wearing a broken horseface in ten or in two years' time. So I pulled one down to try it on. "Whereas fish have no facade, and no horseface," I droned.

"I'm trying to tell you something." Then continuing calmly, "No, not so much of a horseface. They don't experience gravity the way we do. They can float in a kind of middle-world once they've found their level. And their right temperature."

"Tell me," I announce suddenly, "because I'm through with this floating in the middle-world. And it's definitely not my right temperature over here. Do the police have a watch on Kristen, and that's why we were caught?"

"The police have a watch on her. I guess."

"You might have said something about it."

He shrugged and looked away thinly.

"So now I go to the Embassy hoping to retrieve my passport and I'm armed with what?" I waited for a moment. Nothing. "This whole thing is completely out of control." There was another pause. "I didn't get an answer out of Kristen either."

"You didn't, that's good. How would you know if it's out of control or not," he snapped defensively, almost viciously. I'd touched a sore spot for sure.

I took a minute before answering. "I'm going to frighten you by not getting angry and by not replying."

He squinted at me. Apparently I squinted back.

"You're not. That's news."

"Not on the outside, just on the inside…isn't there a song that goes something like that?"

"It has to do with crying."

For a moment I was within a hair of turning them all in. What then? But I could hear them at the Embassy, 'Mr Every no longer has an American passport'. Which I didn't exactly wish to hear.

"Tell them your own suspicions, convictions," Bill continued, still acrimonious, "whichever. They're very close together in any case. Amount to the same thing. Suspicions and convictions."

"In the Orient, you mean."

"In any goddam place," he replied angrily. I'd really gotten to him. "Now go down to the goddam embassy and stand up to them and find out for yourself."

"I won't find out anything there—if it's truly an embassy. Not if I stand on my head. At least not about what I've gotten into, I won't even try to guess."

"I know."

"On the other hand I probably will try to guess." Don't underestimate me, I began chanting inside of myself as if I could threaten the air around me, since I had no one else to threaten. Perhaps my own stupidity from the outset. Now that you've hung me out to dry I'll never give up. I'll never give up. Do you understand? I'll never give up. Of course I spoke it only silently to myself. I'd have to be my only best listener from now on.

"And don't expect any answers from the old guy in the straw umbrella bonnet," he continued bitterly waving his fork, "who gave you the present of the Beretta our first night out. They found him floating face down in the river. If that's an answer for you."

"Well it is and it isn't. He wasn't bathing I presume. He rarely did." I turned to him. "Anyway the last person in the world to get answers from is you. So let's hang it up and proceed from here."

He was suddenly and inexplicably benign again. "Me? I'm the last person in the world to get answers from. You know that by now. We're just two kids on vacation…floating downstream, no not that I hope. Now get thee post haste to the embassy and present thy questions."

I shuddered. Deep down I feared the world hadn't made a mistake after all—it hadn't underestimated me. I was just the type to give up, give in—it's all the same.

*   *   *

I harbored some hope that by mounting a concerted effort, albeit a blind one, just by virtue of its being concerted I might force some of this half-baked intrigue to come clean. But I underestimated the capacity of human nature to prolong mystification, not just for the profit, not just for the political advantage, but for the joy of it.

Sure as shooting I was getting that feeling again of not having any 'back-up'—if you're acquainted with the jargon of law enforcement, at least according to TV. And just now I was not on TV but on my way to the Embassy. I muttered over to myself in review the various appearances as they now stood. 'First Alice, who's somewhat strange, with whom I'd just spent an afternoon insulting the memory of her dead uncle who was not her uncle, then Khao Yai and the ambiguous elephant, then George who's also strange as well as ambiguous, then Kristen with her sharp chin and trapped monkeys and child slaves, who's very strange, and not a Quaker. At least I don't believe so unless they've taken to arming themselves. And finally Bill himself who wants to use an unfortunate peasant floating downstream as an adjunct to a diatribe concerning fish living in the mid-world.'

Before we parted, questionably still good friends, he asked "Why don't you come up north and help plant trees?" Of course he wasn't really changing our deeply shared topic, nor was he addressing any of those we'd raised. "North of Chiang Mai," he specified. You could go a bit further north all right, I registered, but you wouldn't want to go too much further.

Something new was setting up. I groaned in anticipation. "What kind of trees? And why? And why Chiang Mai?"

"Oh teak and mountain pine, mostly, some *cinnamomum cassia* and *adenanthera pavonina.*"

"You're not really going to plant those wonderful Latin names," I was chewing briskly on remnants of charred fish—all of a sudden and for no good reason I felt like taking up the challenge of things mysterious— "up there in that beastly foreign soil?"

"Nope," he replied.

""And you're not going up there to firebomb the opium fields?"

"Put villagers out of business? Nope."

"I imagine you'll just recline on the hillside admiring the immense scarlet-orange blossoms of the *spathodea campanulata.*"

He looked at me narrowly. "The Uganda tulip-vine, flame-of-the-forest. It's widespread up there. Where d'ye get that?"

"I've been reading my guidebook to Chiang Mai. I figured that's where the action would be."

He suppressed a smile. "Damn tourists," he sighed. "Planning on coming up?"

"Kristen up there already?"

"Yep."

I wondered why she was. Leaving me in the lurch, though Bill apparently didn't think so. Something uncertain stirred inside of me once more and dampened the prospect of adventure I thought I was entering. I wasn't very good at adventure. No. But I'd never find out what this was all about if I hung back. "And you're not telling me anything more?"

"Nope. I've told you a lot about fish already." He stood confronting me. "And I'm through arguing. Maybe Kristen can convince you."

"Maybe," I replied. Maybe not, I meant. But I was no longer thinking about Kristen. Why did I need to know what it was all about anyway? I guess I knew why.

Bill regarded me patiently and with some curiosity like his old self as I struggled transparently with these unruly reflections.

"OK I know some one else who'll tell you where to find us, after I've gone. She's in on it too. Dessert or shall we fade away?"

He knew I had no intention of fading away. He reached over and touched my arm, in reluctant congratulation. "Gotta keep chompin', matey." He turned away. "Gotta keep chompin' and never give up, never give up. Even if it turns out you'll never learn to trust any of us."

3

The embassy lady handed me back the slip of brown wrapping paper on which Bill before leaving had scrawled an address. She handled it as if it were loaded with scurvy.

"In most foreign corners in the world," she advised, as if she knew for certain the world had corners. She spoke with a funny nasal accent as if a finger or something were caught quite far up her nose. After all she was from Winnetka, USA, and who wouldn't be somewhat disenchanted residing in this scruffy dump of an Eastern cowtown coming as she did from such a richly cultural metropolis.

What did it matter that she'd read only two books during her entire life and hadn't understood either of them. Her office had teak paneling, book shelves, a capacious dark carved desk with discretely housed computer.

"You can't go around meeting issues like this child thing straight on. You've got to see it from their side." She made a thin smile, perhaps her idea of politely representing their side, while implying any civilized person would look down their nose at their side. At least we agreed there. She was thin, her smile was thin, she thought thin, maybe because you lost a lot of weight in a tropical climate.

"If I saw it from their side, I wouldn't be talking to you now," I remarked. What a world of cliches and fops, I thought to myself. "And further, I wouldn't be an American tourist seeing it from my side, but a Thai policeman who'd already stolen my passport seeing it from his. And then there wouldn't be any cultural exchange, would there? And probably no use for an American Embassy either." I looked at her. "And there is a use, isn't there?"

There was a significant pause during which I unravelled nothing except that I was making more of a fool of myself by the minute. "You've got to go through channels and contact the right people," she scoffed turning momentarily cold, colder, which I didn't particularly care for in a person. "That's our use, if you're interested." I stepped aside a hair to let that cruise missile pass. But I held my tongue. "Trying to break into some one's storeroom in order to take a child you said you saw there…" She fiddled with something on her desk that looked suspiciously like a miniature porcelain lion in the mistaken assumption that it supported her opinion.

"We did," I confirmed pluckily, "try to go through the right channels. Straight through the padlocked door. You know very well every other channel is blocked. With sewage." I was working myself up pretty good, I thought.

"That really makes our job over here very difficult." She turned airily aside, partly in disapproval partly as if she expected the phone to ring. "And our job, you may believe it or not, is to keep American tourists from being victimized by weird splinter groups."

"I'm sorry your job is very difficult. I wish it were an easy job. But I feel much safer now. Actually there's some rumor going around that my so-called accomplice and myself were being watched. Do you know anything about that?"

She glared at me as if she'd pulled me over for running a stop sign in a school zone. "I think I should warn you that your friend already…has gotten into considerable trouble here. Quite frankly we don't want an American citizen to share that trouble with her. If it were at all possible we wish we could take steps to prevent it."

"Why not declare war on Sweden," I remarked placidly, "possibly bomb them. Closer to home, do you have good relations to the police?"

She blanched.

"No one else seems to."

"They're here for our protection," she countered.

"Not mine. They took away my passport. Did you give them authority to do that? I imagine it's been recycled by now. On the open market one might imagine that you did concur with them in putting a trace on us, the notorious Swedish connection. And if so, then why did they confiscate my passport and not hers? Is it so we can be having this present interview?"

As I spoke it struck me suddenly that I was saying something that bordered possibly on a revelation, small as it was and after the fact. I was a point of leverage between at least two parties unhappy with each other. The embassy wanted to put pressure on Kristen through me, and sad to say but equally possible, Kristen's group wouldn't mind for an American citizen to exert pressure on the embassy to loosen up—lay the Keystoners off them. For the moment I wasn't even thinking, no not that again, that the chained child might have been something Kristen knew about ahead of time, and so she led us straight to her. The kid might have been playing with baking soda for all I knew. And maybe Kristen suspected we might be busted, so that here I could stand complaining like a fool. I couldn't tell, I couldn't. I was making up sheer nonsense for my own entertainment. But for sure I felt I stood some-where in a pool of half-truths.

"There are channels for looking in on the welfare of children—your blonde friend should know this, of all people. And yes, we did receive a complaint from the police." She grimaced. "Even US citizens have to learn some respect for authority."

"I don't like the way they singled me out. That's why I'm here. If the embassy has anything to do with it then you're creating your own prob-lems that will come back to roost. One of the first is that stateside citi-zens don't like being followed and set upon. Do you recall that being done in Winnetka? And who told them we were about to free that kid? We could have brought those clippers to prune the garden. It needed it. Fie, t'is an unweeded garden. Recall that one?"

"Considerable progress has been made," she pointed out reproach-fully, not really listening to my jeremiad, "over here in the matter of human rights, since the old regime—since the mid-eighties."

"Yes I can see it all around me. No doubt it's the result of that Winnetka favorite, *Anna and the King of Siam*. Based on the *Romance of the Harem*, 1872. Do you know that informative, indiscreet and insin-cere tract, authored by a floozy?"

"1980's" she corrected, at the edge of deep suburban disapproval which is mighty deep. She looked down at my boots, as if they were the cause of the whole thing. Upon cue the door of the adjoining office burst open, as if it were a scene from a silent film, and a handsome young American male, very cleanly and therefore also from the suburbs I assumed, strode into the room, lifted some papers from her desk, smiled in my direction, and deposited in their place something that looked exceedingly like my passport, but bent and twisted as if it had undergone weeks of torture under interrogation.

"This answers your request about the passport. Gary," our hostess interposed. He started on his way out. "Tell Mr... ah, tell him some-thing about... "

Gary left without telling, fleeing before my savage smile like the self-approving fop he was, recently defected (not that other word) from generation X or Y or Z. She handed me the passport. "As you remarked earlier, this isn't stateside. You're on your own now for the rest…"

I picked up the crumpled passport. "On my own now for the rest of what? You're right though, this isn't stateside. Certainly not here. Doesn't feel like it." I glanced around the room. "Not stateside."

"And as for that address on the slip of paper." Her thin smile, recently restored, confirmed that both it and I no doubt were diseased. I held up the slip in my other hand in order to pollute the room. "It **looks** like it's right around the corner from **your** hotel." She meant something by that. "In Pat Pong, you know, one of those entertainment areas with bars and pick-up places where men go," the disgust in her voice took on that unmistakable tint of intimate autobiography, "mostly married men." I nodded sympathetically as if to say I could see why.

"I see," I acknowledged agreeably, "but I'm not mostly married." I pocketed the slip. "Even though I'm from Illinois. Do you think I'll fit in?"

I turned and walked to the door. She called after me, as if on unexpected impulse.

"Your friend…"

"Kristen. Her name is Kristen."

"Your friend, I think you should know, has done this before. Twice."

I didn't reply. Twice before. Let me see. Did that argue for utter devotion to a cause or utter misdevotion balanced teetertotter on the neck of whoever showed up? I departed, and I still couldn't say for sure whether or not those around me were dreaming to accomplish a small bit of good in the world or were sorely misguided. You remember, those things out there. Good, the world.

4

Evening came and it turned appreciably cooler, for a blessed moment, perhaps under 90. The traffic thinned from its daytime guise of a fat crawling worm. The bars along Pat Pong were beginning to twinkle and chatter dangerously; an occasional tuk-tuk came and went. Up above, the sky was dwindling rapidly into a star-pimpled night. I walked past the street noted by Bill, and dawdled along Silom Road, glancing into the pretentious mausoleumized banks choked with fistfuls, armfuls of worthless five-digit paper currency, the sumptuous silk shops and clothiers all gotten up for show, where you chose from a bolt of wispy saffron material and they could make it up for you, trousers and shirts in some mysterious back room in half an hour. The first place I'd paused in front of—that couldn't have been the address Bill meant to give. Too scruffy. Finally I went into a tidy upscale restaurant where I ate a reasonably good but spicy meal.

I retraced my steps to Pat Pong, unable to put it off any longer. What troubled me, since my debut at the embassy—the more I twisted and turned the more I succumbed to the equal possibility that Kristen had been behind the slave-child adventure from the outset, had telephoned the police when I wasn't looking. Well. Time would have to undo this troubled knot, not I. It was too troubled a knot—I was too troubled—for me to untie.

I neared the location Bill had given me. The street and its divers bars seemed deserted for the moment. Suddenly a couple of scooters, mounting the usual pubescent banditti, barely avoided running over my instep; they sawed and squeaked up to the bar that wore, in English, my address, and two tender maidens hopped off, artfully hiking their short gowns to above their waists in order to clear the seat and show off their red underpants. Their escorts revved up, wheelied, then sawed and dodged away. As if on cue, and I could see why, the streets began to fill.

My two young ladies composed themselves by readjusting their under-garments beneath matching red dresses the length of tennis skirts shrunken in the dryer. Finally they noticed me staring at them. They giggled and jutted their butts out self-consciously as I passed the entrance. They had tiny spirits, I glimpsed, hidden under layers of make-up. I looked at the paper in my hand again, walked to the end of the short street, then turned back and approached the two minute women who watched me now carefully, and not just with their eyes.

"Do you know Alice? Does Alice live here?" I stammered the Thai I had been practicing in my hotel room. They exchanged puzzled looks and burst out laughing. One turned to me, charmingly.

"You, dear. Like fuckee, fuckee? Real good."

"Why would any one do that?" I muttered in mock astonishment. "Unless they harbored a death wish."

The speaker was momentarily taken aback, not registering my witticism. But she chose to persist and in gruesome detail. "Doggie doggie, real good, real Oliental."

"There's that word again," I countered, "oly-something. And it adds another demerit to your overall presentation."

She looked seriously concerned and endeavored now to concentrate on her repertory. "Oh maybe blow-job, no?"

"Same difference," I observed tiredly. "Your ass and your mouth seem to be in the same place."

They glanced at each other in dark silence which made their red outfits appear mournfully out of place.

"You wanna…" The other one was dutifully shouldering the reprise. She weighed about 75 pounds, 60 of which were red lipstick and purple eyeshine.

"I'm trying to find Alice," I yelled in English, not bothering to explain why I wasn't swept away by their proposals. "Is Alice here?" I persisted, a bit more calm now but considerably more stubborn.

"Real good," the other real cute one echoed dimly—she may have been sixteen—"You like fuckee-fuckee Oliental style." I looked at her. She stopped altogether. Her body had an oriental mask about it despite the scanty costume.

"We're not getting anywhere. Sure, on some days. Who doesn't? I'll take it up with my congressman, he should know, and my physician. Now where the hell is Alice?"

They looked at me in sober incomprehension, their jaws working in unison on their respective gum.

"Stop clicking your bubble gum. This is serious."

They stopped, and resumed almost immediately.

"Don't be angry with them," a voice spoke from behind me. I turned and Alice was standing at the door, leaning one arm on the entrance. "They're just waiting out their time, hoping to fall in love with a stranger, and hoping he'll fall in love with them." She paused while I stared astounded by her words and then by her short sequined dress. She smiled. "Maybe I'm waiting to fall in love with a stranger," she offered to my utter amazement. I didn't know what to say.

"Alice for godsake what are you doing here?" I blurted, ridiculous to the end. "In a place like…" At the same time I held out to her the crumpled slip of paper as if it were a traffic summons. She motioned and I followed her inside, past the two suddenly serious Ophelia-like maidens. Alice turned to me.

"Don't be too hard, you say, on them. They're only *bui doi,* what you call it, the Vietnamese have a name, 'dust of the street.'"

"*Bui doi,*" I repeated, "dust of the street."

The room was empty except for the bartender, and too tacky and stale smelling for me to want to remember anything further about it except that the shiny floor I was standing on seemed to be a dance floor. Alice moved quietly and sedately in a short thin green dress; around the collar there was a band of lettering in fine needlework whose characters

I couldn't decipher. A stale human odor hung over the room. And to one side of it, almost annoyingly, I could feel her presence guarding me.

"There's a dove-singing contest tonight, just a small one, down by the zoo. I'd wish we could be there, but you see I work tonight." Again, almost university English. I felt it had been somewhat rehearsed for my benefit.

"Dove-singing contest? I blurted again, unable to stop myself, "but you're working here? You mean you go home with customers?"

She was forming an answer that possibly wouldn't hurt my ears. So if she hadn't been Bill's lover, I reflected, how did he meet her? After all we weren't in Bible Belt, USA, that white bread fortress of fanatics resenting everything that wasn't mashed potatoes and tomato ketchup.

One of the young damsels, tired of draping herself as an advertisement, poked her head through the doorway mischievously. "Bet you do it real good, mister," she giggled. Then seeing that Alice and I were in close conversation she betrayed some embarrassment, yet stubbornly held her ground.

"Don't count on it. I don't do anything real good," I growled in ill temper, "I swore off real good long ago. It's too easy to be real good."

"From behind," she giggled, betraying the slightest tinge of anxiety, but still trapped by her dialectic.

"So do dogs. Bow-wow," I responded ungraciously. "Now go find a fire hydrant."

She was delighted with my universally intelligible animal locutions and used them as an excuse to duck out the door and enlighten her twin. Just then I felt something hard against my chest and looked down. The sturdy bouncer-barkeep, five by five, stood by magic in front of me. I never heard him sneak up. His stolid face was nothing but a question mark, no a demand, though it wore no expression. Questions are the gift of language, and between us we had no such gift.

I looked down at the brown granite knuckles painfully inserted into my breastbone. Maybe bow-wow meant something unpleasant in Thai, perchance an insult to a grandmother or to the evening meal.

"The devil fuck ye," I remarked with no particular animosity, just to clear up any ambiguities in my previous utterances. Alice was still formulating her explanation of why she was in this dump. I turned as well as I could toward her. "Well," I said finally, "well I guess why not.I guess. Go home with them." I indicated with my head the barroom and with it everything that had happened in the past two minutes. "It's got to be better than this hovel."

"I guess why not I guess," she mimicked, needling me.

I shrugged. "Isn't there another way…"

"For you there would be, why not I guess." Again she was proud of her idiom. If not her customers. Very particularly she'd cultivated only an American accent. And she used it pretty sarcastically when she felt injured.

The barkeep had cultivated no accent but had concentrated on tightening his fist on my shirt, possibly, it occurred to me, in the light of my earlier ungentle blessing upon him. Looking me squarely in the eye (in this instance at an upward angle and one brown eye was a shade lighter than its brother) his other hand swiftly seized me by the groin, missing my vitals by small good fortune but snagging me by my unmentionables. By these means, sawing me in the testicles, he lifted me uncomfortably several inches off the floor, while controlling my balance with his first hand.

"*Mon dieu,*" I ejaculated as surprised as pained.

He grinned, one tooth remaining to help the grin along.

"*Ton cul*" he hissed.

I squirmed and twisted. "Oh, my cool." I turned to Alice, indicating my dance instructor. "My cool. Alice put some appropriate music on for this fucking snaggle-tooth linguist."

Alice evidenced no emotion whatsoever. I delivered my partner an ineffectual biff on the nose which encouraged him to grunt and increase my elevation.

"Well how are we doing today?" I myself was now just managing, just barely, to do anything today. I couldn't believe a handgrip could be so remorseless. Nor could I imagine that an individual who had such strength could have room to possess also a personhood alongside it. But the world is strange. Under his grip I could feel my heart laboring like an overloaded jeep engine an entity separate from myself, gurgling and stumbling under the compression. I tried his wrist; nothing happened. It rotated slightly, on roller bearings; no, it was made of iron. Apparently everything on him was made of iron. His forearm was iron—he seemed remotely pleased when I felt it—he was iron all the way up to and including his eyeballs. In recognition of this belated discovery of mine, his right hand smiled to itself and squeezed my shirt-front so hard I farted and nearly popped out of my clothes, like a pea squirting from a pod. I twisted and turned. He frowned, and under the effort of keeping me suspended, his fat lips took on the shine of greasy left-over chicken. Then still with one hand guiding, he swung me in an arc, my toes just touching the dance floor.

I gestured stiffly. "The lights are low. Perhaps you'd like us to dance." For no earthly reason he seemed to think it eminently proper to do so, by way of flinging me about in some jitterbug routine. I on the other hand, in this instance the designated dance partner, preferred to live—it mattered to me to live. It was the first such feeling I'd experienced since arriving in the country and it had to do with recognizing at last what Alice, Bill, Kristen were prepared to do, in order to do the right thing. Which was to feel what it was to live before facing what it was to die.

I tried a few steps on my own, without great success. The owner of the bar arrived from a back office and grinned at the floor show. I grimaced back at him. Suddenly it occurred to me as I swung in my grace-ful arc of circle that I had a right to dance my own dance in whatever land this was, I had the right to speak my own tongue, in whatever land this was, I had a right to have my own voice amid all this babble and to speak it aloud. I hadn't travelled long distances to be just another tourist to be pissed on. Should any one be?

My partner danced me around some more. I noticed Alice standing on the sidelines patiently observing us like a referee. She didn't seem noticeably perturbed. For a millisecond it hurt my feelings. Then as my right foot came up off the dance floor for the seventh time, I stretched down to remove from my boot my recently acquired (yes, from a street vendor), label-brand Jim Bowie knife. I flicked it out and stuck the steel point against his left eyeball. Now here was communication. Instantaneously his other hand came up to my arm, a question sprang to his remaining widened eye then swallowed itself back into the nowhere behind it, retreating into that terra incognita of a different language which had a deeper acquaintance with my own suffering than I ever could suspect.

Well he had his business and I had mine. I shifted the point down to his gullet then a little to the left, in a sudden panic avoiding his jugular vein, and shaking my head at the newly arrived hand, no, no, and pushed in a little. The hand dropped. The other remained in place. I nodded to it since it was still crushing me. The hand remained obdurately in place. My language for better or worse hadn't reached it. "He no letee go," I gasped, "pimp-face," not caring whether that made me a true bigot or not in the eyes of Alice and whatever other spectators there might be. Nothing resulted from that animadversion. "Does he understand English, Alice?"

"Not so much," Alice replied, not overly excited, which momentarily brought back my hurt feelings. "Push harder."

"Well, for heaven's sake." I stuck the point in some more, quite a bit, determined that the playing field should be levelled. At the same instant I became aware that this concept of a levelled field was distinctly not an oriental—to hell with the word—one. A red drop appeared on his neck like an insect bite—good, no I was terrified to have broken the skin— then dawdled its way on a fairly straight red highway down to his collar. His remaining hand hesitated, dropped, and he stepped back, undismayed and holding me flatly and nonverbally in his brown eyes.

There it was: another successful intercultural communication. I returned Jim to my boot, shook myself off smiling and bowing to the owner who, taking a step forward, made a gesture that appeared deeply concerned over the cultural implications of this wholesome American joke. "There's a line between us," I explained to him, recouping my previous use of that phrase to the Buddha lookalikes, "stay on your side of it." He squinted at me like he'd lost a dollar and a half somehow during this impromptu transaction. Alice spoke quickly to the bouncer, and taking my arm led me gently to the door. Then we stepped out past the red twins, who were now draped gawking. And voila, there we were alive amid the evening air and the sky was clear and splendid.

*   *   *

"Excitable, we westerners, what?" I remarked stiffly, slowing pace and retrieving a bit of the conceited self that we all possess in order to stand upright.

"Very." She smiled and leaned amiably against my arm just a little.

"What did you say to him?"

"I warned him not to cut your throat," she replied good-naturedly, "either now or the next time he sees you. Or I'll take my business elsewhere."

"Economic retaliation," I echoed hollowly, attempting to sound casual. "Sounds fair enough." She smiled. Of course it didn't sound fair, not in the least. Her eyes looked into me and saw, I'm sure, what I really felt.

"Thanks," I said in order to sound grateful, but mostly to disguise whatever it was I felt. What I felt was that something had been lost, even in the midst of this small momentary triumph.

*   *   *

Upon exiting the barroom we'd passed the red twins now pacified and staring soberly at us, framed in what they perceived to be some sort of romantic reconciliation against the backdrop of the tawdry street. One twin smiled and hiked her skirt and one leg, showing me her personal engagement gift to us sent special handling—a small dark forest and peeking from within it a pair of surprisingly bright purple lips softly parting under the fluorescent streetlight. Like a kiss hello, goodbye. I pretended a careful examination, in order to cover my embarrassment and also not to appear ungrateful. Then turning to Alice, "I heard that on Orientals the vagina runs horizontally not vertically. You know their writing is screwed up the opposite way from ours. Leastwise that was the rumor when I was young."

"Asians, we don't say Orientals." Alice gave me a shove then followed it to my side. "Where have you been? At the American cinema all your life? Girls are girls. The way the maker made them."

"No they're not," I replied bitterly, waving a farewell to the red girls. "They're something more disappointing than the way the maker made them. If only they meant what they showed," I nodded back at the twins, "it might solve the some of the world's problems. Or even showed what they meant. But I've been told that Thai girls never mean anything they show. And yes," I continued, "I've been at the American cinema all my life. But our lessons there are not so very specific as those I've encountered here."

"A vagina is a vagina, in every part of the world," she remarked somewhat darkly.

"No it isn't," I countered. "It's frequently so much less. That goes for guys too. Even though they're differently equipped. At least they are in my country," I added gratuitously.

"You have more freedom to love than everybody in the world," Alice replied gravely.

We walked in silence, and I felt her strong presence beside me. "What part of me is he planning to cut, if not my throat?" I joked half-heartedly, referring to our mutual dance acquaintance.

Alice laughed. "None, I hope," she indicated vaguely a region lower down, then turning to me. "You're not angry if I take your arm, now you know this about me."

"I guess why not," I joked desperately.

"Now that you know how I..." She didn't finish.

"I dunno" I stalled again, trying to sort out my mixed feelings. "Where do you plan on taking my arm?" Alice thought through the syntax for a moment, then laughed and returned my arm to me, and a second later took it back. We jostled together uncomfortably and were an odd couple as we walked, but she seemed to accept that.

"You're too permeable... I learned that word today," she stated proudly, all lit up again. "It means..."

"I know what it means. Did you meet a raincoat salesman? Would you rather have me impermeable? Like hardened bird droppings?"

"Bird droppings. So you're angry now again," she returned my arm to me; her voice sounded cheerful enough but hurt. "You're thinking of ordering a bombing raid on this whole country?"

I thought it over for a second, squirming uncomfortably. "First, we move the animals out. Then a few people, well maybe a couple more people. Then some temples. Then we bomb it. American tradition. We'll start with Pat Pong," I asserted. She smiled at me a tinge sadly. "Just a small area," I relented, "of town, Fat-Prong, Pat-Porn, whatever that Chinaman's name is."

"That's the western spirit, yes?" Alice meditated, still smiling.

"It's my western spirit. That's the only spirit I have," I answered earnestly. We jostled along. "I'm sorry, Alice," I said.

"I know you are. It's OK, you have a right to be angry. After all I've...Oh my heavens, you didn't forget your sack," she cried anxiously, "did you?"

"No, here it is." I showed her my old green sack.

"I always think of you carrying your sack."

"I carry it," I declared, "to keep my *farang*-ness inside of it and with me, wherever I go." She looked at me shrewdly. "It's my *farang*-sack," I went on. "If you're a traveler, sometimes you must use a sack. It reminds you that you are carrying your homeland within you. If you don't have a sister with you, you carry a sister inside of you, if you don't have a wife, you carry a wife inside, or a brother, or a mother, if you don't have a lover, you carry a lover inside of you." I stopped there.

"If I don't have a *farang*, I carry a *farang* inside of me," Alice imitated dutifully, then added, "even if I do, I carry him inside of me. One special one." Her voice wavered for a moment. "Will you carry that sack when you go back to your country? Should I think of you always carrying a sack like that?"

"Not probably. There would be no need for me to carry it. In America, anyway," I remarked gloomily. "What I've discovered over here is that if you don't have a *farang*, you can find one at the next corner. I guess any one will do. It looks like any one will fit in your sack."

"Not any one will do," she corrected me without hesitation, "only a special one will do," she asserted, "who begins to love me back. Like you do."

I couldn't imagine an answer to that. Something was becoming more painfully true by the moment. "Don't think," she continued, very levelly, "that the things I say are simply from a menu like dishes of noodles you order." She paused, obviously reassured that we both could relate to noodles. "Thai girls are supposed to be that way, saying things off a menu." I mutely expressed my non-opinion on the matter, which ran counter to what I felt. We had reached the end of a long block. Alice turned us around to go back, too soon it seemed. "It's like a game they play, like dishes off a menu." She paused again then went on. "But I'm not Thai, not really; you see the difference in my face. I'm Akha, from up north." She pronounced the *kh* aspirated, not hard, which I could never learn to do properly. Then suddenly proud, "Akha, that's pre-Chinese."

"Pre-Chinese?" I wondered how ancient that might be.

"Yes," she insisted still proudly, then laughed, "as old as the elephants."

"Oh yes," I murmured, "I remember. They're the creatures who can die of grief."

"Yes," she replied. I couldn't tell if she was agreeing or not.

"But no one's that ancient," I objected loudly, and I thought to myself, if they are so ancient as that, then they too will become extinct.

"I suppose you think," she added reasonably, "that no one could be that old."

"I'm not so sure about that," I confessed guiltily, "at least I'm no longer sure. I'll have to tell you someday later. And no, I don't think you say those things from a menu." I fell silent for what I felt was a long while and we just walked. She seemed to be thinking about something else.

"So we Akha go back to the old forms and manners of expression." She waited for me to say something. "Like you."

"Like me?" I asked astonished.

She nodded. "Akha girls go back to the old ways. That is what you find in me." She pulled my arm slightly. "I'm old-fashioned too."

"Is that what I am?" I faltered. "Is that what you think?" We were already nearing the bar. Suddenly I stopped. "How are we, Alice, to live in one world? I mean this modern world. If we are old-fashioned."

She put her hand on my lips so I wouldn't speak any further. "That's enough of modern world for me—to hear you say my modern name." I must have looked astounded. "Come, I must go in now or pay a fine for staying away from the customers." She touched my lips again lightly, then her own, indicating I don't know what, maybe to show we were through talking. "I have one more thing to say, and then I'll cure you headache."

"My headache?"

"The one I give you with all this." She spread her arms outward, no longer smiling. "I'll tell you where they are taking children to sell into slavery from the hill villages near Chiang Mai." I looked at her in disbelief. "It will not be what Kristen did. I know all about that."

"Kristen?" I exclaimed. "You mean you and Kristen... ?"

"Yes. And too I disagreed with the old man and the others at the restaurant that you should be tested with the gun that evening. I thought it foolish, because I knew from the beginning...And now he had to die for it."

"He did, for that? I was hoping we could talk alone..." I burst out in exasperation. "And what can we do with all this..." I waited for a while. "Nobody hears us," I said, "except each other."

She bowed her head slightly and nodded. I wasn't sure she had understood, since I myself hadn't, not entirely.

"Oh yes, your headache," she continued levelly, looking up and letting the noise of my outburst subside, "I'll fix that too." She continued very deliberately, "My cure will be to hold your head all night."

"I thought it was a superstition—belief I mean—that to touch my head would frighten away my spirit and I'd fall ill."

She laughed at my mistaken knowledge. "That's only for children. Children's heads. Or are you still some sort of a child? Maybe you are. My child. Anyway, that happens when you touch a child's head with your hands. I won't frighten away your spirit, only your loneliness." I must have looked puzzled. "Because I love you. You know the sign in your hotel, over the reception desk," she continued. "It says 'Try one of our girls, you'll never be lonely again.'" We'd reached the doorway to her bar. I looked at her flabbergasted. The two young ladies in red surveyed us silently, seriously, their short red costumes a sign of wary attentiveness.

"Never be lonely again?" I protested. Our somber witnesses now stood before us at complete attention. "You must mean always be lonely again," I corrected bitterly. "Always be lonely again."

"I mean never." Alice squeezed my arm and let it go. "Never be frightened or lonely again. I will show. Now you go back and wait for me."

I left, regained my hotel and went up to my room without pausing to read what the sign over the reception desk actually said, never or always. True to her word, when she got off work that night Alice came to my room. And true to her word she held my head all night, amid a dark flavor of the beginning of things. I didn't say in her arms. I didn't say with her hands.

5

Next morning, very early, the sun got up bloodred and pressed a white mist against our window. Just beyond its reach, further down the street, the tall slab of the Shangri-La Hotel stood like a huge black domino waiting in the shadow for me to resume a game I'd no desire to play. Looking down, I saw that only the main thoroughfares had received the sun; the crooked sidestreets remained in darkness. No help there. On the roofgarden of our hotel, just outside our window, a small Buddhist spirit house barely showed itself through the dense white atmosphere, decked out with red tassels and windchimes and Christmas tree lights that winked on and off and tinged the white thickness into whirls of varicolored cotton candy. To one side and above, the greenish mortuary glow of an all-night fluorescent tube.

Alice washed, dressed, told me to wait a minute and went out on the rooftop to bow down before the shrine, kneeling shoeless. I could see her little girl toes and the palms of her feet.

"What do you pray for, I mean toward. What do you pray toward, Alice?" I questioned a minute later, after she'd returned, "when you kneel and pray? You don't have to answer, I'm sorry," I relented, "I suppose I was feeling left out."

She shook her head, thought about it for a while. "You want an explanation I cannot give possibly. How can you describe what you pray for? The words fly up from this world," she considered me meditatively, still holding her shoes in one hand, "and you know I pray for you."

"But why," I persisted like an inquisitive child, "if your religion is so calm and benign, why does it end in general suffering and warfare among you…?"

"Why does your religion too?" she replied. "Why such warfare and suffering, you ask, in all these religions? Well…" I had no notion of what I was about to hear, "maybe it's to satisfy the little tin soldier inside of us." She was already dressed now, and she took my arm. "The little tin soldier inside each of us, you too." We made our way downstairs. She pulled me quickly through the sleepy lobby, past the sign over the desk, betraying a self-conscious haste, then into the street where the mist glowed whiter still and was beginning to disperse.

"The little tin soldier inside of us," I muttered.

"Yes," she gripped my arm very tightly. She matched me step for step, and together we went down the street.

*   *   *

Within the hour we were seated on the breakfast terrace of the relentlessly glitzy Oriental Hotel, if you will allow it, fronting the river, among the early risers.

"The long-tail boats, the long-tail boats," I chanted under my breath to console myself as I watched their rooster-tails lift high and dissolve into a spray of small diamonds.

"Good thing I went back and changed my clothes." Alice adjusted the neckline of her plain loose-fitting dress, glancing around her apprehensively, then diving into a sweetroll, "I would have looked like a whore in this setting." She paused and swallowed. "I *am* a whore." She looked at me then lowered her eyes. She had undone her hair from its elaborate chignon so that it fell along her back. I didn't say anything, but slipped over to her side of the breakfast table the tiny blue and white pottery fragment we had found that first day at Temple Arun, the Temple of Dawn. It sat there on the white table cloth next to her unused fork. She looked at it in silence. The long-tails on the river fired up again, sending up their crystals. She picked up the fragment and put it down the neckline of her dress.

"That is how I keep you," she declared matter-of-factly. "That is probably how you keep a great many," I thought to myself. Then I despised myself for thinking it. We were silent for a while. Addressing the second half of her sweet roll, and giving me a corner of her eye, "Now you'll never be lonely," she smiled, "again. Like me." I looked out at the boats. Wondering which one would be first to take off again. Fly away under its canopy of tears.

＊   ＊   ＊

Finishing her roll, she brought me back with a quick glance. "I know we'd be a good couple because…"

"Is that what I was asking?" I protested, stalling so as to readjust my attention. "I was just watching you eat."

She pretended to swallow again, for my benefit, then she smiled and shrugged. "I know—knew—we'd be a good couple because it's an old Akha belief—superstition, you'd say—that when a young woman and a young man go into the jungle to make love all night…" She stopped right there at the expression on my face, whatever it was. We both recognized silently that she spoke with some experience of the matter. "When they wake up in the morning, if one of them has turned a back to the other, then it won't be a marriage. They shouldn't be married. They can go on making love of course."

Maybe it was the 'of course', but I didn't say anything for a while. She looked at me, anxious and expectant. "And us?" I inquired finally.

"You were facing me, asleep. I didn't let you go till the sun came up."

"But we didn't have intercourse" I objected.

"No. We had something more than that. You became my child, my first—my second child," she corrected herself and folded her napkin carefully, "and now I like to think that my second child is from a different part of the world."

I tried to smile about the different part of the world bit. I found I couldn't eat very much.

"I'll tell you about our religion," she continued, observing my inward disarray, and thinking that to hear more about Akha custom might bolster me. "Let's see. Our people believe in ancestor shrines, but everything is to be venerated for only fifty generations, and then…"

"Then what?"

"Then we must go elsewhere for our religious beliefs. Buddhism, Taoism, even Christianity. Except that the new religion, whichever it is, breaks the old shrines and figures which we've lived with so long." She paused thoughtfully, "We can't go elsewhere for new beliefs because we would leave behind our ancestors whom we've carried with us for generations."

"And so," I asked, "what can you do?"

"So here I am."

I considered it for a while, all the time conscious of her long black hair so different from mine. Our hairs were from different parts of the world. "I hope I'm not an old ancestor you must leave behind," I replied finally, "after fifty generations. That's not so very long, you know, to understand some one so different as we are, fifty generations."

She looked down and straightened the neckline of her dress again. "No, you're the child. I'm the ancestor," she announced with spirit. "Even if you don't believe in me and venerate me."

"But I do believe in you," I answered suddenly, rousing myself. Just then a long-tail growled into life, dissolving my words into nothing—a mere crystal spray drifting toward the orange temple roofs across the river. "I do believe in you," I shouted, my voice misjudging itself and coming down harshly in the silent interval left behind by the fading engine. The solicitous table attendant who had been hovering all the while a few yards away behind a tub of potted hydrangeas, hurried to our table and inquired anxiously, was there anything I lacked, sir, anything I lacked.

CHAPTER FOUR

1

Up and down the hillside, flame-of-the-forest (your *spathodea campan-ulata*) winked out from under the mist of the great tropical canopy. Beneath it, all around us, the smell of camphor wood. Contrary to the sign in my Bangkok hotel, I was lonely again. The forest came alive as I gazed into it, flickering with monkeys and birds too swift and momentary for me to recognize. A brown hawk took flight.

Bill gunned Rover, slipping it out of gear, and we slowed to a halt. The white fog was lifting, a veil dropped by a neglectful dancer then deftly, unhurriedly picked up again. The rest of the mountainside emerged, now dotted decisively with trails of red and orange flame-of-the-forest. Then without warning it was sprinkling on us out of a cloud filled with sunlight. Rover gasped, rattled hard as we pulled over. We had been creeping uphill, and the forest cover was slowly turning to evergreen, still mixed with oak and chestnut and occasional bamboo with carefully pointed leaves, shaped like tools, growing out of the sandy red soil. Rover, Bill and I faced the hillside now; a purple light was on it, and the remainder of the hillside ran up into fog once again. I was the first, among the three of us, to speak.

"It's just struck me," I confided in the direction of the cloudbank which, starting mid-mountain, ran up before us, "that what you see of me, what I see of you, is filtered like the sunlight over there—filtered right through each person's identity. And that identity isn't anything solid, really; it's a cloud, maybe with a mysterious woman within it, or just a vacuum or a hole that needs filling." Bill cast me a significant glance. "We fill it with whatever ideas or agenda we have lying about," I added hastily, "or laying about as most people insist, at that moment." Right there I petered out. Bill looked at me again then turned back to the forest.

"It's just struck me," I continued bravely in the same idiom, gathering strength as if the whole notion were my own discovery, "that whatever I speak, I speak it as if I were speaking in a book. We're all in a book. You too." He let me have a sharp glance. "I know you've already told me what a stupid thing a book is. It pretends to carry another person's words so that we can put them under our arm or in a sack, arrange them on a shelf...generally to puff up our self-esteem or make money..." He considered my oration for a lengthy pause. Two white birds flew up in the distance.

"Besides, the stuff's poorly written, compared to birds," he remarked finally. There was another pause.

"So have I heard, and do in part believe it," I replied tentatively. "I wouldn't want you to think I spoke to you in a book," I mumbled sheepishly, then suddenly emotional, "even if that's what you think... that we're stuck in a book."

"Do you mean to be saying this to me, or to some one else?" He picked up the field glasses and observed the two white birds, now at mid-distance. "Poorly written, compared to birds," he muttered again to himself. I brooded over it for a while. Suddenly Rover honked as he shifted in his seat. "Short circuit," he observed, "sorry." Then touching the wheel, "But I think she agrees with me."

I couldn't say whether he meant Rover, Kristen or Alice or all of them. "I guess books fill the vacuum left by our words," I allowed diffidently. Rover honked again. Bill didn't say anything right off, but jotted a number down on a slip of paper fixed to the dash. Then he looked out again.

"I'm counting Chinese egrets," he reported. I looked out and saw nothing but a curious white mist winding far off amid the dark green foliage. Poking above it and surveying the whole scene, the blue mountains. I listened; it was as quiet as a church. He put down the glasses, slipped Rover into gear, and we lurched forward.

"Honestly prof, how could you imagine I spoke to you like in a book?" We got under way again, hitting every third pothole squarely. "I knew you'd fall for Alice," he yelled in my ear, just above the clanking roar of the engine, and it answered my question. "Who wouldn't? And she wants to see you again when we get back. Whenever."

*   *   *

Kristen stood solitary in the middle of the dusty compound, knapsack at her feet. A bus stop in the middle of nowhere. I couldn't help but feel sorry for her, whatever had occurred between us. The Karen village was an assemblage of rickety huts on high stilts, with long shallow sloping roofs made of thatch. The walls were irregularly cut planks so widely spaced that mice could crawl between them. The cellar beneath each hut, open on three sides, held miscellaneous farming utensils, dried food and its attendant vermin, an occasional three-speed bike. The peak of the roof ended in two thin arms crossed and extended upwards about three feet like sword-blades, to keep off evil spirits, rather than in the single upright sword-blade of Thai construction. Kristen had been crying. Perhaps it was the dust. Or her side of a story we'd never know. The village was entirely deserted. Two amiable water buffalo stood mired in the corner of a wet field and held muddy conference on whether to bid her farewell.

"Every one is out in the rice fields," she nodded toward the buffalo, justifying the desolation. In the distance I could see some children running toward us on the dusty road. It would be a considerable while before they arrived. An unconcerned dog appeared from nowhere, took no notice of us and continued a random sweep for squirrels and mice under the dwellings. Kristen hiked her bag into the back of our truck.

"Hi, Kristen," I volunteered with a view to cheering her up, "want to invite Rover," indicating the canine, "over to meet Rover?" She looked at me suspiciously, as if I knew something about dogs and the local diet.

"No. He and I have fallen out. He ate one of my socks last night. And another article I won't mention."

"Man," Bill sighed, "those native dogs." Rover beeped a hoot of disapproval, and the dog took off. "You haven't made up yet, heh? Well, he'll be burger soon. I guess that's kind of a payback. Anyway, alley-oop now; we're on the way to town. I'm starved." He observed the village meditatively, sensing some of Kristen's melancholy. "Likely we're all starved." On this note we climbed in, fired 'her' up, and got ready to get out of there.

Stepping out of nowhere, actually from behind a great clump of bamboo, a wrinkled old woman appeared by magic, holding closely and protectively in her arms a beautifully plumed rooster. She approached the window of the truck, partially protecting the bird, partially showing it with temperate pride.

"How are we supposed to cook it?" I asked. Silent guffaws from Bill and myself.

"You're not," Kristen scoffed, "she's not giving it to us to cook, and don't touch it; it's sacred to her. She's just letting us see it." We all waited in silence admiring her chicken. The magnificently plumed creature regarded us through one unfriendly red eye. Both woman and rooster hung there unblinking and motionless in time, not letting on that they thought us extremely foreign.

"I wish she'd let us eat it, right now," Bill proposed obstinately, "I'm famished."

The rooster let out an ungodly, egomaniacal screech and twisted its neck through 180 degrees so that the other malignant eye glared at us redly. We drew back, shamed into a few more instants of uncomfortable, silent dialogue with the bird and its owner. Then the old woman's head bowed slightly and she stepped back. Rooster took the cue to come alive and turn his head back the other way, open his hook to screech, but didn't. We nodded to both of them as reverentially as we could manage.

"Say, about twenty kilometers up the road," Bill yelled to us over his shoulder, as we swerved off, hitting the bumps again, "I know of a Musur village—they're reputed to serve really good dogburgers, not this stuff."

"Disgusting," Kristen interjected.

"I've got a couple of granola bars here in my sack," I offered, "two I think.".

"Not as tasty as dogburgers," Bill chuckled.

Kristen turned away, speaking mostly to herself, "No wonder the people in the villages here, especially the children, are all sick," she remarked moodily, "mostly malnourished."

"It's okay, Kris," he consoled her, "I was just kidding. Anyway I never travel without bringing along my mustard and A1." This time Rover guffawed, bucketing over the rough spots and roaring and tooting its short circuit preposterously. I reached into my sack, got out the granola bars, and we all made up as best as times allowed, sharing them. As best as times allowed.

Couple of, three hours later we arrived in Chiang Mai, famished.

2

We drove through the Tapae Gate amid moderate traffic, mostly farm vehicles and service trucks, but interlaced with little bright red mopeds weaving a tapestry back and forth. One, two even three scrawny Thai girls perched on them wearing thin dresses and long orange scarves that fluttered like pennants, while through the blue oily smoke of the exhaust the rear wheels kicked up dust and sticks at our windshield.

Bill turned right, at the moat of the old fortified city stinking of ancient sewage, and dropped me off at my hotel. Kristen and he would stay with friends a little further out of town, near the university. I walked into the garishly modern lobby from which, in its new resurrection, they had forgotten to remove a few pieces of heavy old teak furniture. At one corner some candles burned in front of a little shrine.

Two adolescent girls in ill-fitted low-cut taffeta ballroom gowns, each carrying a corsage of orchids, stood under a sign on the wall whose looped contortions of script looked fine but which probably was a marketing gimmick. They appeared to be part of a packaged tour and had arrived either too early or too late to connect with the customers. I looked at them; they turned away, clouded and ashamed. One of them lifted a brown stubby foot from out of her red spike heels, sizes too large for her. The other foot, upon which she balanced, wobbled precariously. Their faces were of a slightly dark complexion, heavy browed and thoroughly scrubbed, under the luxuriant fine black hair and eyebrows. Their stare remained strong and resentful beneath the cheap gowns and obnoxious cologne. Hilltribe girls, very young. I kept my distance; still they fidgeted, noticing me notice them. Were Kristen and Bill not returning shortly, and had I not needed to settle in and wash up, I would have attempted to explain to them. Explain I was not a customer; that I was not part of a packaged tour arrived in town to make use of them, then leave. But how could I explain that? I feared their muteness—even if we were in bed together—more than the chatter of the red twins at Pat Pong. Probably my efforts to say something would have brought further misunderstanding and indignity, leaving them more miserable than now.

There's a special relation between speaking and loving, that the world never admits. I turned away and headed toward my room. Looking back, I thought one of them began to see me, or rather I hoped one began to see me for what I was.

An hour later Kristen, Bill and I were seated in a tiny but clean American style breakfast nook. The owner had run a laundromat in California for several years. The three of us had two American breakfasts each. Six sets of omelettes with flapjacks. What is this hole in the *farang* identity that requires such filling? I inquired. "You think we can eat," Bill remarked off-handedly,"wait till George blows into town."

"George?" I asked.

"George. He's been in the area checking on what the local inhabitants are doing to the elephants by way of training them, loading the young ones down with immense chains and so forth." I remarked I didn't know that. Training them for what? "Theme Park stuff. They're a sign of wisdom, you know," he confided to us, ruminating over his toast, "the elephants, I mean, not the local inhabitants. They are in India anyway. George says. Here they're being abused by loggers and gawked at by tourists." He browsed a sizeable mouthful of omelette, swallowing with difficulty. "Every time I watch them—the elephants— I feel I'd love to be able to take such huge mouthfuls." He put down his fork and blinked at us.

Two tables removed, a bald, porcine, middle aged American businessman was showing off in front of a young, scrubbed boy he had leased for the week. The youth regarded him politely, uncomprehendingly, as he harangued lavishly upon this and that Businessweek aporia. No, he didn't understand most of it, what it was all about. What precisely was meant to be so impressive? So he appeared respectful and bored, and he glanced furtively at our table. Even at that distance his eyes said yes, perhaps we were the family he was looking for, though right now he was over **there**. Couldn't we? You certainly are **over there**, I thought, breaking eye contact and looking away. Kristen and Bill regarded me expectantly. I was about to mention the two girls in red at my hotel but decided not to.

"Where's Alice hiding now?" I demanded suddenly, as if I were asking all three of us, and most unexpectedly myself. The boy at the other table had turned entirely toward us and was staring, "Kristen," I continued earnestly; she looked up, "regarding Alice… do you think I should…"

Kristen glanced at the other table, at the staring boy, then back at me. "Tomorrow I'll take us to her village, north of here. She's up there, you know." She looked down at her plate, grimacing. She didn't add, like I wanted her to add, "waiting". Because it wasn't so, was it? Or because it wasn't necessary to say it? Or because Alice didn't want her to? Or simply because it would be too hard for me to hear the truth either way.

"She's putting things in order regarding her husband." Kristen peered at me intently. "You can't really believe that I'm the only one who uses people."

✶　　　　　　✶　　　　　　✶

Next morning before we started off Kristen and I paid a visit, as regulations required, to the police superintendent. Short, squat, surprisingly affable, untrustworthy, he removed his cap to Kristen, as if he'd met her before, then glancing at me reasserted it on his thick inscrutable head. No, he advised us, there were no underage girls working the hotels. "But," I said. Yes, the BPP, Border Patrol Police were looking in on the villages to make sure pimps weren't recruiting. I thought the Border Patrol **were** the pimps, I whispered to Kristen who showed no emotion. But it was difficult, he confessed, because there really was no law to prevent families from selling or renting out sons and daughters during the off growing season, especially if the crop (opium, he acknowledged, my, how did he know that?) wasn't good that year. "Ask him about alternate crops" I muttered to Kristen. "You ask him," she replied angrily, "Don't take it out on me." What about reforestation? I suggested to him. Yes, there was much progress being made, especially up here in the north, he made an expansive self-gratulatory motion of the arms which sent me nothing but a warning, would I like to volunteer to help? "I thought that was exactly the problem," I remarked to Kristen. "Reforestation takes opium fields out of use, they can't plant in reforested areas, and eventually the villagers have to sell their children." The Superintendent smiled easily at our telephonic tete-a-tete. Well, it's always been like that, he explained to us mostly showing off that he understood English, and it's just the way of those people. They don't plant rice, they don't own fields. But for sure his men were looking into it. "I bet they are," I said to Kristen as we exited, "Good thing we found out, so we'll be on the lookout for them."

Her eyes narrowed as we walked toward Rover. Maybe she was thinking over my childish protests. Finally, turning to me, "Time for you to wake up. How do you think Alice got into this...? Why do you think she does what she does?"

I brooded for a while numbly. Then pulling myself together, "In order to infiltrate the child slave trade of course. That's why she does it."

"And that's why she'll go back to doing it. No matter how much you talk to her."

"What do you mean?" I cried, lagging behind and uttering almost a child's whimper. "What do you mean she'll go back? To what?" Then recovering, "Listen, I don't give a damn about your agenda—you know, the one you've already got me involved in. Well OK, I'll go it for you. But I don't much care to sacrifice people to an agenda. And I do care about Alice. I won't put the agenda before her." I stopped for a while. "And that's why I went to Pat Pong to find her. And you can ask her about it."

"I have," Kristen replied thin-lipped. "I have."

After a moment I regrouped my feelings. "I thought all this," I gestured vaguely around us "I thought all this...this other world was some way I could change people through writing about it. But I can't, I can't ... it isn't."

She turned and confronted me with a grimace of marked disapproval—whether of Alice's efforts in Pat Pong, or my efforts to change

her, or my rebelliousness in general. I couldn't say which. "Still, no matter how bad it is," I explained now mostly to myself, since in Alice's
absence myself was all I had. I felt her strength invade me, even so puzzled as I was by her. "Still it's the actual moment, not a cheezy journalis-
tic write up of it. It's this moment." Kristen remained silent, shielded
behind a thin deep smile to herself. "Yep," I declared. However my words
sounded, I still couldn't quite bring myself to accept them. "It's the
actual moment." I looked around us once again, my hand on the rusted
green door of our Land Rover, "the actual moment."

Kristen pushed by me and twisted into the driver's seat with an unladylike heave of her rump. She settled behind the wheel, waiting for me
to walk around to the other side. Then with surprising bitterness,
"Words always come too late for life. Eh, professor?"

3

"Here's the marker, don't miss the road George." Bill warned from the
back seat. George was sawing away at the wheel while murmuring to
himself in Bengali, hoping to ward off all mishaps that might arise from
his equivalent of driving.

We climbed the ruts gradually upward, and above us purple light
spread out like a great moist pancake over the heavily wooded hills.
Occasional bamboo huts with steep overhangs on low stilts emerged
from under the mist, lightly dampened by it. "Akha," Bill roused himself. Then around the corner we met again the elegantly shaped bushes
that carried our favorite orange-red blossoms.

Our rut-in-the-jungle ended abruptly. We climbed out to unbend our stiff legs and to set straight the illegible sign which George had used as a bumper post. From there it took another half hour on foot, uphill.

*   *   *

The village gate consisted of a double set of huge log uprights carrying heavy square lintels. The logs were bound together and wrapped with vines; from the lintels drooped clusters of bamboo leaves linked by chains of hanging flowers. Up through the middle thrust a live tree, rooted and growing. Two wooden male stick figures, shaped like slingshots or huge clothespins stood guard outside the gate, their penises erect. A silence told me I should not walk through the entrance. We sat down outside, and waited.

"Kristen," I murmured. A little girl, really a diminutive adult, suddenly appeared from nowhere just inside the gate. In blue and red robes, with white feathers and ribbons in her hair, she eyed us impassively.

"Ta gu, ta gu de," Kristen spoke as she got up from her crouch, rising upward to six feet of blond stranger. "U du tah ma." The little girl bowed her head. "Naw jaw ga la-eu ma—I have come to your place," Kristen translated for us.

"Sure have," I muttered, looking around. "What we need now are the Boy Scouts to help make camp."

"A ma baw ma lo?" Kris continued.

"Something about your mother," Bill murmured aside.

"Do you have a mother?" Kristen snapped at us.

The little girl bowed again, turned and began to run, stopped, got control of herself, turned back and motioned for us to come through the gate, which we did taking care not to touch any of the posts or vines. At the end of a short path we came to a red-earthed village compound. The houses were open-sided structures of logs and poles set on low pilings, with enormous sloping roofs of thatched bamboo and cane. I could see now that the eaves sloped almost to the ground and were propped by additional posts set at an angle into the muddy courtyard. The courtyard boasted a corral of horizontally woven thicket and hollow reed. As we waited, three small pigs appeared out of nowhere then veered away as a woman clad in short kilts and a multi-colored bodice approached us nodding her conical head dress of white beads, bright ribbons and dangling silver coins. She carried a pot and two battered tin cups.

"Have to drink some," Bill commented, a shade gleefully I thought, "whatsomever it is, water, tea, liquor, mixture of all." He acknowledged our silent anxiety. "Goes good with I won't say what kind of burgers, coming up."

"Dogburgers very good," George volunteered abruptly out loud.

We drank, very little, and Bill was able to take over in Thai, explaining that we were friends of Alice. The village women now gathered around us, and all appeared to be about thirty years old, though they were probably ten years younger. They nodded their heads smiling so the wrinkles showed beside their eyes. One gestured toward a second compound behind the huts which were populated, I now noticed, in their lower regions by chickens and pigs. We trudged on to where we were directed. At the center of this compound a young man was standing beneath a tall pole with a rope in his hands guiding something up high. At the far end of the compound another lintel, much slimmer, had been erected as an exit gate, and the dusty steep uphill path beyond was bordered with yellow-green trees.

Whoosh! Alice flew over my head, upside down and smiling at me, her kilts flapping up to her ears, then she swung away on a great arc. She was spinning at the end of a long rope fixed to the top of the pole. Any contact with a tree or rooftop would pulverize her. But she swung freely and exactly, feet together toes pointed upwards, shins covered with black leggings brocaded with bits of red and green yarn, the remainder of her legs bare to the groin. With an instant pang I felt her strength bending over me like a strong pliant reed.

"Halloo Professor!" She whizzed cheerfully overhead and sped away, returning to her orbit, without the least insincerity measuring her own lived time, departing, accelerating, returning, departing on the next arc of a journey I couldn't share. She kept it up for another few minutes. Then she got down, or was lowered down precariously, and she hopped panting to where we stood like a group of humbled spectators who didn't know whether or not to nudge each other, after walking in on a Royal Ballet rehearsal.

"It's not New Year's, and this is a New Year's ceremony," she apologized, breathless, "but I've got to practice and show the young girls how." She dipped her head toward Kristen who stood agape, like the rest of us. "It's part of, what do you say, the fertility ceremony," she added by way of further apology, then addressing Kristen, "do you want to try?"

"No thanks. But no need to apologize," Kristen said, "it was wonderful."

"Come on Kris, give it a whirl. Might come in use. Oh, Swedes don't fly upside down in circles, do they?" Bill observed archly. She poked him. "But I'm sure they could if they wanted to," he acknowledged.

Alice smiled at us. "Please excuse me for a moment," she ducked a curtsy to us, "I have to go to the jungle—after all that swinging." She smiled particularly at me. "We have no toilet." I shrugged in response, not allowing I would have suspected as much.

While she was exploring the jungle I hobbled over to examine her swinging rope. My left ankle, swollen after the hike, made my achilles tendon ache and sent burning surges up my calf. The rope was made of two heavy vines braided or rather twisted together. The young man, observing my limp, held them out respectfully for me as if I might be searching in their anatomy a cure to my lameness. I pretended to look them over, not wishing to embarrass him in his supposition, and after a while Alice crept back to my side, still softly breathless. "Sometimes they break when big girls hang on them," she remarked informatively.

"You're not a big girl," I answered. "Is that pretty child down by the gate your... first child?"

"My sister's," she replied. "Mine died two years ago." I didn't reply, only nodded.

"You see," she looked back and forth between us, in a manner of explanation," mine was not, what do you say, 'legitimized.' They took her away and gave her to a blind man when she was four. He used her to guide him and for begging, up north. But he starved her to death."

None of us said anything.

"Now you see other people taking our young girls and making them work in the brothel until they drop. Organized people. Like the police up here."

I knew that it wasn't the whole truth. Often Akha girls returned again and again to work the bordellos, a primitive way of earning income in order to pay family debts, engineered by landlords. As Bill had implied, it was part of the order of things. A lousy order to be sure. But I was only a farang. Up against a brick wall.

"But now," Alice turned to all of us as if she had been reading our minds on that topic which was so awkward to us westerners, "but now I see the old ways are not good. I am more of you mind." She glanced at me in particular appearing now suddenly puzzled and shy. "My mind is more your mind." She must have perceived the barrier within my eyes. "I am of your mind. If you believe."

I wasn't so sure I believed all the politics and apologies and anthropologies. But I guess I believed her, if not her words. That was the crux of it.

"So I'm your only…" I was the first to speak up. All the while I'd been examining Alice in her native dress. Mixed along with her neckpieces of silver balls and large white beads dangling to below her breasts hung a necklace made of interlaced safety pins. Some sort of girl's gift or token? And now her eye rims were noticeably more almond shaped creating the impression of one eye turning slightly inward. And I'm your only what, I thought. Child?

"But all the children here belong to everybody," Alice confided. "So that you are not, what do they say, an only child. Did you remember to say 'ta gu de' to them, don't fear me, please. So their tiny souls won't fly away?"

"Kristen remembered to say it," I murmured, now understanding her formal mode of address to the child, but still brooding over the strange confessions we had just heard from Alice. "Don't fear me, please" I repeated.

"Oh I don't," she added as a point of information, "You don't have to say it to big children."

"I see," I answered.

"But thank you anyway. My soul will not fly away, even if I must..."

"Alice," I interrupted. But I really had nothing to say. I believe it was sheer instinct to keep her from finishing the sentence, or any sentence that had *must* in it, "What is your real name?" I recalled that I was not allowed to touch her head when it was hiding beneath the elaborate head dress. Yet I felt I had to have some particular part of her to hold to.

"My real name you're not allowed to speak. I'm sorry—I wish you could. My husband's name I'm not allowed to speak," she looked down. I must have all the while been examining her too intently. "And we can't speak the words for twins, flowers and waterfalls. By way of curiosity," she added, "silly superstition, you'd say?"

"Well yes," I replied, "and no. I suppose I regularly think of twins and flowers, and maybe of waterfalls when I think of you. So I end up with no names for you, I guess."

"If you want," she hid her blush—I must have confused her by my joke—and she was offering the next thing she could to remedy the situation, "you can call me Alice-Akha. That means Alice who belongs to Akha people." She smiled a small triumph.

"But I couldn't be Professor-Akha or Doc-Akha, because I don't belong," I remarked.

"Oh yes," she countered eagerly, "we put 'Akha' behind everything that is foreign and yet we feel rightfully belongs to us." She paused, playing with me now, like her old self, "so you could be Doc-Akha, by honor of course," she giggled. "Sounds strange doesn't it? Like one is engaging to sneeze. Doc-Akha. Well," finally after a long pause, "I wish we could share a boiled egg and a hen together." She looked back and forth among us. We remained speechless. Finally I understood. She also was caught between two worlds. That's what we all shared in common. Western, Eastern, city, village, stranger, native. Always two worlds. That's what she and I had in common. Two entirely different worlds. And could any reconciliation grow out of it?

The other villagers were standing around us now, mouths agape as if each word we spoke were something magical that might turn into a bird. Their postures exhibited all sorts of frozen amazement and disbelief of this western interlude of ours. "I have a birthmark," she offered suddenly, for no reason at all, to the four of us by way of general confession before the whole village, "right here." She showed a bluish spot on the inside of her arm. "A birthmark is where God slaps you before you are born and says 'don't come back'" she ended with a laugh.

"So," I murmured to myself, but Alice overheard, "so, we only love each other when we're always being sent away from each other. And that means we can't stay with each other, like we can't stay with God."

"I don't understand your **always being**," she said after a long moment.

I looked around at the villagers, standing in the middle of the compound, all frozen in time. Only the dog moved, unconcerned, sniffing, rooting after some invisible meal. "I mean **endlessly**," I said finally, "**endlessly** being sent away." No one said anything. "Well then, does God send you away because you're a bad girl?" I continued half-heartedly trying to joke our way out of the silence.

"No, because I'm good. Don't you know the difference? And it means I'll live long and work hard." She was so triumphant we all caught the spirit of it and laughed timidly back and forth among one another. The dog emerged from beneath some nearby overhanging eaves to inspect us, as if we'd made a noise he'd never heard before. He eyed Bill suspiciously, who made a gesture of appeasement.

"What happens," Bill examined the errant dog as if it might offer to ease us over the next strained interval, "what happens if this dog urinates on the gatepost. Must you move the whole village location then? After you eat him."

Alice looked at him innocently, then shrewdly. "No. We just move the gateposts over a few feet, and it's a new location for the village." Bill swallowed hard on that. "No dogburgers," she reassured. We all laughed again, this time more loudly and then we cheered. We gathered around Alice and hugged her. There was a lull, during which the villagers stood at first appalled at this exhibition, then relieved, and the dog sensing it had been released from any possible wrongdoing and would not be served up as lunch that day, sat scratching himself and occasionally joining our celebration with a stifled inexpert howl. We stood around a little awkwardly.

"Well," Alice said uneasily, "I'll go get ready." She turned to us to explain. "I came back here, you know, not to go to my husband's village." She seemed to look at me in particular; I glanced around at the village, inspecting nothing in particular. "I don't stay at my husband's village; we're no longer…But I had to come back to pay him back the pigs." She examined each of us, and our glances told her we needed further illumination on that bit of legalism. "I was found with another man, from another village. So I really have no place in his village nor in mine. I cannot invite you into a house. You are disappointed in me?" Her glance included all of us, not just me. But most of this seemed directed to me, as if it were the final explanation I'd receive of why she'd followed the particular path she had. A path she knew I couldn't follow. Maybe that's how she made sure she could love me, while preventing me from loving her. She thought.

"I see," I said, since no one else either could or would say anything, "I see. If I'd known you paid back in pigs," I declared to break another dismal silence,"those little potbellied pigs," I continued then stopped. She looked at me uncomprehendingly. "I would have pursued you more ardently."

"You did," she corrected me. "What is 'ardently'? Anyway you did. But I have no more pigs. You'll have to take me."

"Really?" I cried.

"No," she replied. Then more passionately than any of us, at least more passionately than I was prepared to hear. "But you have to know our custom. Even when an Akha girl says no, she means yes. So, no." We all gazed at her then at each other. "I change my clothes now and come back with you, my second family. No?"

So that was where I stood. At the center of a No that said Yes, or maybe of a No that said No—the same No that hides itself inside of every Yes.

"'No' very big word," George volunteered suddenly out of nowhere, "in Akha. No?" We looked at each other astounded, then back at him ordinarily so silent. He grinned.

*   *   *

The Chiang Mai the bar and cafe owners suffered fits of misgiving and suspicion whenever they saw Alice in our company; they couldn't figure if she were part of a tour package or an independent entrepreneur, or what might be her relationship or service to us. They looked over at us calculating laboriously, as they wiped at the counter, not bothering to pretend they weren't staring. "I really should learn a few words of Thai," I muttered, "so I could tell them where to stuff it."

"You're already certified in diplomacy back in Bangkok," Kristen remarked sourly.

The city was filling with tourists, a great many middle-aged men who this year appeared to favor boy children over girl children. "180 bucks for a kid in Bangkok," Bill remarked, "I mean for that you've bought 'im or 'er, lock, stock and barrel."

"130 up here," Alice corrected him, "probably 40 direct to the parents."

"Positively Oriental profit-margin," I suggested, "even if the merchandise doesn't hold up well."

"Asian, Asian," Bill intervened. "I keep telling you we don't use Oriental any more; it sounds opprobrious."

"I want it to," I grumbled, "in this case. And what the hell are we supposed to call that glitzy hotel in Bangkok? The Asian? Try it. The Asian Hotel, Asian profit-margin," I intoned. "It doesn't sound right. Do you want me to say 'Asian delicacy'? Asiatic? Eastern? The last one isn't bad. If you live in Winnetka and are considering a visit to Martha's Vineyard. But not 'eastern profit margin.'"

Bill and Kristen wagged their heads at me and sighed together in exasperation that I was a lost cause. "Let's ask Alice to decide," they decided together, putting on significant glances, so the rest of us, especially myself, wouldn't have a chance to decide, "whether it's Oriental or Asian." Alice looked at me, shaking her head in imitation of Bill and Kristen. I shook mine back, inwardly tempted to say screw the whole subject and the people who bicker over it. But Alice took up the task so dutifully, twisting this way and that in her little chair (we had landed at a sidewalk cafe), as if she were considering past, present, the future fate of us all encapsulated right here and now, that immediately I relented and awaited her verdict.

The proprietor also waited, for something or other, pretending to wipe down a table with a wet rag while he ogled us, then snapping it at a startled roach clinging to the side of the bar and finally tossing the rag into the sink. It landed on a pile of dishes with a slap loud enough to frighten half the rats in the city. The four-legged ones too. From within the pink shadow of the interior of the cafe, two juvenile bargirls in miniskirts the size of postage stamps materialized like specters out of nowhere already seated at a table against a tawdry pink background, staring blankly at us while they sucked on their iced drinks, frozen in time and space behind their large unreadable eyes. Their thin adolescent legs twirled around each other in self defense, bare to the hip. One girl felt my eyes on her and undid her legs showing me her works. Before I could stop myself a flash of something ran through me declaring I wanted her. But not exactly. The next instant I asked myself, what is the reason behind our being here right now, especially my being here?

"You surely lack Oriental delicacy." Alice observed with polite deference to my scrutiny of the girls' thighs. "But as an Asian I still love you." All of us held our breaths then laughed. Except me truly. She beamed at us.

"Who is the Asian in that sentence, Alice-Akha?" I demanded with great sobriety, "'As an Asian I still love you'. Is it you as an Asian or me as an Asian? Because I'm not."

"You see," she cried, taking my the hand, and at this signal we all got to our feet. The girls stopped sucking on their drinks and twirled their legs up again like rubber bands, as if preparing to propel themselves over onto our table in order to find out what human life was all about. "It says exactly what I want it to. Now," she beamed happily at us, "isn't that Oriental of me? No, Asian of me?" We all laughed, trading hands around. Then we stepped into the street, and a willful stream of pedestrians on their way to assault the outdoor bazaar pushed us apart, separating us. Yes, how Asian of you, I thought as I struggled through the crowd to catch up to her side. And how distant of you, so near.

*   *   *

"No Akha here," Alice interrupted my thoughts as we sauntered through the open-air bazaar, overrun with young children in elaborate and eclectic costumes haphazardly gotten up for the tourist trade. "Look, all the children have washed faces," she jabbed me in the ribs "That's how you can tell they're not really hilltribe." Somewhere in it I thought a note of apology.

Kristen wrinkled her nose in disgust, thinking back no doubt on the child she and I had encountered in Bangkok, or the Karen village she had visited.

"Politics, Economics," Bill reasoned from somewhere behind us. "The whole skin trade is. It's negotiable as to whose poppy fields get turned into Forestry property and so declared out of bounds, or later burned suddenly before the crop comes in." He reflected for a moment. "Frankly some of those villages I've seen are so borderline... they're an apology, not a village."

"But listen. Up there in the hills in June it gets very hot and rainy," Kristen interrupted, "and flame-of-the-forest and jasmine grow on the purple lower slopes while there's rain and mist over the green canopy. The sun is bright orange at sunrise. And the villagers plant dry rice."

"And that's politics too," Bill insisted from behind, "as to which crops they're encouraged to plant by the Agriculture Commission. And after they plant and the crops come in, the market for them is withdrawn, and there you have the same pressure situation...and they sell or lease out the children."

"In August and September the fields are cleared; people collect hemp to tear into strips, and timber, sugarcane, lettuce and corn. Women in the villages with babies on their backs walk about while they weave baskets out of strips of hemp tucked in their belts. And later, in December and January the poppies come in, and again the women with little curved knives harvest the dark opium drippings, basket in one arm and a baby still on the back. If it's a good crop- -for them, not for the western users of it—maybe," Kristen drew in a breath, "Maybe they won't have to sell or mortgage the children, in place of mortgaging next year's crop."

"But in the meantime..." Bill protested, "most of the work is in the sweatshops and brothels."

"In most of the villages I've visited the drinking water is bad." Kristen pondered before continuing. "In a corner of the village compound you can watch children fight off hunger by staging contests for a whole afternoon between their favorite big black dung beetles. In a week there'll be flame-of-the-forest…"

"It's already up there," I interrupted enthusiastically, my admiration for the both of them taking a sudden leap. "I've seen it."

"Kristen meant way up north," Bill remarked steadily, "where you haven't been yet."

"I'm ready," I cried, twisting angrily and pushing back at the pedestrians who seemed intent upon coming between us. Now I was certain where I stood regarding the whole adventure. I couldn't tell whether there was a right and wrong to it, but I wanted to be on the side of doing something and doing it in the company of friends. We returned to our corner of the bazaar to escape the crowded sidewalk.

"Well good, then." He measured his words slowly, facing us. I felt I was about to become either an honorary endangered participant or honorary endangered non-participant in some enterprise.

"And I apologize for ever thinking that Kristen had something to do with orchestrating, setting up that child incident in Bangkok."

"Sure," he replied. "No bad feelings. She did set it up. Not for you, for the police. And to find where the US Embassy stood on such matters. Unofficial, of course."

I stood there glumly.

"Sort of an *agent provocateur*," he declared somewhat haughtily.

"Oh really, that's what you call it. How about sort of fucking over your friends? That's what I call it."

"As I was saying—find where the US Embassy stood. Are they too stupid to see it?" He paused. "I doubt that. Or are they already taking steps in cahoots with the police to maintain the status quo? Which do you think?"

"I don't much care," I announced bitterly. "No one trusts government officials. That's how they keep their jobs. I could have told you that from the outset. They gave me the usual chatter," I waited till I simmered down a bit. This time I was the non-committal one. "The other side to what you're saying," I added "is probably not any more nor less the truth."

"Exactly what I mean. There's always the other side. And which is your side?"

"My own," I replied promptly. "And Alice's." I kept from looking at her.

Bill looked at me approvingly, I thought. "Good answer. What does it mean?"

"It means I'm a dangerous person," I paused. "Are you satisfied? The individual is always dangerous. Because I don't do things for the same reasons that other people do things."

"Kierkegaard," Bill replied.

"No, Kierkegaard says the individual is a basic category. I don't know that he means it's dangerous. Maybe he does. He says the journey toward and within it is dangerous—through a narrow pass."

Bill didn't say anything.

"A narrow pass," I almost shouted.

"The three of us oughta take a trip northwest out of here." He deliberated far off for a moment. Which three? I asked myself. "Just to let'em know," he continued, "that we're out here, crashing about in the wrong area."

"The wrong area? I thought that's where we've been all along." No reply to my witticism. Finally I was to be promoted to an endangered non-participant, whether I was an individual or not.

"Alice and George can get the children and head northeast before..."

"You mean," I cried unable to stop myself, grabbing at their arms as they started to walk in front of me just out of reach. "You mean it's been Alice and George all the while. We're just....we're just a set of fictional ...foreigners."

"Finally you understand," Kristen turned smiling thinly, quietly. She never would forgive my viewing with skepticism her expressions of concern. "You've got it. We're just fictional foreigners."

4

For the last thirty minutes we'd been creeping like snails around a modest but persistent mountain that did not wish to be circumvented.

"Only Oink knows the road," Bill declared, referring half-resignedly to himself in that appellation, "and even Oink might get us…"

When Kristen and I had arrived at the Hilltribe Development Center north of town to pick him up, Kristen was driving, perched high in the tatty overstuffed driver's seat like the reigning peacock commanding a gaggle of gears on the floorboard. Myself was pitiably hunched on the passenger's perch, a plucked rooster with queasy stomach. Bill eyed us suspiciously. "Well," glancing back and forth between us, unrelentingly, "this is nasty business—this feminism." Kristen gave him an austere look. "Fortunately," he continued while Kristen gave him an ominous look and I didn't say anything, "in this corner of advanced civilization it has come to have passed, before it has come."

"I'll say it has," she remarked stiffly, collecting her things. "As in chauvinist oink."

"Seriously Kris, it might be dangerous," he tried to help her to dismount which she refused. Things seemed back to normal, as if our recent stand-off never had happened. And anyway Alice was gone. "Only Oink knows the road. And even Oink sometimes gets…"

'Lost' was the non-fictional word, 'rerouted' the word Bill mumbled out, looking about us much more sharply toward the end of twenty minutes. The hillside was wooded in heavy dark pine, here and there slashed with new bright green foliage and brown spots where the sun had burned it out, or swidden cultivation or illegal logging had fouled it. Thirty yards off our dusty rutted road we glimpsed a few miserable village compounds—two or three huts with thatched roofs and rough plank siding buckled and twisted under the scouring sun, and perched on rotting stilts. Delicate fronds of bamboo stroked our windshield, like the ribbon-fingers of an automated carwash, and then around a corner the road leveled and all at once we came to a clearing.

Several human stick figures rose from the roadside where they had been squatting. Bill slowed. One of the dark stick-like figures waved us forward. Several more stick figures emerged further down the road. We stopped and studied them; in the silence they studied us. One of them raised an arm holding another stick, a curiously recognizable one.

"Forsooth," Bill enunciated, somewhat giddily. "Those fellers look a tad Marxian, don't they? The way they wave around their cheap heaters."

"Cheap heaters," I intoned. Only then it became clear to me that the short sticks were rifles and suddenly I was embroiled now without a flash of warning in something that could be over quite soon, sooner than I could reconcile the Kierkegaard thing, and it was all very stupid, like a brick falling.

"Cheap what?" Kristen demanded sharply. *Assault rifles,* I thought to myself.

"White Hmong. Poppy cultivators," Bill continued.

"Cheap heaters," I mumbled out loud. "That would be Hammett, Chandler..."

"What?" Kristen snapped and turning to me, "Shut up." Bill edged us up to the nearest figure. This one was gunless; he wore a large curved blade in his belt. He shouted something at us, of course.

"Sure, I got ya," Bill yelled back out the window.

"What'd he say?" My voice seemed to issue from my hair, which tingled as it moved about my head. Bill ground us forward a bit.

"I dunno," he answered, which didn't reassure me a great deal. "He didn't speak Thai. But I believe we've intruded upon their opium fields."

"They're Hmong," Kristen declared so openly that it stung, "Green Hmong probably."

"Green? What are they doing over here?" Bill complained. "They're kinda out of place," he reflected, almost academically. "Well, perhaps we shouldn't ask them."

"White? Green?" I burbled, "does it matter?"

"*Moob Ntsuab* as opposed to *Hmood Daub*, White Hmong," Kristen explained authoritatively.

"I understand. Can we get out of here?" I entreated.

"Not to worry. They just make the usual laments and threats," Bill observed mildly, "that the rest of the world likes to feed upon in order to feel concerned and important."

"Don't be silly," Kristen snapped, "and get us out of here before they take us for Border Police."

Three Hmong in the distance now began picking their way toward the edge of the road.

"I thought Border Police were the ones that protected the opium growers," I offered, as if that could help.

"Actually, Hmong call themselves," Bill ground up a gear, and Rover seemed to respond pretty well and got under way cheerfully considering the circumstances, "*Peb Hmoob*. It means 'we three' and it's meant to dispel any unpleasant sense of social competition such as might arise between just 'we two.' Like the Western you and me." The middle man of the three had now reached the roadside. I watched him; his shadow grew across our path, and *pop pop* his AK-47 let off with an unreal sound into the ground ahead of us.

"Jackass," Kristen informed the world, speaking for all of us in plain English.

"Hey, we're getting pretty tired of this shit," Bill broadcasted volubly out the window again, it having entered somehow his mind that a curious, remote dialogue with this not-too-distant fellow might be appropriate. Rover hesitated for a moment, slowing a bit, then at the last instant it concurred with Bill's sentiment by bursting into life—there was a catch in the carburetor—and swerving straight for the man, roaring angrily. The old throttle was on the fritz again, I supposed. The grass soldier hesitated mouth agape at the noise, then took leave flying head over heels into the ditch. "*Peb Hmoob*," Bill continued, wrestling the wheel and bringing us scampering sideways out of the ditch, "has temporarily been modified back to…the competitive Western we two. At least as far as I'm concerned." We skidded around the corner sideways, lost in our own cloud of dust. "Here we are safe again. You may have observed," he straightened us out on the road. From behind us, behind the treeline, several *pops* of a heavy cap pistol.

We assumed once again our somewhat level course.

"There's no more adventurous travel," Bill observed morosely. "There's bothersome, inconvenient, threatening, sinister travel but no more adventurous. Fanatics with assault rifles at airports and such aren't all that adventurous."

"That's because we're no longer allowed to shoot back at them when they get smarmy," I explained. "All that tit-for-tat went away shortly following the sailing ships. Then politics took hold."

"Nope," he replied. He was getting up on his favorite topic, not mine, books, and I would find myself beginning to agree with his diatribe. "It's because of all the goddam travel books. They're cranked out over fifty per minute." He glanced at me significantly. "Every out of work journalist who has a pair of hiking boots, an American Express card and the proper political sentiments…I wish they wouldn't leave home," he mourned, "hobnob with a couple of gurus, urinate in a Nepalese village then hie home and in a week's time do three hundred pages on it." He glanced at me again, momentarily somber. In fact it turned me momentarily somber. "Adventure is one half inside of us, you know."

"And that's what we have to shoot back with."

"Anyway, they've got to write about it. Make it all unreal," he grumbled. "Because they're so damn big white reporter unreal while they're living it."

"Perhaps we should give this inter-cultural thing a rest," I suggested, which was really the wrong thing to suggest given our recent adventure and Kristen's rather brooding take on it. "More time to work itself out. Fact is I don't think it does work itself out, or will." Then as if I'd found a deeper meaning to what I'd just said, "I don't think it'll work out at all. Nor will we at this rate." We bumped along. "I don't think it works," I chanted.

"Shut up," Kristen advised hotly. For the second time. Bill and I traded glances.

Sometime later after we'd returned to town, Bill would confide in me that two years ago Kristen had been attacked and sexually assaulted by a renegade band of Hmong. "She must be a Quaker then," I thought, "to hang around here still. I'd catch me an AK-47 and pop back at them."

She turned on both of us, self-assuredly and seriously angry. "Listen you two, this is the thing itself, not some goddamn song you make up about it…and sing to yourself. You should know that, especially you, professor."

"I don't get what you mean, not exactly" I replied.

She turned and looked out over the hills into the purple mountains beyond. "Perhaps we understand each other too well."

"Perhaps we don't. Has this something to do with my trip to the Embassy? I busted my ass there for you."

She exchanged brief looks with Bill. "You also inspired them…I won't say that. It also transpired that they called the Swedish Embassy which is thinking of sending me home."

"Home's not a bad place. Look at what we've got here." I gestured out the window behind us where the fields lay.

But Kristen was struggling with something else inside her. "I talked with Alice. Maybe you should leave her alone to do her job," she said abruptly.

"You mean let her alone to do your job."

Rover droned on without comment. Things were backsliding again.

"And what job do you think you're doing?"

"To beg her not to sacrifice herself to some risky political enterprise. That's my job. Not to put political agenda over personal relations."

"She doesn't feel that way," Kristen announced crisply.

"I know she doesn't," I fought back, because it hurt. "So what are you worried about? That she actually may love me enough to…what?"

"I'm not worried about that. I'm worried to save you from a disappointment that you'll broadcast to every naive listener when you reach home."

That set me back. She didn't have to explain any further. She didn't, because already I knew she was right. A disappointment. So what? Why should she care? Delayed guilt? Reborn loyalty? And why shouldn't I speak in my own voice when and if I got home. Let the world know it was still an ass sitting on its ass, like it's always been.

Rover jounced and roared, preventing my mind from settling on any reasonable answer. Maybe what I'd been doing all along with my life was just making a song of it. Well then. Bill had said once, we were strolling somewhere along the Chao Phraya checking out the long-tails, it wasn't the truth of it that counted but the song. Out of which, I'd inferred, the truth floated up disguised as a hunk of driftwood or seaweed if it floated up at all. But it kept you looking. And that was the song of it.

The next instant a rut in the road jerked me back into the real world, and the words I came up with sounded like some sort of oblique professorial remark.

"I dunno Kris. Even when you're right you're not totally right. But I blame your religion, not you."

She returned me a sharp look. "I didn't think you ever blamed a person's religion. Only the person."

"We'll have to see." I didn't mean my words to sound like that. And I really didn't want to leave matters on that surly note. But part of me wanted to.

We drove on for a while; it felt different.

"You're a dangerous person, professor," she said finally. "You have your own thoughts."

"I agree. For that I'm sorry."

"A dangerous person. But decidedly very much a person. You act the timorous professor but you don't fool me for a moment."

"Sorry. I wasn't aware I was fooling you," I shrugged it off.

In the gap that followed Bill looked back and forth between us, hoping the battlefield would start to cool down.

"These moments we have here," he began what promised to be a testimonial that was going to take place regardless of the small military inconvenience we had just passed through. He stopped to redirect his thought. "It's these moments we have together that hold me upright. Success, failure, no matter, they're still a kind of song despite what you say, Kris." He paused. "And this person called me whom you have before you is nothing more than a leftover from that song."

So am I, I agreed silently, nothing more.

We were grinding along pretty well now, and the swirling dust we left behind was spreading and filling the lapses and divots in our time together.

Rover clattered and shimmied. A hornbill flew up, wearing its strange armored headpiece of colors, and we slowed for it. Looking westward I could see the whole hillside was dotted with orange bursts of flame-of-the-forest down among the dark pines. Whatever our identities—green, white, blue, red, green—it seemed all we could do, all we were actually privileged to do, was to hold on to one more day for whatever it was worth, together.

5

We got back to Chiang Mai late in the afternoon. I decided I could have done without any of the comical Marxian fireworks, *pop, pop*. Anyway they paled by contrast to the contest that followed.

Alice was waiting for me in the lobby of the hotel. Bill and Kristen drove on. When I entered the lobby she got up from the musty red Victorian couch where the escort service girls would sit rubbing their tired chubby feet.

"I wanted to take you to see this Wat during your visit up here," Alice started, almost formally, as if she were again a tourguide. There was a cloud upon her face. It made me angry; so I pretended not to notice, and immediately I was angry I'd pretended. Then suddenly I was not angry but chagrined, both at myself and at her, and I had to start all over again.

"I've seen hundreds of them, wats," I grumbled, "at least I feel I have." In that instant I intuited finally and in a newly clear light that Alice was beyond the reach of foreigners, of her other foreigners the ones she slept with, and of me her special foreigner, and she'd accepted it, and that put her even further beyond my reach and left me solitary beside her.

"Mostly in picture books," I added in a murmur, trying to soften my statement. With hidden emotion she seemed to accept my words. We left the hotel, following the moat, then turned at the Tapae Gate, and I knew we'd take the long walk to Wat Phra Sing. I saw she wanted us to recapture our first afternoon together at Temple Arun.

"If we had time we could go to where the monks are chanting..." she persisted. "There are many monasteries around Chiang Mai. But it is so late this afternoon. I waited for you a long time."

"I've heard them on recordings," I protested, but actually I was regretting the time wasted on our recent tour through the hills. A stale fecal smell followed us as we walked—the ancient moat—drifting downwind. "And besides, those bass horns they blow for prayer call sound like sick cows. But that's not the real thing, I know." She looked at me quizzically. "The real thing," I started to explain then stopped. What was the real thing, the bass horns or my feelings about them? The sky had turned a deep purple floor over our heads, impenetrable. I stopped and looked up at it. "The real thing doesn't exist," I added, "anymore".

We walked on in silence. A few gusts alerted the treetops that a storm was gathering. We were virtually alone on the street, and the dust chose to blow in our faces alone. Alice looked around us then turned to me.

"I've hidden the children," she said suddenly, fiercely.

I felt suddenly sickened. "Why? From whom?"

"I've got to go back tonight," she continued without noticing, "and get them out."

"Alice, don't". I looked around us. "Listen. Just now we visited some local official's poppy fields, and we're not sure whether that will draw his attention away from you or alert him to the fact…" She accepted it in silence. "What will you do then?" I demanded half angrily.

She shrugged. "Then I'll disappear… for a while." She squeezed my arm. "Just for a while." We were silent. "This is the right time in my life," she added. And we walked in silence for two long blocks.

"You mean the right time in your life is the wrong time for us. Then is it really the right time in your life? I suppose so. I suppose the right time is determined for us by some outside force or situation. Answer me that."

She didn't answer me that.

"Listen good friend," I continued, "I feel so useless here."

Alice's forehead puckered with small frowns concentrating on what I'd been saying. "Useless? But you're not useless. So." She pinched the same arm as if to bring me around.

"So I'm not", rubbing myself where she'd pinched. "So what?"

"It's through you," she surprised me by hugging the arm tightly and the pressure restored some comfort to it, "that all our differences are brought out."

I shook my head. "That's a very thin assurance to live one's life on."

"So that someday, one day I mean not necessarily soon, we will mend them. Our differences." She fell silent.

"Will we?" Looking around I saw how pathetic all these reflections were in the face of the moment. "Love doesn't last very long here among you, does it?" I continued bitterly. "There's always other agenda."

"That is what love does, not last very long. That is not what love is," she answered.

"And maybe that's precisely what it doesn't do—have other agenda."

In answer she looked at me tenderly.

"How did you get into this mess, Alice-Akha?" I said finally. "Pat Pong and all that? Finally me?"

"I said how. Back in the village. You heard." She knew it didn't much satisfy me. "But now you see," she interrupted, all of a sudden sure of herself, "I knew you'd get around to it."

"Get around to what?"

"Get around to what we always do—wanting curiously to live as the other one lives, wanting curiously to speak as the other one speaks. To climb inside each other. Like you did with those small girls at the bar." She giggled. I shook my head in disbelief. "The reason we sound so much alike," she pursued in her relentless fashion, "is that we want to be each other. I do, anyway." She paused for an instant then laughed. "And you do too, when you mis-say my name." Feeling my footsteps falter, she brought me up to speed by measuring hers to mine then increasing our pace.

We walked for a while as I thought things over from the outset to the present. "Do you know," my voice sounded hollower now, "for all the bells and whistles people put on it, there's actually not much real loving over here after all. Not much gaiety either. To hell with all the customs and costumes."

I think she must have understood me by the silent look she gave. "Not enough gaiety to go around a first day kindergarten class. Not enough for the real world. Because the real world needs gaiety."

"Look," she cried, her voice laden with an emotion I couldn't comprehend, because it wasn't a western emotion. Or maybe it was only that I felt she was evading me. She indicated an ancient crone wearing a wide straw hat and carrying a large flat basket laden with tiny wicker bird cages. "Look, there's a village grandmother selling birds in cages so we can release them on the temple grounds. That way we rid ourselves of

our…impurities." She sucked in her breath, as if she were already starting out on that task way ahead of me.

"What impurities?" I demanded, now fully certain that our time was
running out. "And tell me where are you going with the children?"

The old vendor gave us a shrewd look, convinced we were the village
girl in the company of a farang. One of the small birds fluttered in its
tight wicker prison and eyed me with a bright brown pearl. The sky was
darkening further. It was still very hot. A cotton-white mist had fallen
from the purple floor above us and landed along the tops of trees and
buildings. Alice produced her purse, and glancing up at me with a sudden affection, counted out the money. The old crone muttered to herself; the birds battered their wings against the cages as she rearranged
her tray. In another moment each of us held a little clamshell wicker
basket with three sparrows imprisoned in it, crouched tightly together
in the suffocating heat.

"It's silly, this custom, isn't it," Alice raised her eyebrows at me as I
gingerly carried my basket. "No, it's cruel, I mean. Perhaps they're the
same thing."

"Why is our time running out?" I cried suddenly, not giving a damn if
all the temples in the world surrounded us. "Ever since I landed here I've
asked myself how is it that we are to live in the same world, so that together
we can have a world to speak in? Alice, there's your world and there's mine.
Why do you hold yours so far away? Can you answer me that?"

We entered the temple grounds and walked to the center of the
courtyard. "So you can't answer it," I continued bitterly, "or you won't."
I choked down the rest. A steady cool breeze had gathered from under
the dark clouds. At the center of the compound, before a small intense
fire that the monks had kindled, we squatted and set down our cages.
Opposite us, a great tree, a kind I'd never seen before, and next to it the
viharn, the relic-house. Alice assured me that this held murals depicting all sorts of nineteenth century scenes from life, ladies gossiping,
lovers touching each other in favored places while hidden in the

bushes, children playing, and in one corner a full inventory of kitchen utensils. I didn't want to go in. "And?" I said finally, after she'd finished telling me all this.

"What could be more respectful... of each other," she looked around the wat. Nobody was there. Then a monk appeared, sweeping the rubbish from under a building. He nodded to us. "More respectful," she continued, "than our spending our in and out breaths right here now, on these temple grounds with each other."

"Our in and out breaths?" I wavered. It seemed I could recall something of this from an earlier time.

"They're like a family building up around us, father-daughter breath, sister-brother breath, mother-son breath."

"Maybe," I replied. But I must have sounded very dubious. She laughed.

"Well," she offered briskly, "you have your choice of breaths then, father-daughter, sister-brother, mother-child. Which will it be? Which are you breathing right now?"

"All of them," I answered distractedly, "but I guess most of all the last two." She considered my reply for a moment. I went on, "Because those are the breaths the elephants give when they die of grief."

The sparrows fluttered in her cage. I looked around us and at that instant spied the old crone who had sold us the birds peering into the wat entrance. I suspected she wanted to inveigle us into returning the cages to her for re-use. To trap more birds. Something inside of me snapped. I'd never give mine back, deep inside I was sure I'd never give mine back, and I wished her bent carcass on top of the little fire sizzling in front of us for doing that to birds. The next instant I knew I never could live in Alice's country or anywhere near it.

"The in-breath is how we know each other and take in each other and become a little bit each other," Alice explained carefully, sensing my anger. It was really my despair, and I tried unsuccessfully to keep it to myself. "That's the softest, no the richest part of breathing, because it tells us we are young and there is much to do and know. But also there

is the out-breath, which is the letting-go of each other, to make a space."
She placed her hand on mine.

"A space?" I cried. "That's news. For what?"

"So that others can meet and know each other... in that space." She
was slowing the pace of her explanation. "And when they do meet in
that space we've left for them, we can feel proud because that story of
theirs, in that space... we've helped them to it. That's the story we call
the world."

"The story we call the world," I barely managed. "How can that be?" I
protested angrily. "We don't even have the same notion of time. The
same notion of world. My life isn't symbolic or significant like yours is,
Alice, it's just this thing right here, right in front of us like this fire. It's
what I have to offer you. It's the only real thing I have to offer you."

She picked up my one hand and placed it on the other. "The letting-go;
that's part of falling in love too. Maybe it's the duty part, you'd call it."

I guess she was right after all. I may have been right for the first five
minutes we met. But you can be sure that five minutes was all we ever
did have, thank you philosophy, or would have. The choice left open to
me was to act on my five minutes or let them go. No—act on them and
let them go. Stand back and let them go.

I bent down toward the smoldering fire. Worship was worship whatever shape it assumed. The caged sparrows were becoming increasingly
restless as we talked.

Alice glanced down at hers. "Now we release our birds," she said
cheerfully, "and maybe you'll hear them make a small noise as they go
off in this fog, and you'll be able to keep track of them. You see, I think
the mist is beginning to go away. Tell me if you hear them."

We pried open the wicker cages, and the small prisoners took off in a
hurry. But they flew only so far as the great tree opposite us and stopped
there, safe enough for a while. Its upper limbs were still riding the mist,
but the light rain had ceased to drift down on us. At first the soil had
turned a deep red under the rain; now it was drying and receding back

into its brick color. She carefully reconstructed her wicker cage. Then she caught me looking at her, and just as carefully she placed the cage on the small fire in front of us, then took mine and did the same. The fire crackled hot, and they were consumed in an instant. A sweet scent arose.

"Keep your eyes on the tree," she sounded strangely jubilant. "Keep them there. As the mist goes away, bit by bit, each branch will become clear again, with a covering of shiny green on it. Slowly your eyes will move up the tree. And when they reach the top you'll tell if our birds got away." She steadied my shoulder as I squatted, then her hand left with a light push, still not sending me off balance. "Don't speak now," she whispered, "just keep looking. You know," she added confidentially, "it's as if we are looking for the light above each other's head."

The light above each other's head? I almost knew what she meant. I squatted and stared up for a moment. The mist condensed on my glasses. In an instant as I looked up I recognized I couldn't live among highly principled people, religious people, any better than I could look up through smeared eyeglasses. They were all so dangerous, those people. So dangerous to some one who lived only in personal relationships.

I took the glasses off and wiped them with my bandanna. At first the lenses smeared. But after a minute they unfogged and I could see that the mist really was lifting, peeling away from the tree bit by bit, leaving it profoundly and newly green, strangely raw as if in first adolescence. A forest was being born out of a white cloud. The odor of our burning wicker cages still hung in my nostrils holding me back, joined to the strong hand of the damp heavy atmosphere, but I kept shaking them off, my eyes climbing the tree limb by limb. Looking for the birds, to make sure they had got away, was my whole existence now. I was nearly at the summit. The mist had stopped receding, just hanging there for a moment, envious that I was about to reach through it to the highest branch. Then it divided and rearranged itself in parcels as if packing its bags to go. I hesitated; my own voice sounded different, stronger, less wavering, concentrated no doubt by the heavy atmosphere.

"I see the upper limbs now. I think they got away, the birds got away like you said they would." Without waiting for her answer, "Alice-Akha," I reached out to seize her by the shoulders and turn her toward me, rediscovering once more my true voice with which to speak. "Alice, I want us to…" Of course Alice was gone.

                  *   *   *

Next morning I descended to find Kristen and Bill waiting for me. Bill was fingering disdainfully a slip of yellow paper.

"I bet we know now whose poppy fields we discovered, and whose we didn't. Superintendent Supot Kongdee at Fang extends an invitation to come see him—about our little motoring accident the other day. I don't think I'll be able to accept."

"Old Stewpot" I murmured emptily, my mind elsewhere. "I knew he'd show up." To Bill, "Did I get it wrong?" I continued airily, floating beyond the current crisis.

"Of course you got it wrong," Bill jibed acidly. "But don't kill yourself laughing over it. You may have opportunity to do that later. Incidentally it's not like Hmong to complain. They generally discharge weapons in the direction of their unwelcome visitors. More than likely it's his own opium, and he doesn't need us to report to some one in Bangkok that we've discovered his fields." Bill cogitated for a moment. "Right when he may be in the middle of another kind of operation." He paused again. "Whatever he's doing for them down there."

"Who is them down there?"

He ignored my question. "Maybe we can suggest a deal, a trade-off."

"I'm beginning to see why we took that detour. Why is it," I continued sorely, "that we never know what the other person is doing, much less thinking? I mean, even if we're friends, even if we spend life-or-death moments together, we never know truly what the other person is up to?"

"He's the one," Kristen interrupted with discernable animosity, I couldn't tell whether it was directed at Kongdee or myself and my last utterance, "who was caught last year smuggling young girls from China through Burma and selling them to houses in Bangkok. One was killed in a fire while shackled to a bed in one of the houses. Further south somewhere down the peninsula, Pattaya."

"Before that, ivory trader," Bill followed her lead in fleshing out the biography, "illegal animal species, dead or alive. This might be an interesting interview. 'The Mad Mut of Fang,' Get it? The pun I mean, mad mut, fang." He awaited with some pride our responses.

"I'm not killing myself laughing over it, like you warned me."

"Any volunteers?" Bill looked at me pointedly. "Any one of us courageously volunteer to go? Like I said, I'm afraid I'll have to miss it."

"Why," I asked, "must you miss it?"

"Because we're in the midst of doing something," Kristen interrupted angrily, "and you're not."

"Sneck up," I offered.

Bill turned to me, "Besides all that stuff, we know who might volunteer courageously." Both Kristen and he put on significant glances. I didn't know who that might be so I didn't put on a significant glance. Unless they thought it might be me, which was hopelessly off base. I had no reason to go, did I?

"I'll go," I said with an eagerness that at first surprised then appalled me. So I had to go. Not just because they wanted me to, especially not that, but because something inside of me that was not even me said I must go.

And that's the way things got done in the world—by the voice that's not even us, though it must be within us. I wasn't terribly thrilled to be playing the game. Something else was asking me to see for myself… was I an individual, perhaps? One Alice might admire? Or perhaps she was too distant to admire another individual.

Bill pointed at me in triumph as if it were he who had thought it all through, which miffed me even though I knew he was joking. "We'll send our distinguished diplomat here, trained in Bangkok to be articulate in no languages. Sorry. Actually such a non-speaker might be a good play." He seemed to be talking to himself, carelessly spinning my fate as he went along. Who cared, I guess it was just my fate. Actually as a non-speaker I would make at best a good piece of luggage, and that seemed to be my role. I followed the whole thing as dispassionately as I could. Actually I wished I could be sort of dry about things—you know, like an old fashioned Yankee farmer. Not much chance of anything that dry over here. And I knew I was too excitable to be dry, wherever I was.

"Well then maybe I won't go. What'll I tell him anyway?" I looked around at their expressions of amazement, exasperation. "We can't exactly have a conversation." They looked puzzled, disappointed. I was taking on an independent dimension utterly unexpected. Maybe it was a little bit dry. You see the road to being an individual was through a narrow pass that had no calculable dimensions. And it took its course not from a sense of proper conduct or self-regarding etiquette but from its own sense of adventure.

"What's your, I mean our game anyway, may I ask?" Then looking into their faces next instant I felt a mournful chagrin in abrading the surface of their lives, since they'd tried so hard with me. And for the moment I relented, because I'd done the same thing to Alice. But it angered me just the same. "Well maybe Songpot, whatever his name, picked up some English in jail. Where I'll probably end up."

"Jail? Don't be silly. He never went in," Kristen scoffed, her voice not in the least lamed by my momentary falling away. I'm not sure she ever listened to what I said, except when she wanted to. "For those minor offenses?"

"You take Rover," Bill turned to me, instantly back to his old self, "drop Kristen and me out of town and we'll get the bus to Phatao, opposite direction, east, then I'll hitch a ride from there and try to warn Alice and George. Alice is over there now, somewhere, and she should…"

"Warn Alice?" I mumbled mostly to myself. "Could I…"

"No. Go to Stewpot," Bill picked up on my recent perversion of the name, as a sort of honor to me I guess. "Make sort of a tourist nuisance of yourself, not overly smart-aleck." I acquiesced for the moment. "Border Police tend to point M-16's at you and so forth." He said it to strengthen his point, as if he believed that I truly would do something foolish. And that the Police were stalwart enough to lift an M-16.

"I'm used to it. I won't threaten them with my Jim Bowie, if that's what you mean" I continued glumly. Then with a sudden touch of nostalgia I couldn't ward off, "I tried it in Pat Pong and Alice had to rescue me. Anyway I've lost it."

"Just keep him occupied worrying about his opium fields. We'll do the rest."

"I don't think this is a good idea," I objected. "I think he'll see through it. I think you're endangering yourselves and Alice."

Bill wasn't listening, no one was. "Afterwards—after you've mixed it up a bit—go to the Experimental Horticultural Station, just out of town. Ask for the head vegetable grower, Panya, an odd old man. He's Lisu tribe, speaks some English—tell him you know me, you're my friend. Maybe you need to grow some spinach." His face opened in commendation of his own ingenuity.

"Spinach." I repeated. "There's a feeling of unreality about this—like before an accident on an icy road where we get a few cheap thrills swaying from side to side then some one gets badly hurt."

They ignored my analogy. Maybe it wasn't so good as I thought. "It sounds like a lot of horse-piss," I declared striving to drive my point home.

"He'll take you to his village," Bill continued. "He's headsman. Wait for us there."

"I'm listening."

"No more listening. Just doing. Now good luck and take care."

Kristen turned to me and for the first time in a long time she touched my arm almost affectionately. "We've got to go now. What did Alice say about you? It was that you always wanted to live a boy's adventure story. And now here it is."

"Is that what Alice said?" I muttered numbly, more to myself than to her. "Is that what it's been? You mean I've wished…She thinks I've had no other wish for the time we've spent together than to live a boy's life? That's not so. Kristen, when you see Alice could you tell her I…"

"That you're finally leading a boy's life?"

"No," I answered.

She turned toward the door. "Then I'll tell her you love her." She nodded gravely, "However wrong it is." There was a note of resignation in her tone. "However wrong it is. I warned you and I thought you'd understood." She nodded again. "After that you'll have to tell her yourself. Haven't you already?"

Hadn't I? Not really though, not enough. And how could she know, Kristen the know-it-all, that her earlier warning would come true? I'd be damned if I'd let…"Now we've got to go," she declared.

They started to leave.

Of course, I thought. All of us have to go, one by one.

6

Four hours later I was seated at the Ku Charoen Chai restaurant across from the town market in Fang, one of the northernmost villages in Thailand, watching Burmese traders carrying heavy boxes of contraband and whatever else they could balance on long springy poles that spanned their narrow shoulders. Whisking opium and other goods back and forth across the border. Following close behind them and taking me by surprise, a group of Akha women outfitted in the ornamental woolen vests and leggings I could recognize by now, even though it's hot, and tall headdresses tinkling their silver coins. Several have babies slung across their backs, smaller versions of themselves facing backwards; others are lugging net bags filled with gourds and vegetables. They tramp along in their knee-high boots, oblivious of the dustcloud they kick up that follows them.

Other hilltribe groups are present also, Lahu—the Musur of Bill's infamous dog jokes—their women dressed in long black skirts marked with broad horizontal stripes of red, collars of blue and white, large round silver ornaments dangling against their dark blouses. Some of the blouses are outlined along the shoulder seams by what appear to be bright silver upholstery tacks, giving them the appearance of motorcycle jackets. On their heads they wear white turbans. Even the smallest child carries a bamboo basket.

I'd heard from somewhere, Bill I imagine, that Lahu families didn't have proper names, only family histories. They were no-name persons, just histories. How much more difficult that would be—I pondered—perhaps how much easier too, and less painful than a name. Because a name is like a sharp and beautiful desire—say, what you get from a beautiful face, always painful the very moment it has sunk in, sharp and decisive and rarely just pleasurable. Alice couldn't find a name for me the other day when we were walking; in Lisu that would be all right. We'd still make it, if we were Lisu. And Lisu wouldn't feel excluded from her by not being allowed to have her true Akha name. On the other hand, I speculated, how would you ever find somebody? You would go to a village and recite a family history, and some one would step up, "I fit that history, I'm the one you're looking for, no name, but I'll come along with you." "But who **are** you?" I ask. "Well," Alice would reply, "I choose to be the one you're looking for. Isn't that what caring about each other is, a willingness to hear each other's story no matter what the name?" She peers into my face closely, to see if I'm hearing anything. "Would that be anything like spending your life underlining your favorite phrases in books?" I ask foolishly, for by and large that's all I'd done over the years.

"No," she laughs, "that's not it." "You mean recite Alice's story," finally I catch on. Now I know what I've come all this distance to recite. A young woman, totally unknowing of this farang reciter, stands in a shallow stream dipping for fish with her conical wicker basket, no, she's at work bare-shouldered, winnowing paddy, and now she's spinning cotton by twirling a free-hanging spindle while she does a kind of dance back and forth like a young girl playing. She doesn't know there may be some farang reciter of her story; perhaps she wouldn't care. Now she's weaving the cloth; next week she'll wear it at the ceremonial dance in the village, and when the dance is done, she takes a young man from another village into the jungle and makes love on a bamboo mat, one knee lifted high, the other leg straight as an arrow.

"But you know," I say, "I never was permitted to know her real name, only Alice-Akha, a name we made up. I guess that's all we ever have of one another, the stories we make up." Alice smiles faintly, "You're beginning to get a little of the idea, just now, in your story. For however far from the truth it is, it's still a kind of reciting. At least I, or she, have taught you that much." "And will you have a story of me after I go, and we never meet again?" I ask, not angrily, not even disconsolately. "Certainly," she smiles again. "Just because you or I stop reciting the story doesn't mean that the story stops." I'm stymied for the moment. "But I'll not stop reciting yours," I protest finally, "because that is what I've become. My name is 'the one who recites your story. I'll not stop reciting your story.'" "Oh?" Alice resists; she always does, but not deep down. "Oh? Some one else may recite it in the future, as some one, maybe several lovers may have done in the past, or the story will go on reciting itself, even though we can't hear it because we're..." I look at her, "because we're not attending," she finishes. "Or maybe because we are dead."

"Well," I cry out, angry now at that prospect, "maybe you win, Alice, you always do. I don't know what this story I've had spells out. I'll go back to my *farang* friends, and I'll tell them simply that your name is…that you are the one who showed me names are not necessary, maybe not even necessary in order to love some one."

The wrinkled old village grandmother, at whom I'd been staring sightlessly all the while during this imagined conversation, winked a faded gray eye at me, and hoisted up her bundle. She leaned forward and spat ceremoniously some tobacco juice into the dust. I got up.

"Kristen," I spoke out loud right at the old woman, levelly, belatedly, since she was already fixing to go. She gave me an empty gray glance and turned to leave. There was no one else around to listen, and they wouldn't understand anyway. So I called it out loud this time. "When you see Alice, make sure to tell her again…" Then I stepped forward, borne up on my emptily flapping, featherless wings.

*   *   *

Superintendent Supot Kongdee dismissed me with one hand. He had to put down his bamboo fan to do that. So much trouble. Because with the other he was massaging his moustache. His office was surprisingly neat. And he didn't seem much impressed with the story I told of our meeting Hmong on the remote mountain road, the misunderstanding, the mishap. I conceded there had been a language barrier then (as there was now), and accordingly I acted out my part at the imaginary wheel of an imaginary land rover. I attributed the failure of my spirited enactment to the fact he understood and spoke no English whatsoever. Upon concluding I waited, rather pleased with my performance.

"I am told you and your friends wish to kidnap some children and run them away," he said after a while, nearly perfectly, with some effort of precision.

I swallowed shallowly. "Who told you that story?"

He surveyed me impassively. "Your own embassy."

"We all have stories we do not wish to be told about us," I countered finally, but it sounded a bit thin to my ears. His two eyes watched me like twenty. "Sometimes they are true," I continued, "sometimes they're made up just to hurt another person. Now this story you've heard, is it about me or you? And is it true or made up? Are you smuggling children?"

He seemed to think about it for a while. There was in fact nothing in the room except our separate breathings and our separate ways of existing. I counted my breaths in, out, in, out.

"Precious—this breathing," I stated finally without least meaning it as a veiled threat—not consciously so. He drew back as if I'd slapped him in the face and glanced around. His expressionless eyes returned to mine. "I mean," I explained to the eyes, "the story that some one is collecting children to sell on the market."

"Only a fool," some imperceptible movement of his arm told me the fool was me, but I could also sense the outrage in his voice, "only a fool walks in a forest he doesn't know. It was your embassy that warned me about you and the Swedish woman and the others."

I disliked people who kept returning to the same old story, as if in repetition it gained truth. Myself included. But right then I had the spooky feeling that all along the U.S. Embassy had wanted to discredit Kristen and get her sent home in order to protect their hometown tourist citizens like myself from becoming involved in ugly matters. Like I was involved right now. That was the "difficult job" the lady from Winnetka had spoken of. And of course I hadn't caught on. Perceiving me for what I was, they figured they could use me as their avenue to Kristen. And Kongdee had been told not to lay a hand on me, at least I hoped not, as part of that deal. As silent reward he'd regain control of recruiting cheap labor to send down to the big city. I felt ridiculous because I was ridiculous—struggling to enter a game in which so many players were deeply and desperately involved. They knew the rules down to the very bottom of their own desperation. I didn't.

"You're wrong." A voice that might have been mine startled the two of us. "Only a fool thinks he knows the forest he walks in," the voice said, whatever on earth it meant by that. But I was becoming increasingly interested in the silences that occurred between us. The more savage a danger appears, the more we engage in a fruitful silence which makes room not only for that danger, but for our vast freewheeling cogitations by which we desperately oppose that danger.

At present I was meditating on how different oriental, excuse me, silence was from my own.

"What are you so defensive about?" I demanded. "And your words of wisdom. I'm constantly amazed at how goddam knowledgeable every one over here is—hell, skip the schooling, they're just plain knowledgeable. East, west, it's all the same." Of course I was answered by one of those knowledgeable silences. "And you consider me a child. How wise of you. But the child is father to the man. You learn that in school. And to keep a silence that is not merely a silent threat, which is not true silence, you learn that too."

Beneath my haranguing voice a fearful small rabbit, my real self, huddled like a cartoon character under a skitter-scatter of crazy divergent emergencies, the house afire, the cat down the well. Apart from Kristen what did he know about Alice, Bill and George? And where are those others now—and why did Alice take Kristen's place in intercepting the children? Unless, unless. Kristen was intent upon keeping Bill to herself. Despite protests to the contrary, I had no doubt that in the not far distant past Alice and Bill... And finally, when it came down to it, was Kristen only a cigar store Indian, a decoy like myself?

There was another silence. I stepped to the door. At that instant I bumped into the deputy who had been watching me all the while from behind.

"And you had better warn the rest of your friends too," I heard Kongdee's voice, low-pitched, not loud, from further back in the room. "Your criminal friends. The man and the young girl." He knew about them all right. What was the point of pretending any longer? Wasn't open warfare more honest?

*   *   *

That evening at Panya's village, a cluster of low bamboo roofs propped against the hillside by sturdy timbers, I sat cross-legged, reliving the experience. My elderly hosts sat opposite, and rocked back and forth nodding silently to me. The single entrance to the hut gave on to a hearth situated at the center of an uncluttered floor. On the glowing embers, amid the faint, sweet smoke, a battered tin pot of lukewarm tea that never got any hotter, nor cooler. I sat and rocked along with my hosts, rocked away the minutes, which wouldn't come back anyway. The image of Kongdee's deputy rose before me once again.

As I'd stepped past him to the door, a hand, two hands that were cousins of the bartender in Pat Pong had seized me from behind, one by the neck, the other by the belt of the trousers, picked me up and turned me around so that I was facing Kongdee respectfully once again as he finished his utterance. I had a glimpse of strong, brown neck welded to a thick and powerful torso. His broad, curiously troubled brow, primitively troubled, recalled a pirate's face from an earlier age, round-headed, full cheeked, almost handsome except that the sharp brown eyes had no language or cognition in them—those appurtenances had leaked out and left an empty space, or had never been there, and some donation of animal survival, I don't know what had stolen back to fill it. There was no explanation, biological or other.

I turned to my elderly hosts, Panya and his wife who rocked and smoked, nodding to me during my waking nightmare. I wondered what was written on my own strange western pirate face, was it anger, fear, disgust, just fear?

The little fire I sat before, accompanied by my hosts, reminded me of the one Alice and I had squatted in front of at Wat Phra Sing and upon which we had burned our wicker birdcages. Panya's wife had set before me, soon after I arrived, a supper of pork and cabbage and Chinese mustard. We rocked in silence. He smoked his pipe and occasionally passed it to the old woman; he hummed, maybe it was a prayer. From time to time the whole platform shivered as the little brown ponies outside in the yard rubbed their backs against the supporting posts.

In the darkness, somewhere on the village compound, young people were dancing and chanting verses; the young girls would be dressed in blouses with horizontal stripes of red and covered with silver ornaments and a tight black cincture over their full white skirts. All down their backs hung long trailers of colored ribbons ending in pompons and imitating pony tails, as did similar bunches of tassels dangling at the back of their turbans.

Panya traded his pipe again back to his wife who sat bolt upright beside him, nodding to me ceremoniously, first having taken out from her belt a long, curved dangerous-looking knife which she laid to one side, to show the house was safe and protected, and I was too, and they took turns rocking and puffing and smiling at me. Vibrating through the rickety platform on which we sat, I made out the bizarre far-off strumming of the three-string lute, the cue-bue, played by young men courting their mates-to-be, and leaning to one side I could peer out and I thought I could see shadows moving hand-in-hand in an intricate line-dance, like a procession of bodiless pony-tails swaying, always swaying, never stopping. As night slipped on, the dance continued unabated, and my elderly hosts crept up to their sleeping platform a few feet above floor-level and after a while were snoring on their mats.

Alone, I drifted upon the dance rhythms that rose up through the pervasive smell of damp straw under the platform. In the warm night my whole life seemed to drift far behind me. Past scenes in their most intimate detail detached themselves from me and started to drift slowly down a winding river, disappearing, reappearing like sunlight captured on the rippled watery surface. I was listening not to human voices but only to time, to time right now in the warm night. There was only this moment now, and this moment was all I would ever be.

Three weeks later, five of us, Anita, myself, another couple and a spare bachelor rented a cabin in the Alleghenies where we slept scattered in sleeping bags, camp-style. Our cabin was perched on a quiet lake. At one end tall reeds pushed up through the water like a brush-cut hairdo. You could hear fish leaping.

While the others stayed back at the cabin we floated our ancient skiff into the reeds, no firm land there, and made up jungle stories as we lost our way among them. Soon it would storm; the air joining lake to sky turned to tarnished silver. We put in and I built a small fire by a heavy abandoned picnic table, next to it a rotting rowboat overturned with weeds thrusting through the bottom. Anita and I sat as the first raindrops splashed. The fire hissed back gently.

"Moments like this," Anita opened, "it's like you're balancing on top of the world, and you could start life all over again by reaching your foot just a little way down one side of the globe."

We listened to raindrops sputtering in the fire. "My grandfather wrote fishing books," I remarked abstractedly. Just then two, three fish splashed amid the rain.

Anita adjusted her baseball cap and gazed into the lake. "I can't match that. I don't think I had a grandfather."

"They're still highly acclaimed," I continued, regretting I'd opened the topic. "Whenever I look them over…I can't speak back, can't write. They're that accomplished and well written."

With a grassblade she nudged a frog who took several leaps then disappeared into the lake. We were silent for a while. "Come on, tell me about this famous grandfather—no, tell me the favorite books you read when you were small," she reached over and pushed me hard in the ribs, "smaller I mean."

"Boys' adventure stories," I pondered, "late '30's early '40's stuff. I think they left me expecting life to be absolutely true, absolutely heroic, absolutely..."

Anita smiled considerately. "My, weren't you a little man of the world. Scratch that. Child of the world. Weren't you a little child of the world. So I've already told you. And there's nothing like that any more."

I couldn't answer yes or no, so I struggled on.

"Heroic aviators from World War I and II—did you know World War I aces are better," I expounded, "for having been in storage so long? They speak better, crack jokes, acknowledge the enemy can be noble. By 1942 authors are in the midst of the war effort, and all pretense to style and irony is given over. By the way, did they ever come back?" I conclude with a pretty decent flourish.

Anita scrutinizes me carefully. "Did yours ever come back?"

Dave Dawson, Lucky Doyle, Skip Nolan are momentarily taken aback, all of them clustered about in their sheepskin flying togs inside my head. "I...we don't know," they stammer alternately, dodging their feet about and looking daunted at each other then back at me.

"Supposing there's a lull in the action," Anita proposes.

"Go on, suppose it."

She eyes me warily. "At the Front I mean, and the aces are all momentarily aced out."

"Ach ja, right-o, mais oui," I contribute, "you bet."

"So Lex and Terry, Tex and Larry, Dave and Studs (oh!), Sandy and Perry—I'm losing track now—all go off to gay Paree in order to unwind, mix it up with the native citizens, and probably some native citizen wives, have a few drinks at the cabaret and dangle cigarettes out of their faces, hold empty glasses up to their eyes like monocles..."

"So far so good," I observe with guarded admiration.

"Lucky and Tex, no Tex and Perry, or Lex and Terry, wow, think they've spotted this guy from back at the aerodrome, except now he's in civvies. He's liaison to Major Ashcroft, and do you like that?" she demands. I nod approval. "But you know," she demurs, suddenly thoughtful, "this is World War I, and the silent film figures can't speak." I look at her. "They just hold out their hands, you know, flickering, waiting for the printed cards to appear and speak for them." I know, I say to myself but I don't reply or move a muscle. "Anyway," she continues, "Major Ashcroft...well, too many top missions have been going amiss, and this is bound to be the guy who's peddling the secrets—out of envy."

"No," I marvel. "Something about this story sounds familiar, but I'm sure I've never read it."

"Then whad'ya mean no? They spend their leave chasing this bozo all over town in a motorcycle sidecar. Studs and Perry an unlikely duet, on the other hand, get involved with the charity run by the Alsatian nuns for war orphans, flying in urgent medicine."

"And Lucky?" I ask.

"Ah Lucky. Why do you think he's so named?"

"I haven't the faintest."

"Lucky is the one I know about, first hand." She regards me approvingly. "A shrimp about your size, well no, don't puff up like that, a nicer looking shrimp, maybe ten or twenty years younger. There are shrimps and shrimps," Anita appeals openly.

"And stories and stories," I suggest looking down at my bulging stomach. Right then an empty feeling gets started high in my chest. "Don't you think we ought to be getting back to the cabin. Most likely they've got a banquet waiting for us. You know, with unmixed wine and so forth."

"He's pulling people outta burning buildings," Anita pursues relentlessly like she's filling an empty bucket.

"That didn't happen in Paris," I interrupt. She gives me a look. "Well, there was one cannon," I concede, "and a blimp or two." I reach over and tap her leg. "Tossing explosives. Now let's go."

She doesn't flinch. "He finds himself working shoulder to shoulder with this beautiful thin red dress. Oh yes, it happens to contain a young woman." She pauses. "Just think what that means, a thin red dress with a woman inside." She reflects for a moment.

I look dubious. "I'm thinking shouldn't we turn back."

"I thought you might be. They're working together, sweating shoulder to shoulder, like two halves of the same body, the same mind. She's in her cabaret get-up but she pitches in anyway, and hurts her arm."

Instinctively I reach over and touch Anita's arm.

"She turns to him and says 'Why do I need this *me* which is *just me?* My single being goes into the bombed out streets, something in me has been set into motion so that there is no question, and presto I'm sustained unexpectedly by another's touch who is beside me. Another's life, another's death, they take me up...' How'm I doing?" Anita demands self-critically.

"Commendably," I murmur, "for anything short of a philosopher."

"Your hand becomes part of me and together we lift this heavy beam I couldn't lift before. I'm saved by the fluids of your eye to see above the dust, your breath helps me through the cinders; suddenly we're built of each other..."

"How did she learn to speak like that if she's just..." I stopped, "while they're digging through the rubble?"

"She hurts her arm on a jagged beam." Anita indicates, "Right here" She reveals a scar high inside her own left arm that I'd touched without knowing. Now everything in me is listening. "They stand back," she continues, "regarding each other, her regard, his regard." She hesitates for an instant. "You've already guessed it; she's a hooker working the furlough circuit. Part of her war effort," Anita explains modestly. I start to protest. "Anyway he fixes her wound, bandages it up and now they have this blood relation as well as this other relation from the outset." She raises her arm and shows me the scar again. "They don't simply choose each other. Something was set in motion that enabled them to choose." I look away. "They are the two of them both become her, they are the two of them both become him, they have both worked at saving people, among people, they are both each other and both all people." Anita rests for the moment. "They are both people standing at an edge in time, seeing it happen."

"They made it happen."

Anita looks at me undeterred. "And so later, when they go up to her room, they don't...you know, they don't..." she kicks me, beneath the table. "They sit and talk instead. Let's see. About childhood, their plans, their favorite books, growing up, school, loss of parents, of romances, why they undertook the jobs they did. Well it's got to be heroic," Anita ends by protesting. "I've given it my best. But do you know something?"

"No" I confess, "I know absolutely nothing."

"They have so little time. I suppose you know that," she remarks quietly, playing with the grass stem "And one of them must die or go away, if it's to be a true story."

"And it could be either him or her," I add. "That's the normal routine."

"Or her or him," she corrects.

"Anita, we can't just adopt old stories..."

"Why not?" She twitches my mouth with the grass blade. "Is there another kind? So anyway next morning, having talked through the night he gives her that silly key thing he won at college...no, that's wrong. He gives her his brand new golden wings."

"And she?"

"Well," Anita hesitates, then suddenly inspired, "She hasn't anything to give him, having sold all her belongings and herself to boot."

I was silent.

Anita twirls the blade of grass and in a hoarser voice, "I guess all she has to give him...You fill it in."

I remain silent.

Tossing the grass blade away and pulling me up toward the cabin where by now the others surely were fed up with waiting for us. "Dummy. All she has left to give is her tears." She grasps me hard by the arm so that it hurts. "And what good have they ever done?"

*   *   *

Next I knew, Bill was shaking me. There was some early light, and looking out I saw the support posts of the hut opposite mine and clustered around them, head to head, the diminutive mountains ponies under the white mist. A few embers smoldered on the hearth.

"How d'you get here?" I mumbled rubbing my eyes.

"Ponies," Bill replied.

"They took Kristen and threw her in jail," he said after a while. "I didn't think they'd do that, she being Swedish and a Quaker… at that." He paused again, the old joker brooding. "They said they'd beat her unless she gave up the rest of the operation."

I started to get to my feet. "How do we get there?" But he didn't say anything or move.

"Doc-Akha," Bill declared as if about to give a speech, then he changed his mind and just looked strangely at me for an instant. He sat down cross-legged by my mat. I wasn't sure what would come next. Was I to be promoted or put down? The nickname had always brought bad luck, I thought, like a fit of cough. Anyway I hated prologues that didn't cut to the chase.

"Doc," he indicated the smoldering embers before us, "I don't know how to tell it." I arose on one knee then sank back. Down below across the way the ponies nudged each other and tinkled the bells strung along their necks with scarlet cord. In a few minutes there would be cock-crowing. I recalled with a distinct fondness the old village woman and her pet rooster.

"Alice was in the van with some of the kids," he started again, "you know, she was driving them out—she'd collected them. George was in a van following."

"When was this?"

"Early yesterday morning."

Even before I was visiting Kongdee. "Yesterday morning? What do you mean Alice was in the van with the kids?"

"She stepped in for Kristen. Because if caught she might be deported," Bill explained sheepishly. "You knew that." I didn't reply, because I'd harbored reluctantly that thought all along. "Anyway she was pretending to recruit them," he continued, "picking them up. But actually she was getting them out...from... Well, they found out through an informer, I guess."

"The American Embassy if I'm not mistaken."

"Somebody passed the word," Bill added carefully. "Alice and one of the oldest girls were taken out of the van, and they let the girl go after raping her but Alice was shot, executed this morning—as a warning." He paused for a moment. "Supot's way of declaring this territory as his, I suppose," he added inconsequentially trailing off. Bill had the strangest way of trailing off, as if life were a fit of dreaming that would be over soon enough if you were patient.

And I suppose her body thrown away, just like that, I pondered. Executed as a warning. And for whose benefit, or rather satisfaction...? It seemed unbelievable that last night, amid the music, I'd nearly felt like letting the whole thing fade like a dream, Alice, Kristen, Bill, George, the elephants, all of it. Now Bill and I faced each other with our words trailing far behind our innermost thoughts. And it all had happened before I'd ever reached Kongdee's office and acted like a fool there.

"What do you mean executed as a warning?" I demanded stubbornly, not giving up an inch of ground we'd won together even though on all sides around us the territory had been declared lost. "By whom? Tell me, who are *they* that do the executing?"

Bill took in a breath, half-closed his eyes, and slowly let it out. "It means she was killed as a warning, a declaration. Some of the children they tried to take into custody. Some escaped, we believe."

I scarcely heard it. In fact I could scarcely hear any words, least of all my own. "Was she really killed? How do you mean she got killed?" I guess my voice stupidly was repeating. He didn't answer. I guess I hadn't asked it loud enough. I seized his arm; it was as hard as steel, but it gave way to me. "Who is **they** that go around killing Alice and taking her children? What do you mean she was killed?" I repeated distinctly. "All of this does the world a helluva lot of good, a hell of a lot of good."

Bill stared at me in silence. But what else could he do?

"Who is **they**?" This time I articulated clearly, and I thought, How fragile can life be? And why so for Alice, who was the strongest among us?

Bill got up and faced me. He looked pretty pale, and I found myself feeling sorry for him. "They were shot by the local authorities, police, who claimed she was smuggling children and resisted, so forth. Actually, you know, she was subverting their black market. She'd done it before. So this time she was taken and executed to cover up, and also as a warning."

I thought it over for a while. "And if Kristen had been driving? As she should have."

"He wouldn't have figured he could get away with what he did, Kongdee, whoever. Maybe."

"You seriously mean that some inconsequential son of a bitch shot her? Just as a warning?"

"M-16," Bill remarked. "I found some casings. Bought and issued to police." There was a further silence. "George by the way has vanished— he was driving the second bus—they found the bus but not him. Maybe he's ok. I dunno."

"Christ, what a way to run things over here. So much for the global village." I directed these last words to Kristen who was lodged in jail and not here to defend herself. "Screw all the cheap-ass gunners of the world. If they want to issue warnings, I'll issue them back a warning. And a warning to all the pork barrel politicians, spilling their blabber day in day out on the tube, recently graduated from the third grade along with their jackass politics that send our military weapons all over the world, so they'll fall into the hands of insane criminals. And I give warning to the generals and puffed up chiefs and ambassadors and all the self-promoting, ass-savers on this side and every side of the world that grift money and favor by doing that. And every cut-a-deal diplomat the world over who has claimed ever to have done anything except screw the world and all the people in it, screw the animals, screw the trees, screw the waters, and now even screw the stars." Bill blinked at me in disbelief. The stars? "Go ahead," I shouted, releasing my tirade upon the four silent corners of our frail bamboo hut. "Go ahead stewards of the world, find your launching pad and go screw the stars. May the history books pickle your assholes and hang them on display from now to the next holocaust."

Bill reached out and touched my shoulder, as if I were an angry child. "The white man," he recited carefully—it sounded like he was taking it from memory, maybe from a joke played upon me by a certain person not long ago that had made the rounds of our group—"The white man is a burden." He looked at me and blinked. He always was a quizzical duck, I thought. He put his whole hand on my shoulder pushing down gently, demonstrating I guess that he was transferring the burden, her burden, back on me. I blinked up at him. And now the two of us crouched blinking as if we were emerging together into bright sunlight.

7

Alice was lying on a table of rough planks; her hilltribe clothes were fitted on her, vest, black skirt, ornamental leggings. Her feet were bare. Her thumbs were tied together with white cotton thread and so were her big toes. An orange cloth lay folded next to her head, and her head dress showed only three silver pieces left on it; the rest had been removed and placed around her body on the table. "Unless we tie her thumbs and toes with white cotton thread, how will she know she is dead? Now we tie your thumbs and toes, Alice-Akha." Everything was in order and she was fully clothed—except for breathing. Half-visible between her lips, now blue, a silver coin for the boatman, and lying on her collar next to her chin three small sprigs of what appeared to be ginger-root.

I recognized at last how remote and hilltribe her face was, though it had never appeared such to me while she was alive. Faint traces of hair shadowed the upper lip and grew along the broad forehead and full jaw. Now dead, her peasant bones came back to carry her across the river on the long unaccompanied journey. Fact was she'd already departed on that trip before I arrived, and she couldn't take time to turn aside and spend the afternoon with me even if she'd wanted to, and maybe on the other side there were more important things to attend to anyway. We couldn't know. Maybe there was something really important, not just our brief daylight games. Maybe there was nothing, absolutely nothing.

I shuffled my feet, just a fraction. The room seemed empty of life except for my feet. But from the far side of the table, hidden till now, the old dog appeared whom I'd seen sniffing around on my first visit. He padded toward me, neither amiable nor defensive, then stopped. From around his neck a cord led to the table, and its end was tied to Alice's sash. "It's her dog" I said to myself, "when the ceremony comes to an end they will kill and eat him." I looked at the dog and his cord. He showed neither malevolence nor friendship, simply a concentration on his present moment of being. "Right now he's placed here to chase away spirits, her own spirit included, so that she might lie dead all the more easily." Or maybe, it struck me for no justifiable reason, he was there to signify that she had cared for him and that she'd been a good mother to her child who died two years ago.

But now the little girl who had met us at the village gate and brought us in, on our first visit, appeared out of nowhere and observed me looking at the dog and his cord. Quietly she went to the body and unfastened the cord from Alice's belt and started to lead the dog outside. On an impulse I stopped her and acted out that the dog should not be killed. It took a while, but finally she nodded that she understood.

Suddenly some one else was standing beside me now. I felt it before I knew for certain. A diminutive old woman of at least ninety dressed all in black, wearing a black turban on her head, stood next to me, at about shoulder height. She gazed up at me; her front teeth were chipped and stained brown. A strong stench of tobacco floated from out around her, and behind her ear I noticed she had tucked something valuable, a frayed handrolled cigar. From deep among her wrinkles her eyes as sharp as steak knives examined me.

After a moment she passed me a needle threaded with black silk. She made a sewing motion with her hand, then she made it again impatiently as I gaped. What was I supposed to sew? I looked around for a hint. A young woman whom also I'd not noticed enter the room stepped toward me; I was shocked by how closely she resembled Alice. Same symmetrical full cheeks and rich lips, the same black wool jersey over a kilt of the same material reaching to the knees, then the same strong smooth legs bare to the dark leggings ornamented with red tassels. She parted the ribbons on one side of her head dress and exposed an earlobe; this she proceeded to pierce and draw through in pantomime. I stared at her, and her nod returned me to Alice's mute waiting face. So I was supposed to do that. I looked at old grandmother beside me; her regard hadn't moved, and I saw that by comparison with the young woman's her gaze now had lost its edge and turned watery and distant. I couldn't reconcile this gap, the distance between these several gazes, and Alice's not at all and it preoccupied me.

I reached down and tugged aside some ribbons of the head dress that had become entangled under Alice's head. Yes, just as I supposed. A smudge of dirt on the side of her jaw reached all the way down her neck. They hadn't washed the body, and Alice was right to the very end, true hilltribe people don't wash their faces. Holding a cold earlobe between my fingers I worked at pushing the needle through the fleshy part now stiffened.

It required a considerable effort. When I finally got through it, I noticed sweat was running from my cheeks on to my shaking hands and from there on to Alice's face. She appeared to be leaking tears through her mute inexpressive mask. The orange-red cloth by Alice's head, I now noticed, was color of flame-of-the-forest. I pulled the needle through and with it some of the black thread. There was no blood, and through the sweat-tears I looked up at the young woman standing opposite me on the other side of the body. She nodded and made a 'finished' motion with her hand, as if we were working together on an embroidery. I stared at her hand that had finished—everything, just like that.

Then the next thing I realized, I was sitting outside on the porch plat-form, dangling my legs over the edge like I'd seen the children do.

A moment, perhaps ten minutes later, I felt a hand on my shoulder. The young woman who had aided me and who reminded me of Alice held a tray before me. On it a cup of tea, smelling of ginger, a ball of sticky rice, a little thimble of strong smelling liquor and some chicken curry. She indicated I was to taste some of each. Before she left, she bent over me and with a white cloth wiped the streaks of moisture from my face.

After I had finished sampling the foods on the tray, without really tasting them, I realized that I must be becoming an embarrassment to them. I stood up to take my leave. In the middle of the compound the young woman who'd been my mentor was placing a white dove into the niche of a hollowed-out post about five feet high. Of course, the dove-singing contest. But now as I observed the ongoing ritual, grandmother came through the door carrying before her another tray. This one had a small hatchet on it. She motioned for me to take it, then pointed to a cluster of village men who were standing in the compound, all furnished with long knives and machetes, pretending not to notice how ridiculous my little hatchet was that I now carried before me like a child's toy as I stumbled out to join them. Of course, I told myself, we were all going to make Alice's coffin. This was coffin-making afternoon, and it was an honor to me that they included me with them. What Alice must have said to them about me, or might not have said, I'd never know. Maybe they only judged my feelings by their own.

In order to alleviate my embarrassment in not having the faintest notion of how to comport myself, they did me the further honor of investing me with a wicker basket containing a small brown piglet. Wherever we went, it went, offering in advance its not inconsiderable scent and vocal advice. Wherever we foraged back and forth inspecting trees, arguing their length, girth and properties, piglet and I were there in the midst, drinking it all in through the language barrier. I soon got to know my companion, despite a slow start due to his insistence upon orienting his hindquarters to my face. And eventually I became con-cerned that his status should remain that of a totem and not ultimately the main course of a funeral luncheon.

The appropriate tree was settled upon finally, and two equal sections were chopped from its middle. I was entreated to give a few harmless symbolic whacks with my hatchet. The two sections in turn were quickly hollowed out to the rough dimensions of Alice's body, and the outside of the top section, the lid, received extra attention and concern. Each woodcutter chiseled or scraped a design in it, rapidly, deftly, leav-ing untouched a round flat platform at about the spot where Alice's heart would be. When my turn arrived, I could think of nothing to do;

time was a-wasting. Then suddenly the inspiration seized me to incise at about where her feet would be a crude figure of the little pig I'd been carrying around in the basket. I proceeded to do so, earnestly if sketchily. A subtle and scholastic discussion exploded among the villagers immediately following, in which many precepts and opinions were exchanged quite heatedly. It was finally judged that this incised figure was a good omen.

I don't know whether this inspiration from a distant culture made it into their annals, if such there were, but I'm certain Alice would have been amused if not proud of me. She really warmed to such silly occasions as those I was for ever getting into. But the real flesh and blood pig was spared on the spot, I would like to believe through the agency of my inscription; the villagers nodded to each other in approval, the ticklish point of doctrine had been worked through, and as I once again picked up the basket with the pig in it, I realized how small and pathetic a gesture I'd made. My sole accomplishment for the term I'd been in this country was to save a pig. For a while. The two sections of the coffin were suspended by vines from shoulder-poles, held by four men each, and we returned to the village.

All the way back, I imagined Alice in her costume talking to them about me upon our return, loyally explaining and defending my sentiments about juvenile pigs. But stories like that don't translate from culture to culture, she wouldn't do that, and these imaginings of mine were pointless except as a too late token of something I'd never had a chance to share with her. When we'd arrived at the village once more, fearing that the pig might become mine by adoption, I made an earnest show of presenting him or her or it to the village grandmother. Taking the cigar out of her mouth she scrutinized with amazed watery eyes the pig still alive, damned thing, who silently scrutinized her back. Finally she nodded an acceptance, the tension relaxed, and the whole event went down in history, I'm sure. There was, I thought, the faintest trace of a smile on the lips of the young woman who had wiped my face.

It was the moment for me to depart. I pointed to the westward sun. Perched high against the blue hazed mountains, from a distance the terraced fields looked like they'd been combed into the hillside in an immense coiffure.

Then I went in and stood beside Alice's body for a moment. It seemed I had no words to say to her, inside or out. But suddenly, "Ultimately," I heard myself say aloud to her, "ultimately, all these ribbons and customs and hatchets don't do anything about death." I guess I was trying to start an argument, to get her face to say something. Remember how we used to argue? But it didn't change or reply. The issue was all one-sided, not like the old days, and it sounded pointless. "Not the deserving but the elect survive," I said in a last attempt to provoke a conversation. No answer from the other side of the world there on the table. "Not the deserving but the elect," I reaffirmed. Then I turned and left her world behind.

When I rejoined the villagers, all gathered in a group, the children also had joined them. The leader among the men, the headsman I suppose, presented me with something heavy wrapped in a cloth. It was the little hatchet I'd used, if only barely. Some one brought me a tin cup of water. I bowed to them all, to grandmother and her cigar, to the pig, then turned and walked down the path toward the village gate. I was accompanied by the young woman who'd looked after me; I suspect they were letting me know she was my new mother, and the little girl was her daughter, and so my sister.

We couldn't speak our different farewells, but our eyes almost did it for an instant, but for an instant only then they retreated behind the barriers foreign eyes raise up before an outsider. We had our separate lives again. I started down the trail to the dirt road where Bill had been waiting for me all this while in a borrowed Toyota pick-up. The trail darkened as I descended. Looking up into the gathering twilight, it was as if a stage backdrop had been lowered behind the mountains, one I'd never noticed till now, a dark blue cloth suspended on the pinpoints of a million stars and beyond them a million trillion more that had been standing over us invisibly all this while.

Oh yes, the dog went along with me for part of the way to keep the spirits away. That was what I figured, to keep Alice's spirit away. That's what dogs symbolized in Akha funerals. We started our journey back. I imagine it was to keep Alice's spirit away.

*   *   *

We got back to Fang in the dark. Bill didn't take me into town, but to a hamlet some distance off, a Karen tribe's I believe. Even at that late hour they received us as if they expected us. We climbed the ladder and dropped exhausted to our mats with our boots still on. Our hosts had rice with some chicken in it for us, and lukewarm tea. By the side of our mats some one had placed a crucifix. We were being told we were among Christians once again, and already, because of that reminder, even in my exhausted state, I longed for the village I had just left behind. I drifted into sleep, companioned by the sounds of livestock, or of a dog perhaps, rustling under the porch, and I hoped my presence would not disturb them. 'Ta gu, ta gu de,' some voice or other kept repeating endlessly in my head.

I woke to daylight; it must have been as late as six a.m. In a magic reunion Bill and Kristen were seated on the floor beside me, talking softly.

Bill indicated a pale and relieved looking Kristen. "Well, she's a bit pale, but she's back." Bill looked haggard. Kristen reached over and hugged me as I sat up, and bewildered I clung to her momentarily.

"I'm not pale," she protested, "I'm Swedish. Don't listen to him." It seemed like we were starting all over again.

"After a pleasant soiree, while you remained here snoring," Bill continued guardedly, "she's pale. Which reminds me, I might as well tell you now that they'll be looking for her—along with the back wall of their jail." I had a vision of Rover, like a rhinoceros in reverse, stubbornly backing... "You know the ancient Celtic proverb," he screwed his face up into the old Irish muggery, "'If the law is there, it's there to be broken.'"

"I suppose that could pass for ancient and Celtic," I conceded, "but it seems to be the law of every land currently."

"I went up... " Kristen started to explain. I suspected she might offer an apology, a justification I didn't want to hear.

"And they threw her in jail," Bill interceded. "Didn't think they would, but..." he trailed off.

I nodded and said nothing. This was not a conflict that could be spoken; this was not a conflict that could be resolved. And at late last I'd discovered life was not a conflict that could be spoken; life was not a conflict that could be resolved. We looked around helplessly then at one another. "Anyhow," he resumed more confidently "I have a favor to ask. The favor is I don't want you to think we've used you. Nothing could be further...Our times together were more than that."

"They never could become more," I said, "maybe something other and in addition. And isn't that something other what brought each of us here in the first place?"

I looked around. No one seemed ready to agree.

"And if you want to push it a bit further, isn't the whole story, however it turns out, always a reaffirmation of ourselves? For those who survive," I added. "Maybe even for those who don't."

Alice wouldn't have been fazed in the least by my abstract meanderings. So long as they sometime hit the point. Suddenly I missed her terribly and felt alone. But the way they bowed their heads—I was sorry if I'd hurt their feelings flying over them like a jet, or maybe it was simply that they didn't understand me. Alice wouldn't have wanted me to leave them in that state, no matter if she'd understood me or not. "And people like her," I went on since I knew we were all thinking about her, "people like her don't survive for long. No matter how much we need them. Because—you know why. Because we need them so badly."

This time I might have been at least a little in the right. But Bill always patched over my speechifying in order to get us going again, to wherever it was. He usually did get us going. "Could you sort of make a detour on your way **out**," he emphasized the last word, "just to draw their eyes away while Kristen slowly and cautiously, we hope," he glanced at her appreciatively, "vacates this country, in the other direction."

"Were they the ones..." I started.

Kristen interrupted quickly. "Kongdee and his deputy were the ones two years ago...there was an incident involving young Burma girls. And this time, they're getting rid of the evidence...re-establishing control..." She didn't finish.

"Which direction," I turned to Bill, I was still feeling perplexed and empty, "do you want me, to travel... toward?"

"Oh any," he replied, trying to cheer me by carrying it off breezily, "north, east, west; so long as it's not south," he winked as if we had a secret together, but it escaped me what that might be. "As in don't go south, go west young man." He reached out and touched my hand. "Take care now. Go back to the west young man."

"You mean go home. You don't know for sure I'll do that. Nor do I, as a matter of fact. Old-fashioned, aren't I?" I winked at Bill.

We were silent for a moment. Some one had filled a tin cup with lukewarm water and now we passed it around, each taking a sip in turn. I looked into the cup trying to confirm that the old familiar bacteria were still there, as Bill had originally warned me. Invisible. Just an ordinary cup, I guess. They were in there though. How many secrets, I wondered, were still in that cup. I guess it didn't matter. What mattered was we were passing this tin cup around. What mattered was our thumbs and toes weren't tied together with white thread.

"How did..." I thought I should say something, because we were going away for a long time. "How did you get your start in this business, Bill?" I proposed ingenuously, partly to get at the roots of how this whole thing got started, partly to make-believe we were beginning our story over.

He looked at me with sudden affection. "I used to belong to the Working Group on Involuntary Disappearances—UN." So that was at the root of the disaster, I thought. Every one doing good deeds and in total lack of co-operation. He got up, "No more rough stuff now though," he stood stiffly, dusting off his trousers and pulling Kristen up and finally, carefully me as if I were a fragile, even valuable senior citizen. "Well, maybe a little more rough stuff, till we all get settled." We stood around trying to look satisfied with that. I knew they'd wiped their hands of me, and that it was time for all of us to depart.

"Well then who pays your salary?" I quipped, as we started to disengage, "if you get one…"

"Oh," he shrugged equitably, "the world." The last shrug I ever saw of him. He and Kristen walked to the ladder stairs and climbed down. I didn't know where they were headed. Away somewhere. They climbed down just like ordinary people. "Go west," a voice called back. "And remember, keep on chompin."

"I know where I'm going," I muttered. "I'll keep on chompin."

CHAPTER FIVE

1

Kristen and Bill disappeared into the early mist, astride two diminutive ponies. Their feet nearly dragged the ground; they might have been children playing.

So I alone, the leftover, drove back to Fang. You know I couldn't leave the country without a last conversation—I almost said confrontation—with Alice's killers. Maybe Bill and Kristen would approve of me at some undiplomatic level, I don't know.

At the edge of town I said farewell to Rover, threw the keys on the floor and walked on to Kongdee's station. It was quite alright if he wanted to throw me in jail, the three walls that there were left standing of it. He still wouldn't catch the others, and eventually the lady at the embassy would have to do something, if for no reason other than to prove life was making her job difficult again. After all the U.S. had sent them the guns in the first place with which they killed people. And she could damn well spend her time refereeing that mess.

*   *   *

The room was spare and neat and in one corner, most incongruously, an elaborately painted paper parasol, a tourist item, waterproofed through the agency of pig's fat being smeared upon it and left to bake in the sun. When I entered the room Kongdee looked up from his desk as if he'd just at that moment felt my eyes upon him. In reality he'd been watching me the fractured instant I came through the door.

Anyway, the pig-fat parasol. Something about it offended me. I didn't understand why they had to do that to pigs, apart from economic motive, which so far was the only motive that clearly showed itself in the East. No, the Orient. The East. But I didn't see why I hadn't the right to feel the way I did about smeared pigs; the presumption of right and righteousness was about equal on each side, theirs and mine. I wondered if such presumption on each side was, at root, what all this had been about.

Kongdee stirred and my attention returned to him. He knew I hadn't come to discuss global policy. His hand slowly lowered its pen and seemed to move comfortably toward the holstered automatic that hung draped on the arm of his chair. I found myself measuring our disparate existences, so senselessly separated and so senselessly joined at right angles like a Sunday acrostic.

I glanced down at his hand. "If you like warnings, I'll give you a warning." He seemed justifiably put off by my opening in mid-thought, an obscure threat left over from my earlier tirade—and he moved his hand away from his weapon. "The first warning is that women should-n't die—especially like that." It was undeniably my voice speaking but I didn't recognize it, not entirely. "I'm a bit old-fashioned," the voice added inconsequentially. There was an absolute silence as if to say who would deny it. "You'd better learn it," warned the voice.

He answered me with a regard entirely noncommittal on the subject. Why should he learn it? He saw no reason, I saw no reason he should. Had I learned anything about the values of his country? He reached down, slowly took out his pistol and laid it on the table, which seemed to me a rather western stab at interlingua. But, I reasoned quietly, what else could one expect? In a land where the sword was mightier than the pen, and both equally stupid. I approached the table and leaning over—it was rather rickety and spoiled my effect—but he in turn was forced to lean forward to protect his weapon so that we looked like a pair of diplomats, heads together, about to butter each other up and start a war.

Following my own diplomatic cue, I took a sheaf of his official papers and flicked them on his nose. But instead of symbolizing challenge and chaos, they spread out in a spiral of softly falling leaves. Everything in the Orient was so damned artistic, even gravity. But surely I had his full, beady attention now. "The second warning is that since the woman in this case is, was my friend, I'm not so sure that she should have died at all," I continued more evenly. I flicked a few more loose papers on to his nose. "Maybe one of us should die instead." He looked at me not quite certain of my meaning but increasingly certain of my feelings. "It can't be me, because in repercussion your country would run out of arms and ammunition." He appeared genuinely interested in this question of arms supply. "Just another western opinion," I continued reasonably. "But perhaps you'd better consider it." A strange intercultural silence fell upon us. I couldn't discern if he was thinking about it or about anything I'd declared. I imagined I heard footsteps outside the door, but no one arrived. The pig-fat parasol in the corner said nothing. We all agreed upon silence, and it continued for a good while.

"She would have caused you trouble. Your blonde friend knew it; your embassy knew. That's why…" He spread his hands, as if they should his talking. That's why what, I asked myself? She had to die? Had our whole expedition been merely an ill-conceived grandstanding?

He looked at me steadily with no trace of fear. "You westerners," he enunciated finally, carefully, "never can understand. You are so eager and…vulgar about your views."

"I'll tell you why I'm eager and vulgar," I cried, truly amazed at his choice of *vulgar*. "You superficial self-regarding son-of-a-bitch. Because I'm sick of this goddam two-bit country." For some reason he drew back again at that, either surprised or offended not by my personally directed insult but by my simple statement of economics. I was even surprised myself at the novelty of the idea. Two-bit. Very simple. I went on to elaborate. "Every one lives here like a piece shit coming out a half-inch at a time." I leaned over to follow up on explaining that, if it were at all possible. "First you steal or buy cheap the children and make them slaves and whores. Then you order Alice to be executed, to cover over your dealings and frighten others off. Now this is what we westerners feel. We won't frighten. D'you hear? We declare what a brave man you are, Kongdee, you shameless piece of smirking pig-fat." His eyes followed me as I glanced sideways at the pig-fat parasol, which for all I knew he might have been preparing to take home to his family. Maybe he intuited I wanted to melt him down and smear him over something. Not a bad idea. He tensed, then forced himself to relax and become suddenly reasonable.

"Your fellow countrymen may not think so."

"Why should I care what they think? I'm the one standing here and speaking with my own voice. Chew on that, Stewpot."

"Your fellow countrymen may not think so," he resumed with cold impartial menace.

"Fuck my fellow countrymen. And yours. You see, you don't understand the *farang*. You see him only as an American or Dutch or German, a pigeon. But we don't perceive you screened by your nationality, we see you only as an individual and in your case a vulgarly criminal individual."

He smiled as if to calm matters. "It was a person in your own embassy who told us you had tried to kidnap a child in Bangkok," he continued in the same vein of reasonableness. I was impressed again by *kidnap*. It was old news, but that didn't prevent it from enraging me. "We had only to look for you and your…friends. It was they, that young peasant girl in particular, who were collecting the children for bad purposes." He made a gesture of contempt.

"Don't tell me. Everybody was doing me a favor by killing her. I know. It was the lady at the embassy who told you."

Supot smiled sideways, then turned to look mostly right through me, "A young man. Who knew his duty." He looked puzzled at my regard. "I do not understand your…the official people at the Embassy…"

"Really. You mean that pimp," I returned levelly. "I'll explain it to you then. It's greedy pimps like you and him that keep the war going…" His momentary puzzlement asked what I meant by that. What war? "The war between right and wrong. You can dress it up in any political terms you wish. As for the young man at the embassy, I didn't know he was in the murder business. Like you. And if he didn't know it, he'll soon find out. From me."

He looked at me with renewed interest. He raised a hand.

"Suppose this, just suppose," I interrupted before he got started. "The White Hmong will come and burn your opium fields." I spoke now with the joy that fictive invention brings, and he must have felt its vigor. "Unless you turn over the man who killed Alice." I paused. "Whatever your excuses, some empty-headed fascist like yourself pulled the trigger." The threat sounded crazy enough to be believable.

He dismissed any notion of such a dishonorable treaty, tit for tat, but he seemed less certain of himself. "But why?" He tried to look at me coolly. "I want nothing of you. You are free to go." It seemed almost that he was backing down. "You do not seem dangerous. And you have no reason."

"Turn you in because both of you, all of you, are unsanitary decrepit pieces of humanity. That's good enough reason. Do you understand?"

He'd finally caught wind of the gradual change that had been building up in me and spilling over from anger to hatred. And we both knew hatred was the more persistent and deadly.

"Perhaps at first I could not believe it—that makes me believe now you are dangerous," he said after a while.

Did this mean I finally was becoming an individual? Being dangerous? I wondered, my mind skittering all over the place, did all individuals exist as harmful to other individuals in a remorseless free-for-all, no quarter given?

"Don't give me that oriental hokey-pokey and bibble babble false wisdom. Who cares what you believe? You'd better stop believing and move your ass toward a decision, and here is my last offer." I heard my voice strangely rehabilitated into something new. I seemed to have become a politician, the exact opposite I devoutly hoped, to my real self. At the same time I became distantly aware that these western shifts of mood and persona must seem very opaque, very threatening to him. "You send down the…person who killed Alice and took the other children…"

He made as if he were surprised, but he was becoming concerned. "Who is this Alice? What children? There was one woman, a known spy and trouble maker…"

Here we are in Kristen's global village, I thought.

"You send down flat-face who shot Alice," I roared, "or be certain I'll fix it so your opium fields will melt away, your slave-trade, your gold braid, your lendlease machine guns. Add to that, your family, your friends if you have any, your village, your tribe and," I nodded to the corner, "your pig-fat parasols. You venomous superficial son of a bitch."

I had no idea how I might keep my end of this rather ambitious program or any small corner of it. Perhaps the parasol part. I was aware that I'd descended into economic retaliation, that old American standby, but Alice would still be proud of me. My own agenda involved fleeing the country as quickly as possible, and Supot knew it. But he didn't like the possibility of a disastrous commotion, such as only an American tourist can make, which would point the finger at his untidy import business. And then the money…. He blinked, calculating how much economic reality there was behind my words. Or were my words only the shallow, windy bluster that incensed tourists throw off at street corners upon being short-changed.

"Here, I forgot," I heard the same voice, and this time I too detected the suppressed hatred in it that he must have been hearing all along. "You need a bribe. To settle anything." I reached into my small change pocket and brought out the first banknote I touched. I put a crumpled

10 baht note on the table. "Here's your true value, fifty cents. Wipe your ass with it and eat it."

I turned to leave. Instantly I was face-to-face with the deputy. You recall my favorite deputy. He'd been standing behind me all the while, now for the second time. But on this occasion he hadn't the chance to hoist me by the trousers. In an instant my hands reached around his throat before I could stop them, they no longer belonged to my body, faster than either of us could blink. He could have snapped me in two had he chosen to. But at the speed of my strike he froze into an amazed statue of himself. I turned to Kongdee. "Give him up," I croaked hoarsely, indicating the human statue I was holding around the neck like a precious vase, "all the way to his fat lips, or both your asses will be pickled for mankind to sneer at for ever."

I turned back to the deputy. He didn't have two brown eyes as originally I had supposed, but one brown, one gray, a rather handsome combination that now regarded me with surprise, even a certain degree of respect. The gray one flickered. Yes, he was telling me he was distant cousin to the barkeep in Pat Pong. A surge of intimate hatred seized each of us at the same instant—so hateful it seemed a precious bond between us. I spoke earnestly into his ear, closeby, so that each of us might feel and relish this incomprehensible, intimate, brutal bond. "Get you last haircut," the voice whispered hoarsely, "and the devil scalp you for it." I can't imagine what reason I had for saying it or what I meant by it. He nodded solemnly, almost verging on comprehension. I brushed past him, then turned back to say more. But I couldn't. I was all used up.

I started out the door. This senseless life. I turned around. "Do you hear? You took the life that gave things sense."

*　　　　　*　　　　　*

On reaching street level I breathed dense gulps of warm damp air. A storm was building. I turned down an alley and sat down heavily on a wooden pallet, wiping sweat from my brow. Sudden gusts of wind threw red dust at my eyes, and the sand stuck to my boiling face which the breeze then cooled. A violent purple storm was gathering overhead. I was glad for it, for the destruction it might bring. Shops were closed and boarded up. The crowded life of the market street seemed to have been translated into a few broken baskets that the wind lifted and sent cartwheeling insanely about, then after they had come to rest kicked them again as if it were a huge bully chasing children's hoops, knocking them over again and again until they collapsed breathless, but in the next instant they jumped up and fled again from this relentless blusterer's attack, always from a new quarter. Straw mats and bits of refuse joined the chase but they couldn't keep up with the freewheeling baskets. Around and around they flew. I stood up, panting in the empty silence between gusts, then counting the sounds that signaled the bully was starting up again.

From a bend in the alley just ahead, a kind of wind-driven chatter rose up, died out, rose up again with a distinctly metallic overtone. Something told me I should find out what it was; something told me to stand still and not find out. I stepped forward. A swirling gust blinded me and dropped away. Through the settling dust a human figure appeared, moving toward me casually, erratically. I recognized the stocky build, the wide, round head set on a fencepost neck before I could see the face. Then as the windgusts died out I could see or rather I could sense the crewcut, the strong eyebrows and full lips.

In his one hand Kongdee's deputy was twirling two sticks joined by a shiny chain, one of those martial arts fighting contraptions that always looked so improbable in a display case and so corny on the screen. This one appeared heavier than those I had seen, and crudely made. I stood rooted, contemplating this bizarre contraption and its driver, wondering what Bill might advise me to do or Kristen—I'd even settle to be scolded, as long as I could get some advice—as he padded toward me deliberately, more decisively now and his face, I knew without seeing it, was impassive with concentration.

His sticks roared and listened, roared and listened. No backtalk from me. All the empty patter of books blew out of my head in an instant. This was windmill diplomacy, I thought idly. No, it was my chance, or my turn, to tilt at a windmill. No. These notions blew away too. Most likely the fact was Kongdee had given me Alice's killer after all, and I hadn't been ready. Or maybe he'd shown up on his own initiative. But right now there was only this pure, untimed interval in which the windmill roared and listened and in which life roared and listened. And I suspected I might have to experience absolute silence in order to appreciate the sounds of that life. And it was a call for me to begin myself right now, all over again.

Every detail that had happened to me since I had been in Thailand began to run itself fast forward through my head—as if to compute whether or not it were worthy to be included with my prospective dying. And every detail was worthy. I couldn't leave anything out. I had become a word processor reviewing a completed text in short bursts of rattles—there, huge blocks of words were counted in rattles on the screen. But the next instant, everything paused. Wouldn't I ever get tired of myself? I asked. No, I supposed not. I'd never grow tired of myself. Yet it almost did make sense that one could grow tired of that constant voice-in-the-head narrating the story of myself. And if I did, one day, wasn't it a signal that I was ready to go?

A dozen paces off he stopped and nodded to me, our first actual greeting. Maybe he admired me after all, or at least partly understood what was running through my head. His sticks made a plaintive whining through the air, as if they were rewriting our history together. Trivial. He's going to reach over and turn me off, I speculated, that's what he'll do, darken that rattling screen of mine. I noticed the chain yoking the two sticks was shiny and new, like something we'd use on a bicycle to lock it up. All the chains over here had been shiny and new, the ones on the elephants, the ones on the children. And I had not a stone, not a stick, not a solid piece of anything to throw at his windmill.

I reached down and grabbed two fistfuls of red dust, glad to have them. They were the only thing around. We were all dust, supposedly. That made me extremely angry. Yet as both of my hands closed over it, the dust told me what an extraordinary a thing it was to be alive. It wasn't anything I could be tired of or sour about. I wondered how well or poorly, in the scheme of things, Alice and I had done with our time, and I wondered, intensely now, what her existence had meant to her not to me, an outsider, but to her from her side of her eyes, from behind her face. I wanted to ask her that. And I needed her right now to explain again, patiently, the breathing-in and the breathing-out.

Straightening up I hurled my two fistfuls of dust into the space between us. Damn it, I was tired of being at the receiving end of…the world. If the world wanted to cover me with dust then here, it could damn well take some of it back. A strong gust caught my handfuls, and a shower of dirt exploded over both the deputy and myself. "Eat dirt, damn you!" I howled, "all of you." I had the sensation of sinking feet first into the earth amid a dust storm, like an ancient pyramid being ground down by the dust-filled wind. Bending over for two more fistfuls, I heard the whirling clatter of his sticks reassert itself within the opaque cloud and move imperceptibly nearer, then pause upon a high-pitched whoosh of air. I peered up; the dust, our dust began to settle.

He was on the move again, very slowly. As the cloud fell from around him and he emerged, I saw he had found a new weapon—I don't know where he'd collected it—a long cane or pole that he held directly in front of him, around which his sticks and chain now were wrapped. He moved slowly, shifting from side to side and swinging his long stick back and forth like a nasty, swaggering, smoldering child looking for something or some one to strike—perhaps the household pet—trying to clear a path for himself and his anger, Kristen would say, through a dense world that paid him no attention and allowed him no place. "You can see he's a bully, Kristen, and suspects there's no room for him in the world." But it was only my own voice, breathless and piping thinly to my ear. And anyway here he was, doing a good job of making room for himself and coming toward me. And I had to get back to the task of rattling down my text before he reached me.

Amazingly, he had started to make little piglike grunts, perhaps out of perverse mockery, I thought, as if he knew all about the piglet I carried around Alice's village and my aversion to Supot's fat-smeared parasol. That sincerely angered me. How did he know our secret? I scrutinized him again, this time I was going to get a proper explanation from him, maybe throw myself at him and gouge an eye or two in order to compel a proper explanation and make him deny he owned any part of my life's story, or of Alice's either. He answered, rather ineptly, by trying to point his pole at me. Then his steps abated and he halted entirely, regarding me undecidedly and with a frown.

Slowly, gingerly, he seated himself on a half-barrel upended in the dirt. He sent me a curious glance, then smiled to himself and half-dismissed me, turning away in self-absorbed meditation. Then he recalled once again that I existed, and he rotated slightly on the barrel, and as he did so I noticed with remote surprise that he was carrying his pole directly behind him as well as in front of him. In fact it went directly through him. I stood fascinated by this astounding new impossibility. Then I stepped forward; I had a mind to examine this whole inconsistency, but he turned just enough to stop me and keep me in careful view of one eye, like a wary mutt pretending to lie drowsing.

"He likes his pole, no? professor-sahib. Yes, he keeps it, see," George nodded his approval from a doorway.

The deputy lifted his eyebrows, he seemed about to agree with us. Then a cupful of blood spilled from his mouth and never ceasing to look at us he toppled to the ground, curled up like a dog, still keeping us in sight out of a corner of an eye and not ever blinking.

"Beauteous modification, yes?" George gleamed, overcoming his natural modesty. "One pole worth a thousand words, they say, no?"

I agreed tentatively. There was a pause. I looked down at the frayed toe of my old hiking boot, the one Alice had laced for me on our first afternoon.

"We go save the tiger now, professor," George offered, breaking my meditation.

I thought it over for a moment. "How can we save the tiger, George?"

George rolled his eyes, modest once again in the presence of my dense understanding, "Bengal tiger. My home. Very nice. You'll like."

I looked at him remotely, now peacefully. "You're India Secret Service, aren't you George?"

His eyes batted slightly, "Oh no, Bonded Liberation Front. Very fine job. You and I, now we save the children."

"How do you mean that?" For an instant it seemed to me that Alice might be alive, having escaped and now living somewhere, no matter even if far from us.

He demurred, as if he had a confession to make. "No many children in her bus, sahib-friend. No many. We switched buses. Pigs though. Fine pigs. Many escape, very nice. While soldiers chase the pigs."

"And the children?" I asked. But I was also asking about some one else, and George understood. Because now it appeared that Bill's account of the event hadn't been the exact truth. Or perhaps Bill never learned the exact truth. Or perhaps he didn't want me or anybody else to know the exact truth. That Alice had been sacrificed driving a busload of pigs. Or perhaps finally that all these people had been trying as hard as they could, and their miscalculations and theatrical flourishes had to come down on the shoulders of one of us, and it had to be Alice. And I'd never understand why it had to, only feel from now to doomsday the pointlessness of it.

"Children walking now, walking." George eyed me closely. "With Madame Kristian."

Alice and George had known the risk in setting up their operation and had arranged for Kristen to step in if….

"Oh." I dropped my fantasies and returned to the moment. "Oh they are. And Kongdee? What will happen to Kongdee?"

George shrugged disconsolately, then brightened. "Mr Bill, he asked Musur friends to burn his poppy fields. For good."

At least some of my threats would prove true, with no help from me. And characteristically I'd guessed the wrong tribe. "The rest of the children, George, how can we help them from where we stand now?"

"They follow us," he turned his eyes toward our former acquaintance on the ground, "we walk the other way."

"What the other way?" I demanded stubbornly. "Singapore? That's a long walk."

"Very clever, professor-sahib," George regained his courtly composure, preparatory to taking charge of me on our long journey toward somewhere. "Singapore very pretty. No good. Slavery city. To Moulmein, Burma. Very bad place, so they will not follow." He giggled, "So perhaps they watch us, being unhappy, and not watch others." Then adding ingenuously to this load of obscure information, "Burma closed border. They afraid to follow." I nodded in serious consideration of it. Like how could we get through ourselves. "Then later," he brightened, as if to reward us with sunshine at the end of our doubtful journey, "Bengal tigers. We go now, professor, yes?"

We turned away from the windmill deputy put down finally—perhaps we shouldn't have killed him like that I thought, but perhaps we should have—curled and bleeding doglike on the ground. Especially if he were the leader of those who….George read my eyes and deferring to the already derelict shrinking figure, beamed in encouragement. "This elephant-tooth stealer, he's all tuned out."

2

For days at a time we floated downstream on rafts the villagers built for us of bamboo and mixed woods, poling around the bends that doubled back on themselves. Children splashing in the river by their villages waved us by, no richer, no poorer than they. Sometimes we rode Lisu ponies westward and south toward the Burma borders, sometimes we walked from village to village through the hills. No one followed us. No one stopped or threatened us. I wondered that our whole charade was in vain. It was as if the birds had flown ahead with news that two very fragile, daffy tightrope walkers had left the circus for a walk through the hills. In our baggy trousers and straw hats we were two clowns whom the villagers saw as laughable, yet they accepted us. In the evening, their women fed us and cared for our torn legs and feet.

We came to a Shehleh Musur village high in the hills, under the dissolving green afternoon light. Near the shrine at the top of the village, on a level circular dance ground, young girls were dancing dressed in long black coats and white-striped trousers. Tiny pennants mounted high on the thin wooden poles encircled the area and shifted in the wind. The little dancers were dancing on the top of the world on a playground especially cleared for them.

Eventually an old man in a spotlessly white shirt and trousers appeared as if by magic before us, and greeted us. He led us to his house, raised on pilings, and there we were given food and mats to rest on. I recalled why Bill had said he liked Musur so well—he said they were always looking for blessings. Perhaps we were the occasion for a blessing. From our platform I could hear the children practicing their dance steps at the top of the world as evening light came on. Under the cascade of silent trees hanging over us, I watched the straw thatches of the village darken one by one. Then a patch of sunlight slipped through the dark evening clouds and left a momentary pool of white froth on the grass of the village compound, brightening and fading by turns. In the center I could see two little ponies standing side by side, who tomorrow would carry us up the mountain.

George looked at me, looking at the ponies. "This life," his eyes flashed suddenly, "it gives itself to me, this sickness, friend-sahib, gives itself to me, this daylight, this prison, this tree, these ponies, you see," he finished on a lonely half-chuckle.

I thought it over for a while. I had no idea how he had arrived at all this. All I knew was that grief was never lost, not among the elephants, not among people, but somehow redistributed among the trees and flowers surrounding us, to find its way back to us. "How did you get your name, George?" I asked finally. "How did you become 'George'?"

He looked worried for an instant; his eyes batted a negation then twinkled, playing with me, and he solemnly raised one hand as if he were taking an oath, "Oh, George didn't steal it; it was given," he reassured me, "it was a gift."

"I know that; I know it was a gift," I sounded slightly exasperated. "But why did they give you that name?" I waited, thinking of several explanations. "King George? Saint George? Admiral George? Gorgeous George?"

He nodded his head each time in agreement. Peering around his shoulder into the next room I could see the old headman and his wife now reclining on their mats. High over them on the wall a small shelf held sacred objects, the family altar. Beneath us somewhere a pony scratched its back on a support pole, and the whole floor trembled.

George finally allowed it to escape, "Famous actor, great star," he indicated the dimensions of heaven's vast canvas now spreading above us with stars embedded. Millions and trillions of them. His eyes sparkled, sharing his secret with his new childlike companion. "George Burns."

        ✶   ✶   ✶

It would have been more convenient had we been able to continue directly westward to Mae Sot, at the Burma border, and at about the latitude of Moulmein. But we were told that the roads east-west and north-south throughout the area were crisscrossed with army patrols and checkpoints on the lookout for smugglers. Consequently, the smugglers passed a bit further inland, where we joined their flow by throwing a few disreputable light sacks of cotton on our ponies and becoming smugglers for the next few days in order to escape too obvious notice, heading south toward Three Pagodas Pass just north of the river Kwai. It was strange, I thought, that the places we visited, so peaceful, were places where slavery and ethnocide had been practiced, and yet I'd escaped somehow, my whole life long. They had let me pass unscathed; but the downside was that I was passing them without having made a difference to their histories.

We rode past some Hmong settlements; we didn't tarry to inquire which color they were. George took great pleasure in imploring me to repeat once a day the misadventures which Kristen, Bill and I suffered on the road journeying past the opium fields, as if what once was real couldn't be allowed to stay real, but had to be put down into fiction, into the art of history. Now we drifted down through Karen settlements. The larger villages often were administered by ex drug-lords, and we avoided them, sleeping next to our grunting rank ponies under the strengthening stars. For many a mile, in deference to our Hmong story, George would make a gesture as if to jump his pony into the ditch whenever we met along the way a poor, overladen, smuggling soul, balancing on his pole his stolen goods and water bottle. But no one bothered us. The mountains and flatland forests already had swallowed our stories, and we went beyond notice much less recognition.

Finally, just before the last Musur village, where we would have to trade in our ponies and go on foot, we came across a Hmong resettlement camp. All were in pitiable condition. We gave them our bales of raw cotton; that was the most we could do. We rode on.

*   *   *

Kanchanaburi province was more agricultural, more persistently tropical than the regions we'd been traversing. Fields of sugarcane spread over the gentle slopes and depressions of the Mae Klong valley. George and I were transformed on our little ponies briefly into two shabby porters of sugarcane or of the various fruits that grew abundantly in the irrigated fields. George had provided us with a small quantity of raw opium for our travel expenses. Then finally, after we said goodbye to our ponies, we became simply ragged porters carrying the lightest loads imaginable and indulging the incongruous habit, it must have struck a careful observer, of consuming steadily whatever fruit and produce was on our backs.

At an impressively large town market, we shed our wares, purchased some slightly less ragged clothes and took a chance on a *songthaew* heading west and south toward the river Kwai railway bridge, the World War II death camp that never had been destroyed despite the efforts of Hollywood, and now was in process of being refurbished as a tourist attraction. There we joined the general touristic and mercantile flow back and forth between waterfalls, caves and temples. One terminus of the Death Railway was Three Pagodas Pass.

The problem now was that the main and only road to Sangklaburi was interrupted by army checkpoints. We didn't know whether to call attention to ourselves or not. We decided upon not. Whenever we saw one coming up, George rapped on the tin roof of the Toyota, the driver slackened pace, and we tumbled out, adjusting our shielding broad brimmed hats and turning into a field and from there to a next field on the other side of the checkpoint. Then we clambered aboard the next *songthaew*. After a while I lost track, with so much dismounting and remounting, whether or not George was paying for us; it didn't seem to matter. The journey and the company mattered, an osterized, you recall, abundantly cheerful crowd of all imaginable types who accepted us, without seeming to notice us. We swayed and lurched together, and I surveyed the crowded benches and the people trying to hunker between the benches, busily immersed in their lives.

I recalled the story I'd read somewhere concerning the hungry Bedu boy who told his mother that he preferred eating on moonless nights with whomever his hosts of the desert happened to be, because in the dark they would not be able to see what huge mouthfuls he gobbled down, too proud to confess he was starving. His mother, dressed in black and bent carefully over her needlework, replied "Next time you are sitting in the dark with them, take out your knife and a piece of string and use the backside of the knife to cut it." The boy followed her instruction, and as he was sitting in near total darkness among the men of the desert, his took out his knife and, feeling it carefully, started to use the back edge on the string. Three strong voices called to him, "You are using the wrong side of the knife."

I preferred that we keep to the fields and at night shelter under a farmer's porch. It was there I told George the parable of the Bedu boy and his knife. Morning brought a sky already heated to an intense pale blue and cotton ball clouds balanced on the drumlin heads of steeply wooded hills. "Maybe the same eyes do not see so well in daylight," George remarked, struggling to disengage our straw hats from a goat who had found them during the night and now earnestly proposed to eat them, transfixing us all the while with a yellowish translucent regard.

We encountered no one the whole day, save a woman working her small garden. We were climbing gradually all the while, then less gradually, and as we ascended it was as if a backdrop had been cast behind the mountains so that they appeared to be suspended in front of dark velvet. Far beyond the night was swimming with a million stars and, I always repeated to myself, millions of trillions more if you wanted to go there. The earth I stood on felt like a sturdy child balancing its breath against the ancient sprawling universe. That night, without the company of ponies or goat, we were cold.

About noon of the following day we came upon a level field, partly cleared, partly in tough yellow grass, bent pines and a few spikes of bamboo. Toward one end of the clearing somebody had left out three whitewashed sharply pointed spinner tops, children's playthings, emerging fifteen feet from the red soil, inverted with conical tip turned upwards and ringed in tiers as if they had been spools turned out on a carpenter's lathe. One had lost its knob at the end of the stem, but each of the three wore a beaded ring or hoop high on its neck that seemed to have been negligently frisbied over the pointed end and allowed to slip down the tiered, conical shaft. The bases, made of stone and hand-shaped brick, were already crumbling. A stone marker declared something in script. I knew we were standing at Three Pagodas Pass. I shook my head at the whitewash peeling from these strange neglected toys. George drew close.

"Truth, professor-sahib."

"Yes George, what truth?" He seemed anxious and distraught.

"Truth, professor. That she wanted you to take a child with you."

"She had a busload to choose from," I replied moodily. Then I wondered, "Or did she ever have any?"

"Oh no, not true, professor, yours and hers."

"Mine and hers? But we…"

Was this just George being George and comforting me? I wasn't sure Alice actually had said she wanted us to have a child, I wish she had but I couldn't feel certain. I had to settle for something less—that she'd found her own way of allowing us to love her even though none of us, I especially, would ever determine exactly how that might be. I hope she'd found a way, and that some day miraculously we all could read it.

I looked up. A movement in the trees. Then a sudden volley of agonizing grunts overhead. Three howler monkeys leaped into view clutching themselves around their tummies like old men and venting their grief in comic howls that stopped just short of words. George started at the noise then looked over at me, smiling.

"They look like spinner tops," I indicated the three pagodas, "a child's toy."

George nodded confidentially. The monkeys subsided into silence, watching with blinking eyes our every move and waiting for these strange hominids to utter something that sounded like words. "Very big child to play with these toys, professor, yes?" He placed a skinny hand on mine. "Child of the world."

"Yes I suppose, child of the world."

We found a dirt track and started up the hill that marked the Burma border.

*   *   *

About two miles up the path, what we thought at first was a farmer's hut by the roadside turned out to be a local police checkpoint. Of course it had to be; we were hiking on smuggler's way, and there had to be a toll station for local graft. I sat at the edge of the platform, genuinely weary, and George stepped up to a rickety card-table where a stouter, darker relative of Songpot was holding court. "Let us now pause for change of crooks," I muttered to myself.

The lean-to was open at three sides; behind the police officer's chair a frail bamboo wall, and precariously suspended from it, as an emblem of authority, or a souvenir, a kind of African assegai or heavy spear, this one carrying an additional cutting blade at the pointed end. I wondered if a more appropriate symbol might have been the empty hand, palm upwards. The officer's holstered pistol lay on the table and directly in front of him a soiled folder of papers with official red stamps on them. In his right hand he clutched uncomfortably a ballpoint pen, illustrating that the pen and the sword, in this area of the world, always were accompanied by the open palm.

A bench to one side was gallery to three toughs, in varying degrees of undress around the stomach, like our monkeys, and of a frowning surliness, and a very pretty young woman in a blue teeshirt, white scarf and a red fillet in her hair. This completed the gallery. After a long instant of surveying us, the young woman got up, collected a surprisingly smart brown leather attache case, nodded faintly to her compatriots, and bowing appreciably to me, as if in collusion we were honoring together the Stars and Stripes, set off at a brisk pace in her dress shoes down the path we had just laboriously ascended.

George stood before the table in a posture of political humility. Their surlinesses on the bench regarded him with openly manufactured contempt, folding their legs up to make themselves more comfortable while they scoffed. The officer, commandant, captain, local hoodlum, whichever he was, barked some words I couldn't decode, shuffled some papers, barked at George again. My attention wandered. I was damned if we would be stopped after all that hiking, on account of paper work; I was damned if anything in life should be stopped on account of paper work. A red bird called to me from a nearby bush. Suddenly it took flight.

Only then I sensed something had gone wrong. One of the rogues' gallery was unbending a leg and leaning forward. I turned toward the table. George was stooped before it, and the captain was reaching into the holster for his pistol, taking it out, in what seemed to me slow motion. My mouth shaped useless words, no no, soundlessly, then the officer was cocking it, and in an instant instead of speaking I stepped to the edge of the platform.

I slipped open my rucksack and my fingers at their own instigation wrapped around the little hatchet which had been presented to me at Alice's funeral. Suddenly its weight had meaning now, even before I knew what that meaning might be. In one motion I hurled it with all my borrowed strength over George's shoulder and in the general vicinity of the captain's head. It made a whooshing sound tumbling through the air. George ducked instinctively while the captain hung rooted like the egomaniac he was to his own amazed stare at what was coming down the airway toward him. But all this was in milliseconds.

As fortune would have it, I missed him entirely; the hatchet thumped into the wall blunt side first and stuck there nevertheless, about three inches from where his Adam's apple should have been. In a spasm of surprise he jumped back, chair and all. It must have been these successive joltings that undid the ornamental *assegai* hanging on the wall overhead. One end released itself, and pivoting in a half-circle upon its lower fixed point the crude weapon described over what seemed minutes of a clock running backward, a perfect unhurried arc that ended by making connection with the officer's surly bigoted head. There was the whack of a mallet saying howdy to a seasoned melon. He dropped behind the table to the floor without a sound. An embarrassed silence prevailed all around.

George rose from a crouch and peered down at him, then turned to me in disbelief, then down at the recumbent official again. He reached over and picked up the pistol that had fallen to the table and with no more ado squeezed off a round into the thatched roof. I blanched. The projectile detached a sizeable piece of bamboo that in its own lazy turn fell lightly on the neck of the deputy who was the one sitting nearest to us, gawking. In a split instant he leaped off the platform, the devil truly at his heels. The others followed.

"Very nice effect," George remarked happily, dancing around a bit to shake the stiffness out of his legs.

All three of the surlies were sprinting now at a good clip, no need to ask them to pick up the pace. Notwithstanding, George squeezed off another round into the roof, just for effect, and the cheap outdated ammunition, mostly black powder, sent out sparks and incandescent embers that started the thatchwork to smoldering, and scattered little glistening beads of fire in the dried grass around the lean-to, as if an air strike had recently passed over the area rather than a mere pistol shot. They glistened then smoldered out. George surveyed the effect once again, then turning his attention once more to the collapsed, now sighing and whistling police officer.

"Very ingenious, sahib," he beamed at me, falling back under pressure of the emergency into the idiom that Bill had spent considerable time and effort trying to break him out of, but which I felt he uttered to me always with a mixture of irony and sympathy. "Avoid international lawsuits, finally," George theorized, reassuring me that my contribution had not gone unappreciated. "Very industrious clockwork," he indicated the *assegai* now dangling on the wall and swinging idly, just grazing the bamboo organ pipes of the wall and eliciting from them a half-melodious tone. Then stepping back to get the overall artistic effect of it, and to make certain he included me in the general commendation of our exercise, "very industrious conception." He promised to go on dilating praise infinitely as a way of redeeming our long hours of trekking together in silence.

"But George," I protested. "Anyway, it's teamwork, not clockwork."

"Teamwork," he eyed me concernfully, perhaps so as not to lose the chance for extending our dialogue, "professor-sahib, many excuses." He indicated the *assegai* dangling from one end like a pendulum, still playing its tune. "Teamwork." He regarded me for the companionable pedant I was. I stepped off the platform, supporting myself by a hand on his shoulder. No sign of the others; they were far gone by now, but my sweat and fear had added their refraction to the lenses of my eyeglasses and everything appeared in triplicate—for the first time in a long while I noticed the red flowers deep in flame on the purple mountainside. They appeared in triplicate, under the white tropical sun that shone in triplicate. I wondered how they were appearing on the hills above Alice's village.

Murmurs of strife and an occasional explosion from uphill. Whatever was going on, a newly sprouted civil war, seemed to be tumbling toward us. A baggy trousered chap came rocketing down toward the station, waving an assault rifle. He wasn't after us; he was after clearing out of the whole area. I stuck one of the bamboo rafters between his legs as he shot by. He kept right on going, now leading with his head, now with his heels, like a rattlesnake biting its tail and making a cartwheel of itself. I picked up his abandoned weapon.

And just at the right moment. Further murmurs of strife were descending toward us. An assorted, scruffy bunch of more baggy pantaloons emerged from the woods, belonging for all the world to an enclave of swarthy pirates, red headcloths and the whole bit. Who was on whose side? Did it matter? What mattered was that we were caught in the middle. I picked up the AK47, stepped out onto the path and emptied the clip into the ground, a good deal closer to their feet than I'd aimed for, regrettably destroying a certain amount of vegetation in the process. A respectful silence ensued. I'd noticed that crooks and bandits always fell silent after you shot back at them. Something to do with wounded self-esteem or sense of violated etiquette. In unison they threw their weapons into the air and switched into quick reverse leaving a cloud of dust behind.

"Oops, sorry," I muttered under my breath. "On second thought, the devil fuck you gooks," I yelled after them and threw the empty weapon at their heels.

I turned to George, whose mouth hung agape. Half apologetically, I added "I guess it's the little tin soldier inside of me."

"The little tin soldier inside, yes professor."

We picked up our sacks and started to climb the mountain. There are many marvels in the course of each hour. I walk this mountain path, and I am here, and in a single moment I succeed or fail in this enterprise or in this friendship. And I am alive right now. And not with you.

*   *   *

By the old Moulmein Pagoda, lookin' eastward to the sea,
There's a Burma girl a-settin', and I know she thinks o'me.

The song rang pointlessly through my head by the hour. It simply measured the distance between the other side of the mountain, the Burma side, and this side where presently we were clambering over rocks made into slick cannonballs by the icy drizzle of mist condensing on them. Somehow I knew that as we scrambled up the rocks, bloodying our shins and knees, then digging into the red crumbling soil that supported only tough low evergreen, somehow I knew each step was burying Thailand behind us and the people we had known there. It's stupid to sit around and claim that we collect our histories to ourselves, when our histories really are the collection of people and things away from us, leaving us naked like sculptures once clothed by the companionship of others, now waiting to be clothed still once more by the next event, the next companionship.

We were looking down, Thai forests on one side, Burma forests on the other, done in various sculptures of green before us. Twisted trees with gigantic unfamiliar leaves, some sort of oak or chestnut tangled with vines, barred our way, often reaching up out of canyons and crevices that streams long ago had cut into the limestone, so that we mistook them for solid footing and nearly tumbled into them. Then for a spell, for no reason, a damp area filled with ferns and mosses and colorful epiphytes dangling from the trees, Christmas ornaments that had drifted this way from the other side of the globe and had caught in the trees. And not much further on, without explanation a space that moisture had not touched at all, dry tinsel of evergreen and grass.

We had seen no one this whole day; sometimes the trail might have been a trail, sometimes for certain it wasn't. An occasional pheasant startled from nearby brush. Black squirrels kept track of our slow progress, scolding us. I feared a panther might be following us, but it was just the loosened rocks we kicked up as we scrambled along and sent tumbling after us, overtaking us. In one instant I caught a glimpse of a white dog, it definitely was a dog, then it vanished as if it realized that it too was out of its habitat.

George was falling behind further each quarter of an hour. We were at about five thousand feet, I judged, and about to descend the slippery side of the mountain. We clambered along, creeping along at the tail end of our breaths that stretched before us on the cold air. Suddenly George was out of sight somewhere behind me. I backtracked uphill. He'd collapsed by a rock, knees drawn to his chin. His eyes had a shining far-away look upon them with dark circles beneath. I picked up his sack which had fallen a few yards uptrail.

"Go on, sahib-friend," George urged, turning his head to one side. "This George is all tuned out."

"The hell," I said, throwing down his sack and mine too. I half carried, half dragged him for a piece down the trail. Sometimes his legs worked, sometimes they didn't.

"This being saved, oh yes," George rolled his eyes, "very much painful."

"I know it's a pain. Shut up," I gasped, putting him down, "I know being saved is a pain." We kept on. Somebody was muttering through clenched teeth, "You gotta keep chompin'. Never give up. Never give up." It might have been me. At that moment I looked up—I thought I felt another presence near us—and there was the dog on the trail head of me, an absolutely snow-white, thick-coated mountain dog. Was it a Karen dog? I asked myself. Possibly a Musur canine that had escaped slaughter? I was no longer thinking clearly. Or maybe, just maybe it had wandered all the way down from an Akha village far away to the north. Ridiculous. There were no settlements of any kind nearby, none to be seen. The dog sized me up, totally sure of itself, sitting now waiting patiently for me to make up my mind that I knew it from an earlier acquaintance.

"The hell," I droned once again to myself, looking back at the creature, "she's going to show us the way down the mountain. And I don't have anything to offer her." I held out my hand. "Ta gu," I muttered in delirium. The white dog didn't flinch. "The white man is a burden," I chanted giddily, "except when dawn…" The dog got up and turned as if we should follow.

George must have thought I was talking to a specter.

"I'm talking to the white dog," I declared. His eyes bulged incredulously.

"This life, it gives itself to me," he summoned feebly, delirious but still intent on contributing a counterpoint to my spectral dialogue, "this sickness, sahib-professor, gives itself to me," he looked around at the forest as if in confirmation of that fact, "this stone, this tree…" he picked up a leaf no larger than a thumbnail that was near his hand, and his voice trailed off.

Sometimes I carried, sometimes I dragged, often I rolled him down the side of the mountain. The mysterious white canine guided and waited, guided and waited. I followed her directly and as well as my breath would allow. She paused each time I fell behind.

It was toward dusk, to be sure, when we arrived at a small Karen village. I saw the cluster of thatched roofs set high on posts. And it was at that instant that the three of us became two again. The white dog vanished while my head was turned toward the old man and his wife who came forward to help us.

Even at that late hour they had some rice for us and a small vial of terrible liquor which they forced us to drink, like I had to drink at Alice's funeral. But you must understand, I don't believe in reincarnation, not at all. Maybe I believe in something a lot more reasonable and I hope more human. Then next to our mats, the bamboo crucifix once again; they wanted us to know we were among Christians, of all things, and saved.

I laughed to myself, crying on my mat in exhaustion, near to sleep. As if any one name brand of saving were better than another. Life was not a conflict that could be spoken, only sung. And the people who are gone, I thought, could only stay around if we sang to them. I looked at George, asleep now, and tried to balance our moments of happiness against our moments of truth. Then as I sank further down into myself,

'This being saved, very painful, sahib-professor,' I stirred a little in exhausted mirth at that, recalling a whole slew of things ever since my having arrived in the East, as if they were being sung to me over and over in snatches of song. 'Lucky thing Quakers don't fight, eh Kristie?' I crooned silently to myself within my head, wittily it seemed now, wittily. There was a secret smell of mint, and I sat bolt upright. I heard a nighttime voice speak something that sounded like, but I couldn't be sure, 'Ta gu. Ta gu de. Don't go away.'

Come morning George was much better. For better or worse we were in Burma. Whatever unpronounceable name it might hide under. After another day of rest, when evening fell we were on the road again, finally to Moulmein.

3

I looked out on the waves and half-recited, half-sang back at their mountainous indifference:

'Er petticoat was yaller an' 'er little cap was green,
An' 'er name was Supi-yaw-lat—jes' the same as Theebaw's Queen,
An' I seed her first a-smokin' of a whackin' white cheroot,
An' a-wastin' Christian kisses on an 'eathen idol's foot.

A light rain began to fall on us, mixed with the heavy sweet stench of diesel fumes from our decrepit ferry-steamer. I thought distantly that perhaps a rain might be falling on the small intense fire at Wat Phra Sing, putting it out. I wondered about the sparrows, whether they'd been re-captured.

"You know the song, professor, very fine." George could see in my eyes that I was losing something.

"That's all I can remember, I guess." The bottom fell out of the old tramp steamer for a second, then for another second; she paused, then with a smack and a jolt hit bottom and resumed headway. George read the new expression on my face.

"Very safe, sahib-professor, only sink twice a year," he giggled comfortingly.

"I suppose we deserve a little sink," I answered, "what with all the luck we've had." I was about to ask the other question, the one that had no answer of course, but George anticipated me and to my utter surprise gave out in a perfectly acceptable cockney accent.

When the mist was on the rice-fields an' the sun was droppin' slow,
She'd git 'er little banjo an' she'd sing 'kulla-lo-lo!'
With 'er arm upon my shoulder an' 'er cheek agin my cheek
We useter watch the steamers an' the hathis pilin' teak.

"Those elephants you know, sahib," the editorial George broke in to elucidate, and suddenly I recalled in complete detail our first meeting in Khao Yai Park. "Very bad business, teak, destroying all the Burma forests."

"Yes I know," I said. "It was a British consortium—that time." Then I added, "What a rotten history every country of the world has. I wonder if ours is the first age to have recognized it?" It was a fairly foolish question to have asked. Because no one had time to recognize anything or to care about it if they did. I let it go. "Don't you know any more of the poem, George? My brain is all tuned out."

George looked at me with sudden, intimate respect. "No more, professor; that's the most George can do." But suddenly his other voice reclaimed him:

But that's all shove be'ind me—long ago an' fur away,
An' there ain't no 'buses runnin' from the Bank to Mandalay;
An' I'm hearin' 'ere in London what the ten-year soldier tells:
If you've 'eard the East a-callin', you won't never 'eed naught else.

The ship lurched then steadied itself. Burma, the coast eastward had withdrawn from sight; the world's surface is curved, you know, so nothing stays in view very long.

"George, where do you think the rest of the children who were in the buses got to?" Then I added, for it struck me, "There never were children in the first bus, you told me? Just one. And so Alice…was a decoy." For an instant my mind plunged up and down like our tramp steamer in rough water. "Were there ever any children in either of the buses, or was the whole operation just to draw out…?"

George reflected for a while under visible conflict of how to restore me to the present and how to alleviate my suspicions. His face darkened with concern. Were my suspicions so empty, even if unfounded? A good deal, a monstrous deal had been spent for a very little, and no one would admit it.

"Oh the children, professor." He nodded, finally resolved to tie things up. "Oh yes, they're with Madam Kristian," adding a dramatic flourish, "among the aboriginals."

"Australia," I muttered, "of course." But it didn't really settle things.

"Piglets stay back there," he tossed his head eastward. "And maybe later," George now secretly relishing this slice of information so long withheld, "Mr Bill." To my puzzled look he added, "Maybe one day man and wife, as they say, very nice."

"Man and wife?"

"Oh yes. From the very beginning." A new shadow of concern darkened his face as if he felt, rather than knew, I'd been harboring a suspicion that Kristen had stood aside and contributed indirectly to Alice's death. Upon final reflection there was no doubt I'd done my part to damage the comradeship.

But George wasn't remonstrating with me. He was evaluating his own failure. "Pardon my wrong, sahib-friend, but I should have saved one for you to take back. Since Miss Alice…"

"Saved one what?" I demanded, a bit put off by his indirectness. "Piglet?"

"I can get you, sahib-friend, boy, girl, which? two? one each?"

I continued to look at him in utter amazement, then he touched my arm reassuringly. "Very good children, professor, very good. Mother no longer left. Died two year. My own."

I looked out at the slightly curved horizon.

Ship me somwheres east of Suez, where the best is like the worst,
Where there aren't no Ten Commandments an' a man can raise a thirst,
For the temple-bells are callin', an' it's there that I would be
By the old Moulmein Pagoda, looking lazy at the sea.

CHAPTER SIX

1

I arrived at U.S. Customs with extra pounds of luggage, very little of it my own, the rest of it standing upright, solemn-eyed and silent. My actual luggage, most of it, was in Bangkok where already it had been recycled countless times. But these...

"These are just rentals," I remarked to the Immigrations Officer, "I mean loaners. These are just loaners."

She looked at me levelly. "We're all just loaners, if you catch my drift."

"I know," I replied weakly, unprepared for the challenge of the U.S. "Anyway I have to return these in a year."

Once again I felt what it was like to be in a safe country, despite the kibitzing, if not safe at least navigable. Customs officials with braided caps and sheaves of papers waving in hand swam past George's children and myself as if they were sharks with padlocked mouths—our paper work was done—their open-eyed sideways glances admitted as much as they stared at our strange family. And still I felt safe. I thought of Kongdee and the superintendent at the border with a currently sore head. I thought of my Karen hosts and the old woman with the heavy bundle in Fang who had watched me daydream. Bill and Kristen on their mountain ponies and Alice at Pat Pong, walking with me. How fragile all these momentary heroisms left behind…just a boy's adventure story, I guess.

"Now that the paper work is all set…" The Immigrations Officer looked at the two children standing at attention. She looked at me, caught in my daydream, then back at the children. "Maybe in a year's time we'll decide to keep them and loan you back." She smiled, "I'm kidding, you know. Wyoming sense of humor." I nodded, professing to recognize it as such. After all, America was my country too. Then I thought, those who hold their ideals so closely, can they hold people closely too? You're drawn to these people because they seem to offer so much. And they promise they'll not discard you and the other people they love, and they always do.

"Well," the lady in uniform continued, "I've finished all your paper work." She repeated it in order to guide me back, as I stood gaping inwardly at my thoughts, and looking back and forth between us, "I trust you've got some help waiting for you at home." She smiled again, implying we both knew I hadn't thought of that.

"Not exactly," I squirmed, my mind still elsewhere.

"Well," the Immigration Officer looked us over as if this were final inspection at an underwear factory, out of which the customer reaps the benefit of a little square label saying 'inspected by Dora' and then a number, 21. George's kids didn't give an inch, but inspected her right back in utter, open curiosity. "Well," she said, "you'll have to pardon me but I'll say it right out—I'm from Wyoming and we tend to say just what we think." I half-nodded, abstractedly; we'd been through all that and agreed on it.

"But you don't," she continued, as she meant to say it whether I pardoned her or not, "look terribly… so here's my phone number if you need help. Name's Alice, and I wish you good luck." She offered to shake our hands all around but I stepped back in deep dismay. My thoughts had been discovered, at least my innermost misery had been. I murmured a kind of thanks for being back in the States. America was my country too. We collected our few things and walked through the exit into New York, the City.

"Nice score, pop." The voice belonged to a bush-beaten undergrad with Jerrypack and girlfriend-with-Jerry, both mounted on Birkenstocks and freshly soiled from three unsanitary weeks in Nepal. It appeared they were sharing the taxi curb with us. "Scored with the U.S. Government, no less." He winked. His girlfriend smiled and offered all sorts of body signals which I'd like to imagine were positive, just short of modelling nude for me, but which had taken shape, excuse the word, over the months I was gone and which I couldn't decode.

"Indeed," I heard myself say, sounding as pompous and antique as the lions on the steps of the New York Public Library. I looked tentatively somewhere over their heads into the blatant noon air. Then addressing the gray New York day which wrapped itself around us, "Indeed, you wouldn't believe what a marksman I am," and turning to George's offspring, "you see," bending down like a nanny to the level of their rounded, wondering stare. "It's an educational experience just to be in this country. Each minute, believe me."

2

The train back to Chicago would pass through Pittsburgh. I'd made sure of that. And I had time to ponder the crises which the customs lady had anticipated for my benefit. The housekeeper circumstance could be solved, and I knew a few Indian restaurants that could tide us over the meal-crisis. Education, no problem, for the children were smart, and already their written English as good as mine, better. I'd have to relearn Math; terrible things had happened there. I might barely cling to geography, unless it included global economics, and of course diplomacy. Philosophy I couldn't do but it wasn't needed any longer; last month's gingerbread ideas seemed to work fine.

I smiled, the old, comfortable professor was back editorializing. And suddenly I was very lonely and I missed a great many things that perhaps shouldn't be missed: the mountain George and I slipped around on and where we nearly perished, the white dog, the sparrows and the little fire at Wat Phra Sing, our mountain ponies, even the mishap at Pat Pong from which Alice rescued me and then it was not a mishap, and I never could explain these to the people I must live among now. George's children regarded me patiently as I tried to sort out these glimpses and resume a current life. Right away I knew I'd have to take them to Anita. I'd have to take them with me to see Anita. Because that's where I'd been headed, for some time now.

It's Saturday morning, Holy Week before Easter. Waiting for her to reappear, if she's going to. I'm looking down from my window, and I observe the fatman in pink who each morning marches his matched pair of spaniels on leashes that roll up on friction pulleys as if he were holding a brace of reindeer. Do they have free will? I idly speculate. To complicate the question, it's laundry day, and multitudes are hugged by a week's wash stowed in suitcases, baskets, duffels, backpacks, pillow cases, anything. And look, there's Anita right behind the pinkman, making faces up at me. She's wearing tight blue shorts and spike heels, and she's toting a ditty bag stuffed like a great wiener and gazing up at my window. I stumble down immediately.

"You wanted to discuss…" She indicates I might carry the ditty bag, as my part in the discussion, which I undertake with some difficulty. "And why are you lounging out your window? Are you living your own life or everyone else's?"

She's right, I make up stories, conversations lounging out my window—like between her and me. But she knows that already. Is it so wrong? And her story at the lake. Wasn't it the beginning of admiration and wonder? We walk on to the laundromat and begin to unwad things into the machine, shaking them out one by one. Standing at either end of a sheet we flap it up.

She flaps. "Well," she flaps, "have you learned to talk sensibly yet or does that come as a later development like puberty, in your case ?"

"I don't know," I fluster. "I think I can talk." We flap again and a hot pink unmentionable flies upward followed by a hot blue one. Anita snags both midair, "my ass you can" and tosses them into the washer. I think of the moths in the park and everything since. I watch the last one go over the edge.

"Anita, how stupid death is, do you know? I've been thinking." She looks at me a bit steadily and keeps on sorting. "Muslims dream that after this life we're wrapped in bimbo heaven; Christians count on eternal unisex choirs. There are no such things. Only the two and a half minute we're allowed here," I gesture. The machines drown out the rest. "Poof!" I yell over them. Two more underpants sail through the air. We both admire the journey. "See what I mean?" I gather myself.

Anita clicks a thumbnail against a front tooth "At least you're on the right topic—the question of breathing in and breathing out—and not some hokey political junk no one gives a damn about."

"The question of what?" I stammer, staring high up on her legs which have become sort of like home plate. She looks right back.

"People and places slip away, but in part it's so we can have them again. Difficult to concede, isn't it?" Then she adds, a bit acerbly since we both know I'm eyeing the spot and probably grieving over the world's loss of nooky. "If you really want to think about it, it's even more difficult when we're talking people instead of..."

I indicate in sign language that I'm not much relieved to hear that.

"Because for people," she shifts her weight again, and I am newly drawn to her body as an important part of our dialogue, "every new occurrence is a sort of re-occurrence. There's a flickering moment, that's what I call it—in everything new, that indicates it's not necessarily similar to something bygone, but in honor of it."

"In honor of it," I repeat thickly, "that's pretty optimistic."

She ignores my remark, looks down and adjusts her blouse. "This return of things is what enables us to be fully alive, like the nature of our breathing-in and out." She reaches over and tags my solar plexus ever so lightly. "You do breathe in and out, don't you? You've been standing like a petrified comic strip ever since we met a couple of weeks ago." I had, in effect, neglected to breathe in and out during that time. She taps me again gently, same place. "You have this breath you're holding right now—it is not just *convenient to you*, nor is it *just given to you*, you *are* this breath—and then you breathe it out and you're ready for the not entirely new breath that will come next."

She clicks her tooth again, and noticing that my eyes are riveted to hers, she shifts one leg ever so slightly, as if to assure me yes, her body has weight, gravity. She's not just all talk. There is something at the core of her. "Except that you get back a little of whatever it was you breathed out a moment ago—not all of it, not very much, but some— and that's what proceeding by successive breaths is for humans." She rearranges my shirt that she has somewhat disorganized. "Now, have I made myself clear? This needs to be washed by the way. Before you strip let's breathe out after all that." I'm hoping she might at least touch my arm.

She reaches over and briefly touches my arm. "This succession of breathing in and out," she shifts her weight and ever so lightly leans on the arm, "that's all we'll ever be, I guess, until we die—since it's all we were at the instant we were born."

I stare at her, not moving a muscle in order to keep from breathing out.

Anita seizes my arm again, this time more firmly, and holds. "Go on, breathe. You can learn to live without me, you know. You can. You know it."

So that's where Alice got the speech she gave me before the little bird-cage fire at Wat Phra Sing—from somewhere in my own reptilian memory, the breathing-in and breathing-out, the new occurrence in honor of something gone by. Sounds ridiculous, how could it be that she could read my sleeping mind? But there it was. I never got too well the breathing-out part, you may have noticed by now. Maybe it would come in due time, but I wasn't optimistic.

Sometime that spring Anita gave up the discursive side of her existence—you know how people change—and went to live with a good man who was, she told me, a doctor who did a great deal of charity work for *Medicins sans Frontieres*. And that was why she had to leave for a while, and why one day I walked out on the lakefront and met the young shell-collector and why not much later I was on the plane heading East. To the Orient, as I've often called it.

"Nice score, pop." Rajit the lad breaks my reverie. The train apparently had been clattering on during my brief absence. He surveys me with an admiration tempered by curiosity. "When do you show us what's a score, and what isn't, and how to keep it?" No sahib in that inquiry. That went away with Kipling. I don't know, I thought to myself, looking at him blankly. "Don't ask me of all people," I finally stammer under his inquisitive gaze. "I suppose it's given to us like our breathing."

3

The address Anita had given me on the phone was in a modestly fancy district that looked down on the joining of three rivers, high on the embankment where three years ago we'd met and shared our different worlds. The happy couple had the entire top floor of a white stucco moderne house, glass block skylight at one rounded corner, and an enclosed porch on the roof with some tubs of evergreens surrounding it and a rooftop patio spacious enough for shuffleboard or start-up rollerblade.

"Welcome to Pittsburgh, and the USA," the good doctor addressed the kids since he knew I had already been here, in body and spirit. Gaya gave him a rounded stare as if he'd added "chaps" to his salutation, and she held out her hand. He was quite a bit younger than I'd imagined, and considerably taller and more ivy league—he made me feel awfully tattered—I caught myself checking the bagged out knees of my trousers I hadn't bothered to replace. There was something unexpectedly, but not disagreeably Anglo in his demeanor. Maybe it was in the reddish whiskers, light blue eyes, and a curved stem pipe. The last item set me back on my heels as I contemplated it, like I'd stepped from the unreal world of cheroot-smoking grandmothers backward into my 1930's picture-adventure books, in which the sandy haired explorer, having dismounted his camel or biplane, points at mysterious treasures with his curved pipe. I could imagine what Anita might see in him. I guess. Then I pondered whether the what in itself mattered at all, just the seeing.

He led us upstairs to the rooftop porch, himself carrying both heavy bags, and out on to the patio which now showed itself to be full of pale spring sun drawn from the northern hemisphere. Long garden boxes traced its perimeter like a pathway in a park, containing seedlings recently set out. I peeked over the edge and down at two of the silver rivers. "Anita will be out in a minute," he said, reading my thoughts as I leaned over gazing. Then he poured some lemonade from a pitcher into two blue-and-white striped tumblers and presented them to the children. They carried their lemonade carefully to the porch furniture and sat down.

"Well," he turned to me, and there was the slightest hitch of embarrassment as he looked directly at my gray hair. "Well," he caught himself and continued in an affable, businesslike manner, "I understand that you are the child of the world."

Tears sprang to my eyes for no apparent reason and prevented me from answering either yes or no. I felt very tiny, like I did at Three Pagodas Pass, and looking up at this large, friendly man and his pipe, "I am?" I queried uncertainly, scarcely breathing in or out. He surveyed me benignly without adding anything further. "I suppose I may be," I confessed, "I don't know why." And then inanely and entirely out of place, "Are you and Anita planning on having children?" He looked at me and weighed all sides of the question that had just tumbled out of my gray head. I kicked myself for having asked it. I could hear the echo of what I'd just said bounce back and now there was a foolish voice that was also mine adding more to it. "That would be nice," it said, in spite of my efforts to suppress it. "Among the Akha," I continued as he turned to retreat to the screened porch.

"Among the Akha?" he asked. I couldn't explain who they were, or why, just then. George's children regarded me with silent eyes, absolutely silent for I imagine George had told them, but all the same politely awaiting my explanation of the Akha. Or perhaps I was plain demented, and George might have warned them of that too.

"Among the Akha," I repeated, "a girl child is said to reside in the stem of the day." He nodded enigmatically and stepped warily off the patio and into the apartment. "I don't know what they mean by that," I shouted after him and turned to George's children as if I should apologize.

"If you used your head you might see they meant that out of the stem, leaves and flowers would come," Anita spoke quietly from behind me. I turned, and she saw in an instant that the face I turned was creased with shame and grief. No need for me to speak at all. "You don't have to yell in any case," she advised less severely, "I can always hear you." Then she embraced me very hard. "Wherever you've gotten yourself to." I continued to swim voicelessly inside of myself. I'd not expected an embrace at all, not really. She stepped back to survey my disarray, then waited for me to bring myself up to the present moment.

"How could I know," she said quietly, "that you'd take life so hard? And so far away? Fighting yourself on a foreign land. But apparently you did." Then after a pause, "Don't use your head much, huh? Tried to teach you." She turned to the children, who had set down their lemonades, and having risen now stood transfixed and gawking at the mysterious melody of this western discourse known as love. I glanced aside at them to see how they would take it. Anita was wearing the outfit she had worn the first day we met.

"Gaya and Rajit," I stammered inconclusively, "they're on loan you know…"

"You mumbled all that on the phone," Anita remarked, moving toward the children and taking each by a hand. I listened for something to happen in her, like the old discoursing tone of voice—unjustifiably I suppose—it should have been gone by now.

"I brought one of each," I explained earnestly, repeating George's phrase.

"I see," Anita smiled, letting go of the hands. The children remained stiff and dumbfounded cardboard figures stolen from the Ratchawong and delivered to the Queen of the Faeries. "You're getting quite a bit more perceptive to have observed that." He eye caught mine. I must have been staring at her intently. "Well," she continued, "for sure you were somewhat occupied, fighting against yourself on a distant field." I guess she was trying to get me to smile, and she couldn't. She brushed back her hair and held her face toward me for inspection, then relaxed. "Go ahead, look it over. Same old stuff. Nothing has changed much."

I stood all jumbled inside my silence. Old events kept playing randomly inside of me. "I have three eggshell lacquer boxes—they're round—that Kristen gave me to keep." I remarked inconsequentially to Anita and the children, "Now they're yours to keep."

No one could answer that one, not directly. "Well I have to admit you're bringing back with you quite a sizeable inheritance," Anita replied, the faintest bit drily.

"I wish I were part of it," I blurted. "Why did you send us off from each other? I wanted to stay."

She reflected briefly. "Your education was floundering, foundering. Which is it?" I shrugged, I didn't know, or care. She clicked a thumbnail against her tooth, and watched carefully to see if I could smile. "And I was pretty sick, you recall. So we couldn't have the children you wanted. Not right away. I didn't want you to wait around and watch me being sick like that."

"I could wait," I declared, "I'd be able to do that." We fell silent. I don't know what came over me. "Alice," I started.

"Who?" A gray eye scrutinized me, then allowed it was all right.

I closed my eyes, and faces ran across the darkened screen. George's exhausted face as we climbed the slippery rocks, Alice's distant face with the black thread in her ear, the patient eyes of the white dog. Life was something that only could be sung. I couldn't explain that either.

"I'm sorry. I'm just confused." It was up to me to save the moment now. "You were right about the breathing-in and breathing-out," I managed. "I heard it again."

Anita smiled.

"But I don't know what to do about it. I don't know what to do."

There was an awful silence, and her smile started to descend into something more serious. Alerted at the same moment by some signal the children took a step forward, already on a mission to extricate me as their cardboard father according, no doubt, to instructions from their true father. "Anyway, my promise," I declared looking around me then finally to them, "my promise to George, that's their dad," pointing to their solemn faces, "was to do the best for them I could, as he did for me. And you are the best I know." I returned her scrutiny. "I mean, the best at letting me come to know the best."

"Hmm," Anita allowed impartially, evaluating my declaration like a customs officer. She took each child by the shoulder. They resisted slightly, like children do when they are plucked from their private limbo of yearning to be free. Then slowly under her touch they began to give way. "And these two," she asked, swaying each in turn gently, "have been consulted about it of course?"

"Of course," I lied. "I always consult children about everything." Then I recalled the young boy on the beach collecting shells. "Why would I stop now?" I looked at Gaya and Rajit; they nodded silently, declaring they were game for whatever bizarre scheme I could invent. "Unless," I continued, squinting up into the pale preciseness of the sunlight that fell blanketing the terrace, "unless your husband might object."

"My husband?" She mused. "Marry him? Now why would I do a thing like that to such a nice man?" I shrugged. I didn't know why not. She went on, "About the only doctor that deserves getting married by me is not a useful one like him but a nitwit like yourself." I started to apologize for that, not knowing what else to do. "Who needs steering." I apologized and agreed. "He," she indicated the vanished pater familias, "is busy, unlike you. He not only does doctoring, but he's an editor of the *Contrary Opinion Newsletter*."

"That must be a pretty thick publication," I mumbled, "I mean, pretty thin publication." She looked at me. I looked back. "That's just my contrary opinion." I waited. "To show I can do it too." Anita responded with a sharply raised eyebrow, and shaking her head walked over and hugged the children to her.

"He'd love to have them here. And where will you be?" she inquired equitably.

"I'll be somewhere nearby. Not too far, I guess. Do you know," I added, indicating George's kids, "I believe I'm finally being promoted from out of being the child of the world. Your husband, ah, you know, called me that when we met. You must have told him."

"Told him what?" Anita looked at me sharply and drew George's children close to her. "What do you call these?" She looked back and forth between them then at me.

"Kids. Children, I mean."

"These," she placed a hand of demonstration or was it of protection, on the head of each of George's kids, children I mean, "these," she declared, ignoring my questioning regard, "are **children** of the world. You're the **child**."

I pondered the difference, whatever it was. Maybe it was that tiny huge difference between breathing in and breathing out, the stuff stories were made of, day by day. One day the breathing in and out would stop. But the whole story would keep going because then it had room to, having swallowed our individual stories. And maybe it would use parts of ours in some mysteriously ordinary new story.

There were barges on the water that evening, each with a light fore and aft, pointing toward evening, morning. We walked in an area where no one would find us.

It was our first night alone really, after all the weeks we'd known each other. There seemed to be no beginning to the barges, but there they were, coming from some place upstream and waiting out the night, each one a life. They floated slowly past us on the water putting in on our side somewhere safe we couldn't see them.

Anita reassured my arm. "Nothing will come of this. But heroes will keep coming, changing, remaining, no matter how heavy the disguise."

"All the more reason for us to believe in just us," I objected. "We made this story and therefore I am, you am, we am."

We were quiet for a while. "Where's you baseball cap?" I asked suddenly. "I always think of you wearing your baseball cap. And the green sack you carry." Then after a bit, "The person behind the story always dies," I continued evenly, "and it's too damn bad, just when we're getting to know them. Will you wear your cap after you've...?"

She examined her thumb, biting it to make sure she had a decent respondent this time. "Not hardly," she directed at the thumb. "People don't repeat themselves, not as whole persons I don't believe. But heroes keep popping up, like I said, changing their disguise. Bits of them get recycled into the world, kinda preserved that way.

Undercover as it were," she added archly. "Maybe all of us creatures aren't immortal, but we may be slightly more than just mortal. What do you think?"

"I don't know," I shrugged, "for sure I don't." Suddenly I grasped her arm, the one with the bitten thumb. "On second thought maybe I've got a glimmer of it. A story like ours keeps going for just a short while. Well, maybe for a short while longer."

I decided I ought to go back and find the young scientist I'd left collecting clamshells along the deserted lakefront a month ago. Check in to see if I'd heard him correctly. And see what further advice he might give. If he was still there.